THE HAT SHOP
ON THE CORNER

MARITA CONLON-McKENNA

BANTAM PRESS

LONDON · TORONTO · SYDNEY · AUCKLAND · JOHANNESBURG

F 146,821

£ 13.95

TRANSWORLD PUBLISHERS
61–63 Uxbridge Road, London W5 5SA
a division of The Random House Group Ltd

RANDOM HOUSE AUSTRALIA (PTY) LTD
20 Alfred Street, Milsons Point, Sydney,
New South Wales 2061, Australia

RANDOM HOUSE NEW ZEALAND LTD
18 Poland Road, Glenfield, Auckland 10, New Zealand

RANDOM HOUSE SOUTH AFRICA (PTY) LTD
Isle of Houghton, Corner of Boundary Road and Carse O'Gowrie,
Houghton 2198, South Africa

Published 2006 by Bantam Press
a division of Transworld Publishers

A catalogue record for this book is available from the British Library.
ISBN 9780593056097 (from Jan 07)
ISBN 0593056094

Typeset in 11.5/15.5pt Erhhardt by
Falcon Oast Graphic Art Ltd.

Printed and bound in Great Britain by
Mackays of Chatham, Chatham, Kent

1 3 5 7 9 10 8 6 4 2

Papers used by Transworld Publishers are natural, recyclable products made from wood
grown in sustainable forests. The manufacturing processes conform to the
environmental regulations of the country of origin.

Marita Conlon-McKenna is one of Ireland's most successful authors and her books have been widely translated and sold internationally. Both *The Magdalen* and *Under the Hawthorn Tree* have been number one bestsellers and other novels include *Promised Land*, *Miracle Woman* and *The Stone House*. She lives in Blackrock, Dublin, with her husband and family and is the current chairperson of Irish PEN. She has also won a prestigious International Reading Association award.

Also by Marita Conlon-McKenna

In memory of a wonderful aunt,
Eleanor Murphy,
and her little shop on South Anne Street.

Acknowledgements

To Bridget Higgins, milliner and hatmaker extraordinaire. Thank you for the wonderful day in Galway, showing me your craft and sharing with me the secrets of a milliner. Your passion is contagious and I fell madly in love with your wonderful hats.

To Philip Treacy. Thank you for the beautiful hat, the warm welcome in Elizabeth Street, and the constant inspiration of your stunning designs and exquisite creations.

To my mother, Mary, who when I was a little girl would lift down her hatboxes and with a rustle of tissue produce a gorgeous hat. So began the magic, as I watched her dress up to go out to the races or a stylish party!

To Dublin, my city. Your streets burst with life and energy and your big old heart is so full of stories – it's no wonder you are a city of writers.

To the Royal Dublin Society Horse Show and Ladies' Day. What a perfect day – sunshine, hats, frocks, champagne and horses and all the excitement of the competition.

To the Mansion House, Dawson Street, Dublin.

Thanks to The Mad Hatter, J. C. Brady, Halo and all the other wonderful hat shops that I visited.

To my editor Francesca Liversidge, for making writing such an interesting pursuit, and to Nicky Jeanes, Deborah Adams, Vivien Garrett and all the team at Transworld.

To my agent Caroline Sheldon. Assembling a hatbox is the very least of it! Thanks.

To Gill, Simon, Declan, Geoff and all the team at Gill Hess, Dublin. Your hard work and good humour is much appreciated.

To the Irish Booksellers who have cheered me along and been there from the start. Thanks. Your support is brilliant.

To Anne Frances Doorly and 'les girls' – Ann Lawler, Grace Murphy, Yvonne Taylor, Karen Quinn, Helen O'Dowd and Mary Joy. Thanks for all the years of fun and friendship, girls' nights and that special trip to Barcelona.

To all my friends, old and new, and my lovely readers, thanks.

Last but certainly not least, to my tall, dark, handsome husband James and my children, Amanda, Laura, Fiona and James, and son-in-law Michael Hearty. I couldn't do it without you all.

Chapter One

Ellie Matthews's heart was heavy as she joined the rush of early morning workers making their way across St Stephen's Green. She ignored the clouds racing above in the blue sky and the rows of bright red and yellow tulips that lined a pathway through Dublin's city-centre park, and she barely glanced at Jimmy Byrne, the park keeper, already busy with shovel and hoe planting out wallflowers. Crossing the old stone bridge, she paid no heed to the ducks dabbling on the lake below as she approached the main gate.

Crowds of commuters stepped off the Luas city tram line and, joining them, she headed down Dawson Street. Cars hooted and the traffic roared as Ellie turned into South Anne Street – the street she had known all her life. She stopped and, rummaging in her handbag, pulled out the key of the shop, turned it firmly and slipped inside the door of number 61. Her heart was racing and she leaned against the wood to steady herself.

It was almost six weeks since she had last crossed the threshold of the small milliner's shop her mother owned, and in those six weeks her world had utterly changed. She tried to compose herself as she touched the counter, the display shelves and the hatstands.

Forty days ago, Madeleine, her mother, had finally given in and agreed to be admitted to hospital. Once there, she had slipped away from the pain and fear of her terminal illness in a cloud of morphine and gentle acceptance that Ellie still struggled to understand.

'I am not afraid,' she had insisted, 'so you must not be either.'

The days had run together far too quickly as she watched her beautiful mother pass away to that other world she believed in so strongly.

Her aunts, Yvette and Monique, and Monique's husband, Uncle Jean-Luc, and her cousins had come over from France. They had gathered together, along with close friends and colleagues, for a funeral mass in Clarendon Street Church, her mother's favourite city-centre place of prayer. Afterwards, with the simple grace and style she had exuded throughout her life, Madeleine Matthews had been laid to rest in a pretty plot in a graveyard in Wicklow. Ellie sighed, assaulted still by the pain of it.

Two of them! There had always been the two of them against the world, mother and daughter, best friends, companions, much more than that. She had never imagined a life without her mother – and now, for the first time, she was alone. There had been no brothers and sisters, no huge extended family to call on, for Madeleine Matthews had raised her child on her own. Ellie knew her mother would have loved to have more children, a family of dark-haired, wide-eyed boys and girls, but it was not meant to be: a little less than three years after her whirlwind wedding to Philip Matthews, he had walked out of the tempestuous marriage and left her with a small daughter to raise.

Ellie glanced round the shop, which was dusty and in need of a good hoover. The doorway was filthy, the windows needed a wash, and the back of the shop was filled with hatboxes and bags of sinamay, felt, satin and gauze. Unfinished pieces of work cluttered the surfaces, along with offcuts of petersham ribbon. She studied her mother's huge cork noticeboard arrayed with photos, coloured drawings, samples of fabric and unusual patterns and designs, and wondered where to begin.

The shop was shut but no matter, it should still be neat and clean, the way her mother liked it. Ellie slipped off her red beret and black coat and, with a piece of ribbon from the counter, she briskly tied back her shoulder-length black hair. It was high time she began to tidy up. Wrinkling her nose in disgust at the sour-smelling contents of the half-open milk carton on the shelf and a stale packet of biscuits, she began to bag some rubbish. Next she got the brush and mop and bucket and washed out the tiled front entrance to the shop, keeping her head down and ignoring passers-by. A small black cat appeared and tiptoed across the wet tiles, trying to slip between her legs and into the shop.

'No, little cat!'

Ellie shooed it away with her brush, before going back inside and turning her attention to the hoover. She had just started it when she heard a knocking on the shop door. Surely they could read the 'Closed' sign?

There was a man standing at the door. Switching off the noisy hoover and smoothing her hair, she ran to see what he wanted.

'I'm sorry to disturb you,' he began.

'We're shut,' said Ellie firmly. 'I'm only here to clean the place.'

'Oh, then forgive me. I was looking for Madeleine.'

'Madeleine's not here,' she explained slowly, trying to compose herself. 'She passed away a few weeks ago.'

'Oh . . . I'm very sorry. My condolences on her death,' he apologized. 'I knew she was ill but I didn't realize the seriousness of it. I've been trying to get in touch with her.'

Ellie could feel pinpricks of tears behind her eyes as this tall man in his expensive suit stared at her.

'Madeleine was your . . . ?'

'My mother.'

'There is a resemblance,' he said gently. 'And of course Madeleine told me about you. We've been in discussions regarding the sale contract for these premises. You probably know about it.'

Ellie shook her head. Her mother had barely discussed the business over the past few months. She had been too ill, too weak to waste her energy on such material things.

'Please, come inside. I'll just put the catch on the door,' Ellie said.

'I should have introduced myself properly,' he offered, his eyes serious. 'My name is Neil Harrington – from Harrington Smith, the law firm.'

'And I'm Ellie,' she replied firmly, wondering if he knew that the business was now hers.

'We represent Casey Coleman Holdings. They are one of Ireland's largest property companies and have invested heavily in property on this street, which they intend redeveloping to provide shops and offices and accommodation. I had drafted a contract of sale on their behalf with your mother with regard to number 61.'

'My mother was going to sell the shop!' She couldn't disguise her surprise. Ellie would never have imagined her mother willingly agreeing to the sale of the business she loved so much and had worked so hard to build up.

'Yes, we had discussed the sale. She felt circumstances were changing. The street – well, it will be radically altered with this new plan, as I said, and I had already drawn up the contracts.'

Contracts. Ellie couldn't believe it. Why had her mother made no mention of any dealings with the serious dark-haired lawyer? Her mother had bought the shop thirty-one years ago and had worked here almost every day since. It had been far more than a business to

Madeleine Matthews: it had been her life! She would never have considered selling it if she hadn't fallen ill. But perhaps the man standing in front of her was right? Perhaps her mother had been more of a realist than she had imagined, planning for the future. A wave of emotion almost overwhelmed Ellie. She was adrift, like a cork bobbing on the ocean, not knowing where she was going to end up.

'Miss Matthews?'

'I'm sorry, Mr Harrington. I knew there were plans for the re-development of the street, but I wasn't aware that my mother had already considered selling the business.'

'I suppose, under the circumstances,' he said, looking at her with what appeared genuine concern, 'she wanted to do what was best.'

'The best!'

Ellie swallowed hard. She felt hurt, threatened. Who could say what was best when her mother was dead and buried and she was the only beneficiary of her will? A simple document, the will included the shop, their second-floor apartment in a Georgian building in Hatch Street, and a small savings account that had already been depleted by the costs of the funeral.

'I have no wish to intrude at a time of grief but I will leave you a copy of the contract to read.' He withdrew a large brown envelope from the leather briefcase he had opened on the wooden counter. 'If you want to discuss it with me or my partners over the next few days or weeks, whenever, we are at your disposal.'

Ellie tried to control the tears welling in her eyes. 'I'm sorry,' she said.

'Bound to be an awful time,' he murmured. 'I should go. Here's my card if you need me and once again my sympathy on your mother's passing. She was a lovely woman.'

Despite his stern expression he seemed kind. Glancing at his card, she could see he was a senior partner in the law firm. He was young

– thirty-five or thirty-six – for such a position. She wondered if her mother had liked him, trusted him.

Ellie walked him to the door, saying polite goodbyes, before watching his tall figure in the dark grey suit turn back up towards Dawson Street. She fingered the envelope. No, she'd read it later when she went home. For now she'd concentrate on getting the shop spick and span, even if it included tackling the massive spider web up in the corner near the top shelf. She'd better get used to doing such things, for now there was no one else.

Hot and tired, she had an immense feeling of satisfaction after a few hours' cleaning and tidying and washing down dusty paintwork. For once she had not dissolved with grief and she had actually lost track of time. Except for a break at lunch when she had slipped across the road to buy a sandwich and some milk, she had been permanently ensconced in the shop.

Suddenly she realized that someone was knocking loudly on the shop door. Was it that Neil Harrington again? Perhaps he had forgotten something. She tried to tidy herself, then stepped forward and opened the door. It was a customer.

'I'm sorry,' she apologized, 'but we're closed.'

The determined middle-aged woman on the doorstep paid absolutely no heed and brushed past her to stand inside the shop.

'Where's Madeleine?' she demanded. 'I have been trying to contact her for the past three weeks. Twice I've been to Dublin but the shutters were down. I tried phoning, I—'

'I'm very sorry,' explained Ellie. 'My mother passed away two weeks ago. She had been sick for a while.'

The woman looked pale and for a second seemed to reel with the news.

'Oh my God! I can't believe it, poor Madeleine!' she gushed, fiddling with her handbag. 'I just can't believe it. I was here with Madeleine only a couple of months ago ordering a hat.'

'A hat?'

'Yes, it's for my daughter's wedding.'

'When is the wedding?' asked Ellie.

'It's on Saturday,' wailed the woman. 'That's why I came in today to collect it.'

Ellie felt an instant of panic. She hadn't noticed any completed hat ready for collection either in the shop or in the small workroom out the back.

'Sorry, I only came in today to sort a few things out and tidy up. Perhaps you could give me some details of the hat you ordered?'

'It's a sort of dusky pink, with one of those big wide brims with a slight upturn. Your mother had found some fabric in just the right colour to go with my outfit and she was trimming it with silk flowers and a swirl of ribbon.'

Uneasy, Ellie was almost certain there wasn't a hat of that description anywhere in the small shop. She'd check every box and bag to be sure.

'Listen, Mrs . . . ?'

'The name is Maureen Cassidy.'

'Well, Mrs Cassidy, would you like to sit down while I just check my mother's workroom and storeroom?'

'Oh, that would be lovely, dear. My feet are killing me from walking all round town.'

Ellie settled her mother's customer with a copy of *Vogue* before trawling through all the boxes stacked on the floor in the back room and making one more round of the hatstands. There was one hat crown in a rich, deep rose colour on a block. She had to find her mother's hard-backed notebook to see the order, the rough design she had been contemplating. At last under a pile of tulle and organza she found it. There, in her mother's fine writing, were the order and

15

the rough sketch for Mrs Cassidy, with a completion date of two weeks ago. What was she going to tell the customer? She went back out front.

'I always love reading these stylish magazines,' said the woman, smiling up at her expectantly.

'Mrs Cassidy, I did find your hat on one of the blocks in the back but I'm afraid it's not finished.'

'Not finished!'

'I'm sorry but it must have been one of the last things my mother was working on before she went into the hospital.'

'Not finished . . . but what am I to do? Lucy's wedding is on Saturday. It's all organized. I have my dress and a little jacket and the most darling shoes and a handbag, but I have to have a hat. I'm the mother of the bride . . . What am I going to do?'

Ellie stood there feeling awful, unsure of what to say, for not finished was an understatement: the hat was barely begun.

'Not finished, you say?'

'Not even near being finished,' she admitted candidly.

'But couldn't someone else finish it, do the rest? There must be someone?'

Ellie shook her head. 'This was my mother's business. She employed no one else.'

Mrs Cassidy looked as if she would burst into tears.

'There must be something someone can do? Where else am I going to find a hat that will match my outfit at this late hour!'

Ellie felt guilty. Her mother had prided herself on never letting a customer down, on always having the work done, the hats and ornamental headpieces ready on time to be collected by her clients.

'I can finish the piece,' she volunteered, tilting the notebook in her hands as she considered it. Was she talented enough to step into her mother's shoes, to continue her mother's work, to finish off the piece

16

to the customer's satisfaction, to create something with the style and panache that Madeleine Matthews always did?

'You?'

'Yes, I am also a milliner, trained by my mother. I've spent most of my childhood and growing years in this place and have often helped her with her work. I studied art and textiles in college and have a very sound knowledge of design. Besides, my mother has left a copy of the design here in this notebook.'

Maureen Cassidy studied the coloured drawing. 'Are you sure you'd be able to do it?'

'Of course,' Ellie assured her. 'I have worked on many hats.'

She simply couldn't let down her mother or this nice woman. Whether it was out of loyalty or love or the big soft heart her mother and friends were always teasing her about, or some moment of utter madness in her bereavement, Ellie found herself promising to complete the hat and have it ready for the customer in less than twenty-four hours. It was a promise she had every intention of keeping.

Chapter Two

Ellie couldn't believe that she had made such a rash promise to one of her mother's customers. What had possessed her? However, holding the stiffened rose-coloured crown in her hand she knew that it was the right thing to do. She wanted to protect not only her mother's reputation but that of the hat shop. Maureen Cassidy deserved the very best and Ellie was determined to work all night if she had to, to achieve exactly the design her mother had sketched out so precisely in her notepad. She would simply finish the job. She had grown up with the world of millinery, shaping the materials on the hat blocks, sewing and stitching and steaming, bending brim wires and covering them, hand-rolling silk petals and flowers, trimming feathers, fixing ribbons; from her mother she had learned all the skills needed to create the perfect piece of art that was a hat. A hat that would make Mrs Cassidy shine at her daughter's wedding in three days' time!

The street outside was quiet, a few passers-by gazing at the window before hurrying on their way to the bus or the Luas tram as the town began to unwind and the shops shut. She watched as the newsagent's and Scottie O'Loughlin in the old toy and joke shop pulled down their shutters for the night. Mr Farrell from the antiques shop five doors down checked his keys as he locked up, the newspaper under his arm as he headed up the street. Over the past two years South Anne Street had changed. Property prices had sky-rocketed and some of the shops had been forced to close down. A few landlords had refused to renew the leases of their existing tenants, knowing they could sell to the developers for a huge price. The woman from Killiney had closed up her beautiful gift shop further down six months ago, and it still lay idle along with a few others, their shopfronts empty and neglected. Ellie remembered South Anne Street as a bustling thoroughfare with a range of shops run by a myriad of characters, everyone knowing everyone else. It was a shame the way things were changing.

The street-lights flickered on as one by one the rest of the shops and businesses in the street closed for the night.

I'd better run out and get something to eat, thought Ellie, pulling on her coat. She raced to the deli near Duke Lane to buy a roll and some soup and a wrap, for she intended to work for the rest of the evening. She was trying to balance her purchases and open the shop door when she noticed the little black cat again, miaowing for attention.

'Scat! Go on, scat!' she called, trying to shoo it away. But the cat pushed its way in between her feet. Terrified that she would hurt it, with her key stuck in the door and her soup carton wobbling ominously and about to spill all over the two of them, Ellie found herself lurching forward and landing in a heap on her own tiled doorstep as the shop door opened. The soup was saved but the bag with her supper in it lay beside her on the ground. The little cat tilted its head curiously at her and a second later pulled out a piece of chicken from the fallen wrap and gobbled it up.

'You, you!' she threatened.

The cat stood for a few seconds as if trying to make up its mind. Its small black body tense, it stared at her then stepped past her into the shop and jumped up into the chair with the blue cushion near the window.

As she stood up, Ellie burst out laughing, something she hadn't done in weeks. She was tempted to scoop up the small creature and bury her face in the comfort of its warm fur, but she was afraid to scare it. Inside she sat down in the tiny kitchenette and took out what was left of her supper, holding her breath as the cat appeared again. Minouche, the street cat her mother had adopted, knew the shop well and settled itself patiently to watch her eat.

'I suppose you're hungry too.' She tossed it a bit more of the chicken wrap, which it delicately chewed. The cat eyed her intently as Ellie poured it some milk in the lid of her empty soup carton. Whether she wanted it or not, she guessed she had company for the night.

Ellie concentrated for the next few hours, discovering there was a bit less of the dusky rose pink sinamay material than she needed. She would have to be careful or there would not be enough for the trimmings. She cut delicate pieces of the fabric and folded them gently over the fine wired shape she'd created, concentrating as she didn't want the material to tear before she lightly stitched and glued it together. She counted each shape, laying them carefully on the table before she began to search for the perfect piece of gossamer silk that would cover the joins and create a rim of colour round the brim. She wished her fingers were as deft in working the fabric as her mother's and berated herself as part of the sinamay tore and ravelled. There definitely wouldn't be enough. What was she going to do? She had three or four more loops of petals to form and she had run out of material. She could feel a sense of panic invade her as she knew there was no guarantee she could match the colour, let alone order more in the next day or two. She would have to be inventive, perhaps use a different colour or shade for the underside, and for one or two rolls of heavy rose petals. But what colour? Another pink, a cream, green? She worked carefully and, finding a piece of pale pink and a piece of cranberry, she tried them. The cranberry was too strong but the paler pink would work. Grabbing some cream the same colour as the trim, she twirled and fixed it into position. She worked for hours, and realized that the sense of pleasure she got must be akin to the feelings experienced by her mother when she was creating her millinery confections.

The hat looked beautiful. It was perfectly balanced from all angles, with a medium brim and the ideal height.

When Ellie realized that she was totally satisfied with it, she gasped with surprise to see that the clock on the wall said twelve thirty. Even the cat over in the corner was fast asleep. She put everything away neatly, pins, scissors and needles in a safe place. Proud of her work, she placed the hat on a stand.

As she locked up, the cat suddenly pushed out past her.

'Going on the prowl!' she joked, watching it slink along the pavement and disappear into the darkness.

She decided to walk home along by the Shelbourne Hotel and up around the edge of the Green, the fresh night air filling her lungs.

At home, the flat seemed strangely silent. There were a few messages on the answering machine from her friends Kim and Fergus, checking that she was OK, and more letters of condolence from old family friends. Ellie would deal with them later. First she was dying for a mug of tea and some nice buttery toast: the work had made her starving.

Curling up on the sofa in the sitting room, she finally got a chance to study the documents that Neil Harrington had delivered to the shop earlier on. She was careful not to smudge them with her buttery

21

fingers but even a very quick perusal seemed to indicate that he and his clients were offering a good price for the property that Madeleine Matthews had been wise enough to buy outright. It was a tempting offer and she could understand her mother's readiness to negotiate with them. The small business she had started was now worth quite a large sum.

Ellie was too tired tonight to read the minutiae of the contract but she promised herself that tomorrow she would read it properly, for the proposed sale of the business would ensure a far greater inheritance from her mother's estate than she had ever imagined.

All night she tossed and turned, her sleep disturbed both by the exciting prospect of having a large sum of money at her disposal and by guilt about selling the hat shop, the business her mother had worked so hard to build up. Her mind was in utter turmoil as she imagined the shop finally closed down.

'Oh, it's a miracle. I am so pleased! I can't believe it!' confessed Maureen Cassidy the next day as she tried on the dusky pink chapeau with the slight upturn and the silk peony roses with their paler pink and cream petals lolling against the crown. 'Oh, I do love the way you've used the cream ribbon and petals to show off the pink!'

'It's a beautiful hat, Mum,' complimented Lucy, the bride-to-be. 'It's exactly what you wanted and the shape suits your face perfectly. The colour is just right for your outfit.'

Relieved at seeing such a satisfied customer, Ellie began to relax.

'You saved the day, Miss Matthews. Thank you. I know your mother would be very proud of you, very proud,' gushed her client, taking out her credit card as Ellie gently placed the hat in a pale blue hatbox, easing a light layer of tissue over it for protection.

'I'm glad you like it,' she said, smiling.

'My other daughter, Jenny, is getting married early next year,' confided Maureen Cassidy, 'and of course there will have to be something totally different for that wedding!'

'Another new hat,' joked Lucy, throwing her eyes to heaven.

Ellie was about to say that completing this commission had been a one-off and that the shop was likely to be sold in a few months' time, but instead found herself biting her tongue and saying nothing.

'I see the little black cat is back,' murmured Mrs Cassidy.

'The cat?'

'Yes, your mother always used to say that cat brought her luck. Used to come and go as it pleased.'

'Mum, you are so superstitious,' joked her daughter.

Ellie said nothing as she stared at the cat, which had somehow manoeuvred itself into a snug corner near the window.

'I am eternally grateful to you, Ellie dear, and I see you have the same wonderful talent as your mother!'

Ellie blushed as the Cassidys said their goodbyes. She wished Lucy well with the wedding, and was filled with a strange sense of satisfaction and yearning as she watched mother and daughter walk away arm in arm, the pale blue hatbox swinging between them.

She was about to put the latch on the door and close up when her best friend, Fergus, appeared.

'I called to the apartment and when there was no reply I guessed you might be here,' he said, hugging her to his skinny frame. 'You OK, El?'

'Yeah, just a bit emotional. I've been clearing up and cleaning out. Sold a hat to one of my mother's customers for her daughter's wedding on Saturday.'

'Hey, that's great!'

'Yeah, I suppose, but it made me think of Mum.'

'You poor old thing,' he said, holding her close. Ellie was comforted by his warm embrace and thoughtfulness. Fergus Delaney and herself had been close ever since they met up at Irish college when they were both thirteen years old. Over the years Fergus had always been a shoulder to cry on, a sounding board for mad ideas and the best friend a girl could have. The fact that Fergus didn't fancy her in the slightest, and had told her when he was nineteen that he suspected he liked only men, made her love him even more. With his roaring red hair and pale skin and freckles, Fergus was one of those Celtic men who stood out from the crowd and was always loyal and true to his friends. Madeleine had adored him and insisted on trying to feed him up whenever he called to the apartment.

Over the past few weeks he had been a huge support, visiting her mother in the hospital, helping with the funeral arrangements, checking in on her constantly and holding her hand when she felt scared and sad, telling her she was not alone.

'What about lunch?'

'I was about to take a break,' she admitted, yawning, 'though I have a load of paperwork I have to read thoroughly.'

'I've had no breakfast yet.' He gave her one of those pleading looks that are irresistible. 'I'm starving.'

'Let's go eat then.'

They got a table in the corner of Ryan's Café, where Fergus opted for the all-day breakfast, loading his plate with rashers and sausages and pudding and a big helping of chips and beans.

'I don't know where you put all that.'

It wasn't fair, thought Ellie, for Fergus seemed to burn food like a fire, stoking up energy. She chose the cheesy pasta and a side salad.

'So what's this about paperwork?' he asked, munching.

'You won't believe it, but Mum was talking to the developers about selling the shop,' she confided. 'Their solicitor called yesterday with copies of the contracts that had been drawn up.'

'And what do you make of it?'

'I don't know. I suppose it's a bit of a shock. I always imagined the shop and my mother going on for ever. You know she was really opposed to the big shopping scheme they are planning, and I guess that's why it was such a surprise that she was even negotiating with them. I'd have thought she'd have sent them packing.'

'Given the circumstances,' prompted Fergus gently, 'Madeleine was probably thinking of you.'

'I know. It means she realized all along that she was dying, that there was no way she was going to get better.'

'And she knew you were settled and happy in your job and the money from the sale would be a real inheritance. Dublin property prices have gone through the roof and a shop just off Grafton Street should fetch a fortune.'

'Fergus, she was thinking of me. She always did. But still, Mum adored the shop and . . . well . . .'

'You shouldn't sign or do anything with that contract until you get someone to read it.'

'You could read it!' she cajoled.

He threw his eyes upwards. 'Come off it, Ellie, we're both shite at figures and legalese. Someone else, promise!'

'I promise.'

'You do want to sell it?'

'Yeah, I suppose so. It's just all happening so fast. Losing the shop will be like losing another part of Mum. Part of what I've grown up with, what I am.'

'Then don't do anything hasty. Take your time. Don't let the big boys bully you into something you're not sure about.'

Ellie took a deep breath. How was it that Fergus was so wise and always gave such good advice?

'Are you going to eat the rest of that pasta?' he enquired, staring at her plate.

'I've had enough,' she said, passing the dish over to him.

'You know, it's a great little shop in a wonderful location,' he

25

mused, spearing a piece of creamy penne, 'and you don't have to sell if you don't want to. Think about it.'

Fergus had walked her back to the shop and then taken off on a mission to meet up with the new graphic designer who was coming on board the small advertising agency where he worked.

Ellie let herself in and sat behind the counter watching the street outside. The distant sounds of traffic and the rumble of the city were strangely comforting as she tried to pretend nothing had changed in the small millinery shop, and that her mother might appear in the doorway any minute.

She sat there for hours, remembering her mother, always charming and bright, making magic as she worked, singing softly under her breath, as Ellie played dolls with the polished wooden hat blocks and learned in time the essentials of hat-making.

Chapter Three

Over the weekend Ellie decided to trawl through her mother's old bank statements, cashbooks and accounts for the shop. Reading Madeleine Matthews's perfect writing with its odd fancy curl invoked a strange mixture of emotions: sadness and a certain pride in her mother's achievements. She remembered the large clientele and all the commissions her mother had worked on over the years. There had been the sparkling production of *Pygmalion* at the Abbey Theatre and a very stylish *Importance of Being Earnest* at the Gate Theatre. Her mother had created headwear for a huge number of stage productions over the years. Then of course there were all the fashion shows: Madeleine Matthews had worked with so many designers on hats and headpieces for their collections. But the mainstay had been her loyal clientele of stylish women of all ages in search of the perfect hat for a special occasion.

Going over the old cashbooks and accounts revealed the delicate balance of their financial affairs in a confusing array of debits and credits. Her concentration was suddenly disturbed by the mad ringing of the doorbell as Fergus and Kim dropped in to see how she was.

'Ellie, it's the weekend. Why don't we all go for a drink in Hartigan's?' coaxed Kim, glancing at the array of papers and books spread all over the table and couch.

'I can't,' she moaned, 'I've got to try and read all this stuff from the shop.'

'Do it another night! It's Saturday,' begged Fergus.

Ellie refused. Besides, she wasn't exactly in the humour for a glass of wine or a pint in a noisy pub. She'd far prefer to stay home and try to get to grips with the finances of the business before she made any decision.

'Leave her alone, Fergus,' argued Kim protectively. 'Just because we want to go drinking doesn't mean Ellie has to. OK?'

Fergus looked instantly apologetic. 'Do you want us to get you anything?' he offered. 'A takeaway, a pizza, chips on the way home?'

'You have eaten?' questioned Kim, her blue eyes serious.

'I was going to make myself a sandwich later.'

'You have to look after yourself,' she scolded. 'You've been under a lot of stress. I'll make you something before we leave.'

'You two sit there and I'll do it,' insisted Fergus, disappearing off to the galley kitchen, banging around and talking to himself, as he made toasted cheese sandwiches and coffee.

'There's so much to go over,' confided Ellie to her oldest friend. 'Tax returns, accounts, though everything seems up to date.'

'Is there anything I can do to help?' offered Kim.

For a second she hesitated. Kim and herself had started school on the same day and despite being total opposites – one tall and fair and sporty, and one small, dark and arty – had become instant best friends. In senior school when a crowd of thirteen-year-old girls had begun to tease Ellie unmercifully, it was Kim who had told the bullies to leave her alone. In turn, when Kim had admitted she hated French and was bound to fail it in her Leaving Certificate exams, it was Ellie who insisted for the following four months that all their conversations were held in French.

'*Non, non, non*!' Despite Kim's protests it had worked. Following a degree in commerce, Kim, who was a whiz with figures, now worked in Davy's stockbrokers. She was a numbers expert but it wasn't fair to ask her, when she was all dressed up in her flirty red skirt and black boots, to give up her Saturday night to pore over account books.

'Maybe next week, some night after work, if you've got the time you could run over everything with me?'

'Sure,' promised Kim.

Ellie hadn't realized how hungry she was until she devoured Fergus's tasty grilled cheese sandwiches layered with onion and Worcestershire sauce.

'Bit of energy for the night,' he teased.

'Listen, thanks, you two,' said Ellie, half tempted to abandon the work and join them. 'I don't know what I'd do without you.'

'See you next week,' they both promised and she listened to them tramp down the wooden staircase of the tall Georgian house, slamming the door as they left.

Tucked up in bed later that night with a calculator and pen and paper, she thought about Fergus's assessment of her. Perhaps she was a little crazy, totting up figures like a lunatic instead of being out with her friends. She pushed the thought away as she studied the blue ledger. Her mother's business seemed to have gone up and down like the proverbial roller coaster for a number of years. Some months were busy and others deadly quiet. Times when Madeleine had large sums of money on deposit in the bank and other days when they were almost broke. Yet her proud mother had never alluded to a shortage of money. Never said a word. Why had her mother hidden so much from her, especially during those precarious patches? Ellie frowned, wondering how she had persisted in her childhood assumption that everything would always be all right, that her elegant, capable mother could resolve any problem.

As she trawled through the accounts Ellie realized that, despite everything, her mother's hard work and the small hat shop had for the past twenty-five years kept them both. Paid for their spacious first-floor apartment just off Leeson Street, and her private education with the Loreto nuns on the Green. Funded her through years of college and her post-graduate year in Paris, provided holidays in Provence and kept them in a style that few single-parent families enjoyed.

Falling asleep, she tried to imagine her life without the shop. She would return to her job as a buyer for Hyland's, the busy textile importers down near the Quays. Her boss had been kindness itself, giving her an extended period of leave during the final weeks of her mother's illness and putting no pressure on her to return to the office until she felt ready. Her mind was racing as she kept thinking of the small shop with the hatstands in the window, unsure if returning to Hyland's was what she still wanted.

Her heart sank when she saw the state of the shop doorway on Monday morning. She didn't want to imagine what someone had been doing in it. She fetched the brush and mop, pouring a good dose of disinfectant into the water as she washed down the tiles, the cat looking disdainfully at her as it slipped inside. This morning she intended going through her mother's order book, checking for any outstanding payments, trying to discover if there were any business matters she had overlooked. She was typing letters to customers who still owed money when the phone went.

It was Neil Harrington, enquiring if she had managed to read through all the documents he had given her. Was she ready to sign them?

'Yes, I have looked at them, but I've been so busy with the shop and sorting out my mother's affairs that I haven't studied all the clauses,' she admitted, feeling like a guilty schoolgirl who'd been caught bunking off.

He began to ask her about one of them.

She had to put her hands up and confess to not understanding it. 'I did try. It's just that I'm not very good at these contracts and things.'

She could sense his disapproval at the end of the line and before she knew it she found herself accepting his invitation to a lunch at which he would run through his client's offer in layman's terms.

'Thank you, that would be very helpful.'

Putting up the 'Closed' sign on the door as she went to meet him at the Hibernian Club, Ellie wondered if she had gone mad. She had passed the large, imposing club on the Green a million times over, and was curious to see inside. A man at the reception directed her to the reading room, where Neil Harrington sat behind a copy of the *Financial Times*.

'I'm glad that you could join me,' he said, folding away the paper. 'It's a bit more private here than most restaurants.'

He was wearing a grey pinstripe suit, she noticed as she followed him into the high-ceilinged dining room. It had a perfect view of the park and the waiter seated them at a discreet corner table.

Ellie fought to control her embarrassment at realizing that, except for a very elderly woman being assisted into a seat by her son, she was the only female in the room. She buried her gaze in the menu.

'I can recommend the lamb or the steak and kidney pie.'

Neil Harrington waited while she made up her mind. Ellie decided on the monkfish and he opted for the steak and kidney pie.

31

'Would you like some wine?'

He ordered a bottle of Chablis, and Ellie promised herself she would sip her one glass slowly. Over their starters he told her about the law firm where he worked and the kind of clientele Harrington Smith had built up over the years.

'So it's your firm? You don't just work there?'

'My grandfather founded it sixty years ago and my father built it up!'

'Family businesses are special,' she mused aloud. 'It must be great working alongside your father.'

'My father died eight years ago,' he said abruptly.

'I'm sorry!'

'He was a good man, respected by everyone. It was a huge loss.'

Ellie cursed her own insensitivity, realizing that he had pulled back from her and was trying to control himself. She of all people knew what it was like to lose a parent. Without thinking, she reached for his hand. Neil Harrington's gaze met hers.

Grey-blue eyes under heavy dark eyelashes. Momentarily her hand lay on top of his, before, embarrassed, she pretended to scramble for her napkin. There was an awkward silence between them.

'If you want, I will talk you through the documents and then we can have a look at the paperwork.'

'That would be grand.' She smiled, relieved the tension between them was broken.

He talked slowly, making sure she understood, as he explained about the wide-ranging plans for the street and where her property came into it.

She watched as he tucked into the pie and three roast potatoes with gusto, noticing he had no wedding ring on his finger. Maybe he lived alone and needed a bit of sustenance. The fish in its creamy sauce was delicious, especially when washed down with another glass of the perfect Chablis.

She forced herself to concentrate on what he was saying as he went through how the contract could be structured to be tax-efficient for both parties.

'You will of course have to employ your own legal adviser,' he said.

'Can't you do it for me?'

'Conflict of interest,' he responded.

'I'd like to have you looking after my interest,' she said aloud, suddenly appalled at herself when she realized he was studying her face as if she had two heads.

'I mean someone like you,' she mumbled. 'My mother's solicitor, Tom Muldoon, must be eighty if he's a day and I'm not sure he'd be up to all this.'

Oh God, she was making it worse, she thought, noticing the creases round his eyes as he ate his sticky toffee pudding.

'Did he handle your mother's will?'

'Yes, of course.'

'Then perhaps you should go along to see him. Age really doesn't come into it.'

That was her put back in her box.

'Perhaps I will.'

'But first, how about we take coffee in the lounge? We can spread out the papers there and I'll run through a few things with you. Have you a pen? You could make a few notes about what to ask Tom.'

Sitting in the magnificent red-painted room with its leather couches and comfortable chairs, she felt her head swirling as he began to talk her through paragraphs and clauses. She downed two cups of black coffee in succession in an attempt to sober up quickly so she could focus on his explanations.

'You do understand what I'm saying?'

She nodded, wishing that, like the little black cat back in her shop, she could just curl up on a cushion and sleep. She forced herself to concentrate and began to scribble notes, hoping that she would be able to make sense of them later.

A middle-aged man in an immaculate navy blazer and yellow-patterned cravat approached their table.

'Hello, Neil! Good to see you,' he interrupted. 'I was hoping we'd run into each other.'

Neil politely introduced her to Jerome Casey, the proprietor of Casey Coleman Holdings, the developer who was offering to buy her out.

'This is Miss Matthews.'

She was momentarily taken aback.

'Hope I'm not disturbing anything?' the newcomer asked.

For some absurd reason Ellie began to blush, drawing even more attention to herself.

'No, not at all,' Neil assured him. 'Ellie and I are discussing business. Miss Matthews is one of the proprietors on South Anne Street to whom we have issued contracts. She has very recently inherited a property there.'

'Well, Miss Matthews, you will see we have made a generous offer for what has become essentially in property terms a bit of a backwater. As you can imagine, the redevelopment costs are enormous.'

Ellie had no idea what to say and could see that, under his charming veneer and polished appearance, Jerome Casey was a tough businessman, used to getting his own way.

'Neil, once everything is to Miss Matthews's satisfaction I will leave it in your good hands to conclude negotiations as quickly as possible.'

Neil said nothing.

'Perhaps when you have finished,' suggested the older man, taking his leave of them, 'we could meet in the reading room as there is something I want to discuss with you.'

Neil cast a glance at his watch as Jerome walked away over the plush carpet.

Ellie felt guilty, conscious that she had taken up far too much of his time. 'Neil, listen. We can finish up now. I'll talk to my mother's solicitor like you said.'

'I hope that I have been of some help,' he said, standing up politely as she gathered her handbag and notes. 'But once your Mr Muldoon has looked over the documents perhaps we could meet again soon to get the contracts signed and finalize the property sale. Casey Coleman Holdings are anxious not to have any further delays on this project.'

Ellie took a deep breath. It was important that she remember that to someone like Neil Harrington she was nothing more than a little glitch in his tightly arranged business schedule. Something to be smoothed over so as not to upset a client like the mighty Jerome Casey.

'Thank you for the lovely lunch.'

'All part of the service.' He smiled as he grabbed up his paperwork and briefcase and insisted on walking her to the door.

'I'll let you know what Tom thinks,' Ellie said, reminding herself to be as professional as he was.

'Then I look forward to hearing from you, Miss Matthews.'

Out in the fresh air Ellie took a deep breath, aware of the tall figure in the window still watching her as she turned towards Dawson Street.

Chapter Four

Tom Muldoon, the balding seventy-seven-year-old lawyer, had enjoyed a long friendship with Ellie's mother, and was delighted to be of help to her daughter. He insisted on studying the contract in great detail and reading aloud every line of the legal document for the proposed sale of the shop.

'Everything seems to be in order, Elise,' he said, polishing his gold-rimmed glasses. 'There is a pretty standard six-week closing period when you have to remove all stock and clear shop fittings from the premises. The amount they are offering, while not substantial, is very generous, as the shop is not being sold as a going concern but more as a vacant property.'

'Mr Muldoon, what is your advice?' she asked, honestly.

'This is exactly the question your mother asked me a few months ago,' he admitted, 'and I am afraid I will have to give you the same response as I gave Madeleine. If you are happy to sell, see your little hat shop closed down and hand over the keys to these big property people, then do it. I don't believe you will get a better offer. However, if you want to keep trading and making those beautiful hats of yours that my late wife used to yearn for so much, then you should sit tight. Legally there is nothing they can do. You own the building. They can build their big fancy stores and malls around you while you keep trading, and perhaps some of those new shoppers they attract will find their way to your shop also.'

She listened carefully to what he was saying, asking him, 'What did my mother think?'

'Madeleine was unwell and hadn't the energy to continue,' he explained. 'She didn't want to burden you with the business or force you to stay in Dublin.'

'I do travel overseas a bit with my job,' Ellie admitted, 'but Dublin is my home.'

'Madeleine thought that if the proceeds from the sale of the shop were put on deposit, they would give you a very secure income and provision for the future,' said the old man, staring at her kindly. 'You know she always had your well-being at heart.'

'I know she did,' admitted Ellie, 'but I'm still not sure what to do. My mother loved that shop and I guess I do too.'

'Then take your time,' he advised. 'You young people always think you have to rush into everything. Believe me, time is one thing you still have on your side.'

The elderly solicitor was right. Ellie phoned her boss, John Hyland, a few days later and told him about the shop and asked for a period of unpaid leave of absence.

'Are you sure I can't tempt you with this buying trip to China in a few weeks?'

'I don't want to let you down, John,' she explained reluctantly, 'but I do need the time.'

Ellie decided to clear the shop's remaining stock, for if she wanted to sell the business the shop needed to be empty and if she decided to keep it she would have to make space for a new hat collection. She placed the last of her mother's marvellous creations in an enticing window display with pink and yellow tulips she had purchased from the flower seller at the end of the street.

To untrimmed straws and brims she had added ribbon and flowers and feathers, even edging a boring brown felt with pink ribbon trim. The remaining feathers and flowers had been pulled together in a rather eclectic mix of headpieces in wispy styles that would suit most women. She was pleased with the results and the constant trickle of customers who were happily buying and depleting the remainder.

'Are you selling up?' they asked. 'Moving somewhere else?'

Ellie maintained a sphinx-like smile, not knowing the answer herself.

Francesca Flaherty and her sisters Louisa and Mimi had just completed a shopping assault on Brown Thomas and a number of exclusive boutiques around the Grafton Street area. They were laden down with bags when they spotted the hat-shop window with its gay display of colours and a 'Sale' sign in the window.

'Look at this, Frannie!' squealed Louisa, a leggy blonde sporting a geometric print jacket and co-ordinating skirt. She pulled open the door and immediately tried on a red felt slouch with a black leather trim.

Within a few minutes each of the sisters had added to their purchases with a bargain hat and colourful headpieces.

'Would you have anything to go with this?' asked Francesca, as she eased an exquisite pale pink suit from a Design Centre bag and laid it across the counter.

Ellie shook her head. 'No. Nothing that exact shade, and you should try and match it. It deserves something special.'

'Well, what would you suggest then?'

Before she knew it Ellie found herself chatting about the merits of different styles. The three sisters confided that they were off to the races to support a darling horse called Polly's Party that Francesca's horse-mad husband had recently bought.

'She's a real chestnut cutey with a blaze on her forehead and good form,' admitted Francesca.

'So fingers crossed she'll be lucky,' chorused Louisa and Mimi, 'as we are all putting bets on her.'

'Would you be able to make something to go with this suit, something a little different?' asked Francesca. 'I don't want anything run-of-the-mill. I want a one-off "wow" of a hat.'

Ellie laughed. At least the customer was being honest: she didn't want simplicity or classic low-key elegance.

'Actually, the business is winding down,' she said softly. 'That's why I'm selling off all these.'

'Just our luck,' moaned Louisa, pouting her full lips, 'to find this perfect little shop when it's closing down.'

'But would you be able to make me a hat before you do?' Francesca persisted.

'I'm not sure,' she said, being honest. 'When do you need the hat?'

'In just under two weeks.'

Ellie took a moment to consider. What would the harm be in accepting a last minute commission? Her mother had always trained her not to turn away business and to grab opportunities whenever they came. Besides, she was already getting an idea in her head. Yes, she agreed and immediately began to show Francesca a range of styles that would create the necessary 'wow', though the colour might have to be hand-dyed.

'If Francesca's ordering a hat we will too,' insisted Mimi, 'but of course they must be very different.'

'Though we don't want to clash,' Louisa reminded the others.

Ellie found herself caught up in their excitement as she

enthusiastically agreed and began to show them a range of designs and colours. She watched as the three sisters decided who would wear what. It was another hour and a half of measurements, styles and colours before the trio had finally chosen and in a flurry of high heels and handbags made their farewells.

Upturns, chapeaux, sidesweeps, toppers, down-brim, picture hats, pillboxes, cartwheels – her head was full of millinery styles as she considered the use of straw, sinamay, satin or organza for the three hats she had just been commissioned to make. She had taken down her mother's order book and written in the orders along with a few simple sketches of what each sister required, relieved that the youngest, Mimi, had opted for a simple straw in lilac.

To tell the truth, she experienced a frisson of excitement as she took out the wooden blocks and began to shape some material. When she was small, these blocks were like dolls to her: she used to call them Jacqueline, Anouk, Brigitte and petite Poppy, and play with them while she did her homework and waited for her mother, telling them her secrets. Now she ran her fingers over the round shape of Anouk, feeling the smooth wood, curving edges as she gently fitted a navy sinamay tip and crown, pinning it into shape with great care. As she smoothed the material into position, she experienced a thrill the same as any artist or sculptor would as they began to create a unique piece.

Neil Harrington had left two messages on her phone and she was embarrassed when he arrived early on Thursday morning at the shop.

'I see your sale is going well!' he said. 'Good to start clearing things out!'

Ellie sucked her lip and took a deep breath. 'I spoke to my lawyer as you advised, Neil. My mother always valued his wisdom. He told me to take my time and to think about things.'

'Was he happy with our contract?'

'Oh yes, of course. The contract and terms were fine. The thing is I haven't decided yet about selling. I'm still not sure what to do.'

'If you are looking for a higher offer,' he warned, 'I guarantee my client won't budge.'

'No, that's nothing to do with it,' she insisted. 'I just want to consider all the options, sell up or keep the shop and continue with the hat-making as my mother did.'

She could see he was most put out by her delaying. He no doubt wanted everything signed, sealed and delivered straight away without any complications.

'I understand, Miss Matthews,' he said coldly, 'but I will await your call.'

Francesca Flaherty tried on the curved navy crown with its stunning brim, a huge ripple of pink curving pleats.

'Oh, it's lovely!' she enthused. 'It's so amazing. I can't believe I'm actually getting to wear it.'

Ellie looked from every angle, checking the size was right and that it wouldn't fall forward on her client's head. It had turned out even better than she had imagined, the pink a perfect match for the figure-hugging suit with the detail kick-pleat on the back of the skirt.

Thirty-five-year-old Francesca with her green eyes and flashing smile was certainly going to turn heads at the races.

'I can't wait for Paddy to see my new Lucky Hat.'

Her sisters were equally pleased with theirs. Louisa was wearing a jaunty fuchsia-pink disc with a single black feather trim and Mimi's lilac and cream was the perfect complement to her outfit.

They all thanked her profusely as they paid, Francesca reminding her to put a bet on Polly's Party.

'You might be lucky!'

Ellie laughed, watching the three of them pick up their hatboxes and leave. With every day she was realizing that creating hats and headpieces and simple balanced designs that accentuated a woman's

41

bone structure and lit her face was fun, and something that gave her a unique sense of pleasure and satisfaction.

That evening Ellie phoned her aunt Yvette Renchard in Paris, her instinct telling her to talk to a woman who knew more about the millinery business than anyone she knew.

'Are you OK, *cherie*?' her aunt asked worriedly.

Ellie reassured her before telling her all about the little hat shop and what was happening.

'What do you want to do?' Yvette asked, direct as always. 'Is this little shop just bricks and mortar and money to you or is it more? Your home, your soul, the place you work and feel true to yourself? *Ma petite* Elise, you must decide what makes you happy. You work for someone else, do a good job, come home at night and put your feet up, watch the television and forget about it, or you have your own business, a little shop, you work far too long, sometimes with crazy people who make you want to tear your hair out, but it is yours and you never forget that.'

Ellie smiled: that was exactly how her mother had felt about the shop.

'But what about hats?'

'Hats are hats. Things of beauty to enhance and charm and disguise if need be. You know about hats, you have been making *les jolies chapeaux* since you were small. Madeleine and I used always to say that you had the great combination, "the eye" and "the touch"!'

Ellie giggled, knowing that her aunt was paying her a huge compliment.

'I am a fussy old French woman,' said Yvette candidly, 'but much as I adore you, I cannot make this choice for you.'

'I know,' said Ellie softly, 'I know.'

'But I will come and visit you soon,' promised her aunt.

Ellie sat in the dark afterwards, mind buzzing. She was beginning to wish that somehow the little hat shop on South Anne Street could stay open.

Chapter Five

Francesca Flaherty surveyed the crowds gathering to watch as the racehorses were led round the parade ring. Paddy was deep in conversation with Terry Sullivan, his trainer. She smiled and tried to look relaxed, knowing that this little horse was Paddy's main chance to make some money and get them out of the precarious position their accountant kept on talking about. In her high heels and her pink suit with the magnificent hat that she'd had made by that new young milliner, she felt a little like a racehorse herself.

Before they left for the Curragh racetrack, Paddy had kissed her and told her she was the most beautiful young thing he had ever seen. Looking over at him with his grey hair and intense expression, his mouth taut, Francesca realized how serious he was. She knew that over the past few days he had put a number of very large bets on their horse, spreading the money. Gambling was serious business and not for fools, Paddy had explained to her often enough. It was about working the odds, interpreting the horse's form and having the contacts within the industry, jockeys, apprentices, stable lads. She herself had put a fifty-euro bet on just for luck and had the ticket stashed in her neat navy handbag.

She watched as the other horses were led around. Firelady and Mercurio, both huge brown horses, were nervous of the noise and the crowd. Polly's Party looked smaller and calmer as she tossed her brown mane from side to side. Paddy was right: she was a real cutey. She longed to pet her but Jackie, the stable girl, had told her to wait until after the race was run.

'We don't want anything to spook her.'

Mimi and Louisa appeared back from the champagne bar with their men in tow, giving her a thumbs-up as she posed for a photographer. The pink had been a perfect choice – and the hat! She just loved the way the pink pleats rippled as she moved her head for the camera. Minutes later they left the ring as the horses began the long canter down to the starting line, with Timmy Young, their jockey, in Paddy's orange and black racing colours. Paddy came and slipped his arm around her, Francesca urging him not to worry.

'How can I not worry!' he almost shouted. 'You have no idea how much money is riding on that horse.'

Francesca swallowed hard. There was no need for her husband to be so tetchy with her. It wasn't her fault that Paddy wanted to treat her like a doll and not involve her in any serious aspect of their lives. How could she have any idea of the money involved if he deliberately chose not to tell her!

'Paddy, she's going to win.'

He threw her a despairing look. 'If she doesn't, I'm broke.'

Francesca could see he was serious. For once there was no mask of joking or wisecracks – Paddy was telling the truth.

'Almost every penny we have is riding on her.'

Francesca was speechless. Broke? How could they be? Paddy had always been successful, a winner. Hard work and business savvy had turned his small photocopying business in Talbot Street into a chain of budget computer stores across the country. Following the sale of the company five years ago he'd invested his money, moved it around, bought property, shares, horses, hotels, even a stake in a basement nightclub. She knew that a year ago he'd been refused planning permission for an apartment block on a site he'd paid a fortune for in the hope of doubling his money. But surely he still had his other investments and interests? She knew that her husband, one of life's movers and shakers, had over the years tended to sail close to the wind, trading shares, dabbling in investments, playing the stock market – but to gamble so much on a horse? She couldn't believe it.

Lately there had been letters from the bank, problems with credit cards, even talk about downsizing to a smaller house. She didn't want to think about it. Not today. Paddy would sort things out.

She looked over at Louisa and her sensible husband Matt, a dentist from Celbridge who spent all day fixing up kids' fillings, and Mimi with her big heart stuck on her boyfriend Don. He lectured in Irish studies at Maynooth College and after eight years together he wouldn't even commit to buying her beautiful sister a ring. And there was Paddy, whom she had fallen for the minute she'd laid eyes on him.

They'd met literally by accident, on Camden Street, when Paddy had shifted the automatic gears of his Jaguar into reverse instead of drive and hit her precious green Mini. Shocked and outraged, she'd intended giving him a piece of her mind but had burst out crying instead. Paddy had soothed her and wrapped her in the cosy warmth of his navy cashmere coat. Three months later he had asked her to marry him and replaced the battered Mini with a sleek silver BMW.

The thirty-year gap between them had never mattered, as Paddy was the most interesting man she had ever met. Taking a gamble and marrying him had been the wisest decision she had ever made. Some said she had married him for his money but they were wrong. Even if he hadn't a penny to his name she would still adore him and fancy him like mad.

'Paddy, stop worrying!' she beamed, putting on her widest, prettiest smile. He always loved it when she smiled. 'That little horse, she's a real little goer. And besides, I'm wearing my Lucky Hat.'

'Lucky hat?'

'My new hat! It's lucky, I can feel it.'

The group made their way quickly to the owners' enclosure, watching as in the distance the horses were loaded into the starting gate.

'I'm so nervous,' confided Louisa. 'I don't know if I'll be able to watch the race.'

'We have to watch,' urged Mimi. 'We've to let the horse know we all believe in her. Positive thinking.'

'Hope Polly's OK,' murmured Francesca aloud and silently praying.

They stood together, breaths held, as the starter gun went and the horses took off, Mercurio with his jockey in green in the lead. The pace was fast and four horses clumped together at the front as they came round the bend. Timmy Young was looking for a gap to go through, Firelady huge and strong ahead of him.

Francesca stole a glance at her husband's face. It was grey, every line and wrinkle obvious – he suddenly looked an old man. Their horse was falling behind, Paddy's eyes downcast as her sisters went silent.

'Come on, Polly!' Francesca urged, praying that the small horse could somehow quicken her pace and break through to leave the rest of the field behind her.

Suddenly the mighty Firelady slipped sideways, her jockey using the whip like a madman as Polly took her chance and edged her pretty little nose through, Timmy determined as she challenged Mercurio, the two of them racing neck and neck. Would she ever do it? Francesca could feel her own heart pounding as she held her breath, the crowd roaring around her, Louisa jumping up and down and going almost purple in the face like she used to when she was a kid.

Polly's Party was pushing forward, her small head down, concentrating as she left the bigger horse behind and pounded down to the finishing line, the crowds ecstatic as the complete outsider won. Timmy stood up in his stirrups to give a victory wave to their supporters as he was cheered to the winner's enclosure. Her sisters were like madwomen as Francesca fought to control her tears. Paddy reached for her hand and they fell into each other's arms and laughed and cried and hugged with utter relief. They were both aware of how close they'd been to ruin.

'I told you she'd do it,' smiled Francesca. 'I was wearing my Lucky Hat!'

Chapter Six

Ellie watched as Kim sat peering at the accounts, punching figure after figure into her black calculator with a purposeful look and scribbling notes on a pad. Ellie did her best not to disturb her friend's concentration except when she was asked to pass something or find some important receipt or invoice.

She held her breath as Kim stopped and looked up, pushing her fancy red-rimmed glasses up on to her head.

'Well?' asked Ellie nervously, feeling a pit of dread in her stomach at the thought of impending bad news.

'It's a healthy business,' grinned Kim, ' a good sound investment.'

'Are you sure?'

'Yes. Sales figures and accounts and bank statements don't lie.'

'So does that mean you think I could make it work as a business?'

'Yes!' said Kim firmly. 'Ellie, you've no idea how many people are trying to set up businesses, invest in new companies or get start-ups going. Here you have a very viable business which you already own. It's a great opportunity.'

Ellie almost danced with relief as Kim confirmed her own gut instincts. 'Obviously the redevelopment will have an impact during the building work,' cautioned Kim. 'But once the new shops and hotel open it should attract even more visitors to the street.'

'What are you saying?'

'I'm saying that your mum's shop is a good solid business with existing goodwill. It will need further investment, upgrading – all businesses do – but in the long term it should really be worth it.'

It was exactly what Ellie had hoped to hear and she could feel herself getting more and more excited at the prospect of a little hat shop of her own!

'Kim, what would you do?'

'El, I'm an accountant,' she said seriously. 'I come from a long line of accountants and bankers. But having said that, I'd finance someone like you.'

'Well, I hope the bank agrees with you because that's what I'm going to do! Try to get some money together and invest it in the shop.'

Ellie threw herself back on the couch with a rush of excitement, and a feeling of sheer joy and inner clarity. Her mind was made up, the decision made. The little hat shop was hers and she intended to keep it.

'Oh my God! This is great!' Kim hugged her, getting equally excited.

'Let's open a bottle of wine!' giggled Ellie, jumping up and running to the fridge, 'to celebrate Dublin's finest hat shop!'

'Well, I'm not surprised,' Kim said later, munching cheese and crackers and contemplating the future. 'You've always been great at making things. Remember the skirt I was meant to make for sewing in school and you ended up making it for me?'

'Sssh,' teased Ellie, 'that was our secret, remember? Mrs O'Malley thought you made it yourself and gave you top marks in home economics that year.'

'And that great hat you used to wear in fourth year, made from old wool. Everyone wanted one,' Kim went on, helping herself to another glass of wine.

They sat up talking till long after midnight, planning all kinds of things for number 61. Both agreed that a complete change of style and décor was needed if the faded and rather outdated hat shop was to be considered the chic new millinery establishment Ellie intended it to be.

Within a few days Colm, an architect friend of Fergus's who specialized in shopfitting and offices, had drawn up a rough plan, with an estimate of the costs. It was more than Ellie had budgeted and she wasn't sure she had the courage to go ahead with the project. There was the expensive German lighting, which he considered essential for the job, and exquisite Italian panelling and display systems. A quote from two firms of decorators had also left her reeling, as no matter how many times she calculated and recalculated there was no way that she could afford it. If she wanted to keep the business and have some money to live on, she would definitely need a bank loan.

On Kim's advice she set up a meeting with her local bank manager. Sitting behind his desk in his grey suit, Bill Daly seemed accommodating and encouraging of her artistic and entrepreneurial spirit, saying the bank were always pleased to foster the expansion and upgrading of a small business. She began to relax as he touched the keyboard on his computer and called up her account details.

Ellie had put on her dark suit and most serious expression and pinned her hair up to try to impress upon him that she was a good investment.

'Good location. The shop is just off Grafton Street,' he said drily, studying the screen. 'South Anne Street, where the development is starting.'

'Yes, my mother bought the building years ago. The shop was hers but now I intend to take it over.'

'Indeed,' Mr Dunne soothed. 'I know, it's all on the file.'

She sat back in the leather chair, trying to seem nonchalant as he perused her current and savings accounts and the special account she'd set up for the transfer of her mother's finances.

'And you have left your previous employment?'

'Well, for the present I've taken leave from my job at Hyland's.'

She was beginning to wonder if the man across from her was listening to anything she said as she had already explained fully that she was going to run her own business. All she needed was for him to approve her loan so that she could get on with it. She watched his expression as he touched the keyboard again.

'Now that we have had a chat about it, it's a matter of getting your signature here on this form, then I can pass it on to our lending department. It will take a day or two but they will come back to you as soon as possible with their answer.'

Strange, he didn't sound as enthusiastic as he had at the start of their meeting.

'I thought you would make the decision, Mr Dunne,' said Ellie, confused.

'In some cases I do, but most things go up to the lending department for approval. It's standard practice.'

As she said her polite goodbyes a few minutes later, Ellie noticed on one side of the corridor a big copy of the slick marketing poster for Casey Coleman Holdings's South Anne Street project. The bank was named as one of its lenders. It was no surprise when three days later she got a negative letter from the bank with regard to her loan. They would approve a short-term loan for a much smaller figure or an extension to her overdraft facilities, but not the amount she had hoped for.

Her attempts to get a loan with another bank were equally negative. Ellie was disappointed – but it was strange, the more obstacles she encountered the more determined she was to hang on to the business. The temptation to take the money and run grew less appealing. The little shop with its faded carpets and polished counter and mirrors had too much of a hold on her for her ever seriously to contemplate leaving. Maybe she was crazy to turn down the pile of money she was being offered but she had to listen to her instincts.

'What are you going to do?' Kim asked, sensing Ellie's disappointment when she called over to the apartment after work.

'I'm not going to hand the place over to Casey Coleman Holdings and take the money and walk away,' said Ellie fiercely. 'The bank where I have my savings account will give me a much smaller loan but it's on good terms, so that's something. I can draw it down as I need it.'

'Great,' cheered Kim, 'though people are going to call you a Mad Hatter for turning down all that dosh!'

'Let them,' laughed Ellie.

The fridge was empty of wine so they resorted to the chilled remnants of a bottle of vodka and a carton of orange juice topped up with ice as they considered an alternative strategy.

'The shop doesn't need that much doing, surely?' said Kim encouragingly. 'Nothing major anyway?'

'Colm feels moving the internal wall will help. It's only a partition wall so it shouldn't be too expensive. Then there's stripping, painting, new fittings, new floor, mirrors, chairs,' listed Ellie. 'It's going to cost a fortune and take almost every penny of my savings too. Remember I'm going to be officially unemployed and have no salary.'

'Poor you!' teased Kim. 'Then we'll just have to do it on the cheap.'

'We?'

'Yeah, I'll help you. I know we're not professionals but I'm sure Fergus isn't too bad with a paint-stripper. Mary-Claire is always boasting about that course she did on distressing furniture and Polo is doing bloody art and design so he should have some ideas. We can all give a hand.'

'Are you sure, Kim? It would be at the weekends or after work and I can't really afford to pay people.'

'Plenty of drinks and sandwiches! Anyways, what did you have in mind?'

Ellie couldn't believe it. Kim was willing to give up some of her precious free time after hours from her busy job to help her.

'Actually I'll show you.'

She got up from the couch and rooted around for Colm's plans plus a folder with ideas and rough sketches that she had put together. She produced the pad with her drawings of what the shop could look like, interior and exterior sketches with the shopfront and walls painted in various colours and with slightly different treatments.

'Wow, Ellie! These look great. It's going to be beautiful – the kind of place anyone would want to shop.'

'I'm still not sure what colour scheme to use but definitely nothing too harsh or strident. What would you think of a cream or ivory or primrose yellow?'

'What you need to do is get some of those testers and try them out on the walls to see what works best. That's what Brian and I did when we were doing up our apartment. Remember how the place looked like a rainbow for months?' Kim stopped.

Ellie automatically stroked her friend's arm and shoulder. It had been so hard for Kim when Brian and herself had broken up after two years. Kim had accepted their incompatibility but she still really missed him.

'And I thought if we took up the carpet we could either sand or bleach the floorboards,' continued Ellie.

'Yeah, that awful old grey carpet of your mother's has got to go.'

Ellie hadn't the nerve to tell Kim that the carpet was meant to be a pale blue and it hadn't been changed for twenty years.

'And what about the counters and the shelves?'

That was Ellie's quandary. The fittings had been specially made years ago and were still in perfect condition. It was just that the dark wood managed to make the shop seem cramped and old-fashioned. New fittings would cost a small fortune, something she definitely didn't have.

'I have to think about that,' she admitted.

'Anyway, the little hat shop is here to stay,' said Kim, fixing them a refill.

'Yes,' Ellie said triumphantly. 'It's going to be Hats! Hats! Hats!'

The next day she phoned Neil Harrington. He was away but his secretary gave her an appointment for early on Thursday morning at his offices on Lower Fitzwilliam Street.

Ellie put on a simple pale blue suit for the meeting. Sitting in the waiting room, she noticed the wonderful Louis le Brocquy and Donald Teskey paintings on the wall. They were two of her favourite Irish artists; he was obviously a collector.

'Miss Matthews, he'll see you now.' His middle-aged secretary led her into a beautiful room with magnificently decorated plasterwork on the ceiling, and tall sash windows overlooking the long narrow stretch of garden at the rear of the building.

Neil was wearing a white shirt, tie loose, collar open. Freshly showered and shaved, he looked good.

'So you've come with the contracts.' He smiled, indicating the chair in front of his cherrywood desk.

She glanced nervously at the bookshelves beside him – law books,

Irish law, international law, reams of them. Photos in polished silver frames on his desk, and on the wall more art, Markey Robinson, O'Connor and a Yeats etching.

'Yes, I'm returning them.'

'Your signature needs to be witnessed on each copy,' he said affably, lifting the brown envelope off the desk. 'I can ask Jean to do it if you wish.'

'That won't be necessary,' said Ellie cheerfully.

'Good, then they are signed and witnessed already.' Neil had spread the papers on his desk and was looking at the blank part at the end of the contract. 'But it's not signed?'

'No. I'm not signing it,' she said softly, almost afraid to look at him, 'because I'm not going ahead.'

'But I thought we had agreed, that you understood everything,' he said slowly, 'that it had all been explained to you?'

'I do understand,' she retorted. 'It's just that I'm not selling.'

'Not selling?' His voice rose, annoyed. 'I thought you were going to honour what was discussed and agreed with your mother? Jerome Casey and I were both under the impression that you were prepared to accept our offer.'

'I changed my mind. I'm sorry,' she apologized. 'I didn't mean to mess you around and waste your time. It's just that I don't want to sell the shop.'

'Please, Ellie, reconsider,' he remonstrated, standing up and coming to sit on the corner of the desk in front of her. 'Get some good business advice. My client is making a very generous offer. Think what you could do with the money.'

'I just want to make hats,' she said softly.

'If you are determined to continue with your hat-making, perhaps you could relocate? Find another shop or studio here in the city. I have a number of auctioneering contacts who I'm sure could help.'

Ellie Matthews pulled herself up to her full height of five foot three and stood straight in front of him, dark eyes serious.

'I'm sorry, Neil, but the business is not for sale.'

'I am . . . I mean my clients will be very disappointed,' he said coldly.

'Thank you for all your work and the advice but I've made my decision,' she said, sensing his annoyance at her for wasting his and his clients' time.

'So you are turning down their offer, rejecting it,' he said dispassionately, facing her squarely. 'Was it the money?'

'No.' She shook her head. Avoiding his eyes and the fact that his legs were almost touching her, she concentrated on the framed photo of his father on the desk. 'It's a family business, Neil. My family. I thought you of all people would understand that. I just can't walk away from it.'

'What will you do?'

She smiled for a second, thinking about it.

'I will make hats!' she said defiantly. 'Hundreds of them.'

Trying to control herself and not give in to the absurd shakiness that was threatening to overwhelm her, Ellie reached for her handbag on the floor, flustered and nervous, as Neil tried to step out of her way. Shit . . . her beautiful blue willow-pattern handbag burst open on his carpet, spilling everything she possessed on to the floor under his desk. She scrabbled to pick things up – her mirror, keys, wallet, phone, diary, a notepad, her perfume, two pens and a pink highlighter, a mini toothbrush, dental floss, a hairbrush, hairgrip, cotton buds. Neil Harrington looked appalled as her bright pink lipstick lay exposed on the carpet. He bent down to help her, the two of them almost colliding as they both reached to retrieve it. Grabbing the lipstick, Ellie bumped against him and the bright pink tip smeared his pristine laundered shirt. Ellie searched uselessly for a tissue to wipe it. His hand caught hers.

'It's OK. I'll get it cleaned,' he said politely, surveying the vivid stain.

For one mad minute she pictured herself helping him to unbutton it, discovering if he was really as stuffy and old-fashioned as he seemed.

'I'm sorry, Neil,' she apologized. 'I didn't mean to.'

'It's all right, Ellie, I always keep a spare in the office.'

Embarrassed, she tried to smile, and wished he was ancient like Mr Muldoon instead of actually rather handsome and attractive. She suspected a few items had rolled right under the desk but to get them she would have had to kneel right down on the floor in front of him. No way. They could stay where they were. Hopefully his secretary, Jean, would retrieve them.

'That's it.' She smiled.

The two of them somehow managed to say a polite goodbye, Ellie knowing that despite his good manners he was furious at her change of mind.

Outside on the street she checked her bag. Her raspberry Juicy Tube, her mascara, her lucky old Irish twopenny piece and a Tampax were missing, probably lying somewhere under his desk, at Neil Harrington's feet.

Chapter Seven

A ragged-looking crew of her friends turned up on Saturday morning in old clothes and grungy boots and trainers, ready to work. Fergus, unshaven, with his red hair standing on end and looking particularly rough, was brandishing a paint-stripper. He began to attack the shop walls with it.

'Keep out of the way!' he warned as he swung round and began to strip away the layers of blue paint. Over the next few hours they all worked like crazy stripping the old paper and paint until there wasn't a hint of blue anywhere.

'What we need to do now,' suggested Polo aka Peter O'Leary, a friend she had got to know in art college, 'is put up lining paper, so the walls will be good and even before we paint them. That's what my da always does.'

Mary-Claire, the sweetest girl with a sexy husky voice and cropped hair, who'd hung around with herself and Kim and done daily battle with the nuns over a tattooed shoulder and a pierced nose, ending up as one of the brightest copywriters in a top Dublin advertising agency, was dispatched immediately to the nearest DIY shop down in Capel Street, with Polo going along to make sure she got the right thing and enough paste.

In their absence Fergus, Kim and Ellie got to grips with the ancient carpet.

It was thick with dust despite all the hoovering, and was almost stuck to the floor. 'Dump it,' ordered Kim as they hacked strips and chunks of it away. To Ellie's joy, underneath were almost perfect floorboards.

'They're just beautiful!' said Kim admiringly as they bundled the carpet into the skip they'd hired.

'A brush and a good hoover first,' declared Ellie, trying not to cough as she set to straight away, clearing everything up as an exhausted Kim and Fergus declared an immediate lunch break.

They were studying the floorboards and demolishing thick turkey and stuffing sandwiches when the others returned.

'A good sanding and a few coats of varnish and that floor will be like new,' said Polo knowledgeably. 'The old man did ours at home and made a grand job of them.'

Ellie couldn't imagine Mr O'Leary, a usually fastidious insurance manager, suddenly becoming such a do-it-yourself expert.

'When did he start all this?' quizzed Fergus.

'Well, the old dear has been on at him for years, but since he's retired and people were going on at him about having a hobby he decided to have a go. Did an apartment in Sutton last week. I could ask him to have a look at your boards, El, if you wanted. I'm sure he'd do the job for you.'

Ellie felt like hugging Polo for even considering asking his father.

She wasn't sure about bleaching the floorboards or whitening them. With the dirt and dust from the street, they'd probably look filthy in no time. But the natural wood colour could make the shop warm and more spacious-looking. Yes, sanding and varnishing them to show off the quality and character of the wood was best. Fingers crossed that Mr O'Leary would agree.

They worked until it was dark, peeling away what was left of her mother's imprint on the shop until they had a blank canvas and were ready to start over again.

'What about the colour? Have you decided yet?' prodded Mary-Claire, gazing at the spread of pastel shades along the wall behind the counter.

Ellie nodded. 'Yeah! It's going to be a pale primrose yellow – soft but warm. What do you think?'

They all gathered round the sample.

'I like it,' Kim declared loyally.

'Bit girlie if you ask me!' joked Fergus, before she took a swipe at him with a paintbrush.

'I think it will work well,' mused Mary-Claire, 'and reflect more light.'

Polo nodded as if he was an expert. 'What about all your fittings?'

'New ones cost an absolute fortune. I can't afford to change them, I told you.'

'Well, you can't leave them the way they are,' insisted Mary-Claire. 'It will take away from everything, dominate the space.'

'You've got to do something with the counter and display shelves.'

'With the shelves you could remove the middle one and just have a top and bottom, which might be more dramatic,' suggested Polo. 'It's lovely wood so it would be a shame to just dump it.'

'What if we painted it?' suggested Mary-Claire. 'I know it's sinful to paint such beautiful wood, but if we don't it will only end up getting thrown into a skip. What do you think, Ellie?'

Ellie tried to imagine the counter in a soft white or pale wood colour and knew immediately that it would work better with what she planned.

'Yes. I agree.'

Before she could change her mind, Mary-Claire and Polo had decided that they would tackle the job, promising that in a few weeks she wouldn't know the place.

Six weeks later Ellie twirled round her premises. She felt like pinching herself as number 61 looked totally different from what it had been. She had taken Colm's advice and gone with the German lighting. It had transformed the place. She had also reluctantly followed his suggestion of moving a partition wall to make the front of the shop slightly bigger, although she had lost space in the workroom. A wall-to-wall workbench had been built against the back of the new wall. The sad, tired look of an old hat shop had disappeared and been replaced with a pale yellow shopfront that brightened up the whole street. A friend of Polo's who specialized in signage had written *Ellie Matthews – Milliner* in a looping black scroll above the doorway. The floorboards looked almost like new and were perfect against the colour of the walls and the hand-painted, slightly distressed-looking counter and display shelves. The tiles in the doorway were shining and through the sparkling glass she imagined her hats enticingly placed in the shop window to attract the customers' attention. The pretty striped canopy added a final touch.

Mary-Claire, using all her advertising contacts in magazines and newspapers, had insisted on doing all the publicity to help launch the chic little hat shop.

'Ellie, I promise, everyone is dying with curiosity. Of course they'll come!'

Tomorrow there was the official opening with fashion journalists and magazine editors invited plus some of the social diary journalists. Many of her mother's regular customers were coming, and a few of her own: Francesca Flaherty and her sisters and nice Mrs Cassidy and her two daughters. There'd be champagne and canapés and she was thrilled that Dominic Dunne, one of the country's leading designers and a friend of her mother's, had agreed to do the opening.

Kim had begged her to ban the black cat, Minouche, from the shop.

'The thing is half wild,' she warned, 'and God knows what dirt or diseases it's carrying.'

Ellie looked at the green eyes and little black nose and saw that Minouche was determined to come in and explore its new surroundings. She ignored her friends and the cat curled itself up in its usual spot under the window. As she looked around her she realized that the shop was perfect, just as she had pictured it a hundred times over in her mind. Now all she had to do was make and sell enough hats to keep the business going.

'Pasta for everyone!' she offered, leading the way to the Italian restaurant up the street after the grand preview for her friends. She was delighted that Colm and Mr and Mrs O'Leary had joined them.

'It's my treat!' she insisted as they ordered huge bowls of creamy tortellini carbonara and spicy chicken and tagliatelle. Fergus opened two bottles of Chianti to go with them.

'I just don't know how to thank you enough for all the work you did.'

'Go on, try,' urged Fergus. 'Try.'

Sometimes she could kill him for the way he wound her up, but thinking of all his effort and hard work over the past few weekends she chose to kiss him instead.

'You are the best friends in the world and I don't know what I would have done without you all over these past few months,' she said, overwhelmed. 'You've been so good to me.'

She could see that Kim was trying to contain her emotions too.

'But helping me to fix up the shop so that I can reopen it – well, that's the best ever. So thank you, and Polo, thank you to you and your dad for doing the floor.'

'No problem, my dear,' responded Mick O'Leary, who truth to tell was beginning to enjoy this new career he'd fallen into.

'And here's to Ellie and her beautiful new shop,' interrupted Kim, raising her glass to toast her. 'From tomorrow the whole of Dublin will be flocking to her to buy their hats.'

'I do hope so,' said Ellie as she glanced round the table, choked up by the goodness of these people whom she was lucky enough to be able to call friends and who had insisted on not charging her for all their hard work and time.

'To the shop,' they all chorused. 'Ellie's hat shop!'

Chapter Eight

Creating her first collection of hats was a daunting prospect but a trip to the millinery wholesaler's in South William Street and a delivery of essential materials from the Milliner Warehouse in London and Beauvoir's in Paris had ensured that she had everything she needed to begin. Despite the shop renovations and the sanding and the wiring of the new lighting, she had worked night and day to design and make hats that she hoped women would consider both irresistible and delicious.

The city was awash with cherry and apple blossom, the country-side and gardens covered with white hawthorn blooms and with every breeze the drifting petals covered the pavements and paths. She herself was nervous, adrenalin flowing as she covered reams of white paper with sketches and rough drawings of what she wanted. A Japanese print of a cherry tree on her mother's noticeboard – thin trunk and slightly curved branches reaching skywards, its starkness softened by a spray of blossom – inspired her, made her giddy with excitement, as she too strove like the unknown Japanese artist to create simple shapes, black, white, red, jade green and a pale pink. She put each design up on the block, taking her time, as the materials stretched and developed the shapes and curves and lines she wanted. She held her breath as she took them off. Checking how each would sit on a head, she added brims to some and painstakingly worked with fine wire and silk to fashion each individual petal of blossom, perfect orbs of white and pink and black and a creamy rose to contrast with and soften the crowns and brims. Each hat was different, and the eight headpieces with their simple wraparound wire-covered shapes that clung neatly to the head, all with a bold dash of colour, had also somehow managed to retain the Japanese influence that had inspired them. Overcome with sheer joy as she finished her 'White Blossom' collection, knowing that each hat was as individual as she could make it, Ellie was nonetheless filled with trepidation as she put five of the pieces on hatstands in the window.

The opening of the little hat shop was a great success. The place was packed out with well-wishers, wine and champagne flowing as journalists and fashion stylists chatted and good-naturedly admired her work. Two of Ireland's newer designers vowed to remember her when they were showing their next collection. Her ears were red with all the praise and flattery bestowed by Dominic Dunne on her work and the refreshing new look of the hat shop perched on the corner of South Anne Street.

'I can't thank you enough,' she said afterwards, 'for all your kind words and for taking the time to come tonight and do the opening.'

'Ellie, it's a pleasure and the very least that I could do,' he said, kissing her cheek. 'I just wish Madeleine was here with us both to enjoy it.'

'Maybe in some way she is,' whispered Ellie, conscious of a reassuring sense of her mother's presence at this time when she needed it most.

It wasn't a large collection – but Ellie had put her own stamp on each piece. The hats were original, beautiful, each a small, delicious individual work of art. Seeing the admiring reaction of her guests and the photographers pleased her enormously.

'Ellie, everything is gorgeous enough to tempt anyone to spend a fortune,' declared Francesca Flaherty loyally as her husband Paddy insisted on buying his lovely wife the most expensive hat in the place, saying the glinting green silk matched her eyes.

Ellie was brimming with happiness as people admired her work and Kim made sure she mingled with everyone. Some strange temptation had made her send Neil Harrington an invitation. She wasn't surprised he didn't show, but had to admit to being disappointed. It was daft, for she didn't need his approval.

The chic little shop on South Anne Street quickly attracted attention as the bright window displays of colourful hats and unusual head-pieces enticed women of all ages to step inside. The 'Blossom' hats were greatly admired and sold quickly. Variations on them were ordered. A glowing mention in the weekend section of the *Irish Times* helped, as did the use of two of her hats in a fashion shoot for *Image* magazine.

The young milliner concentrated much of her efforts on creating just the right atmosphere, for the purchase of a hat was such a personal affair. There were mirrors and good bright light and two re-covered comfortable chairs. A large glass vase was constantly filled with fresh flowers and greenery, which added to the gaiety of the place, and outside two cream-painted stone urns of violets welcomed customers as they stepped through the door. Clutter was kept to the minimum, as it was her hats that she wanted people to notice.

Interiors were one thing but providing a unique collection of hats that appealed to a certain type of customer was essential. Ellie decided also to create a fun range of gay hats in strong colours, yellow, pink, red and orange, using tulip-print material that she had ordered in from Amsterdam, and another based on simple straws with big print bows and dancing yellow, orange and red silk flowers.

Women of all ages loved them and in no time Ellie found her order book beginning to swell.

Standing outside the doorway of number 61 and seeing her name written above it, Ellie experienced a sense of joy unlike anything she had ever known. She was proud of the shop and proud of following in her mother's footsteps and continuing the tradition of hat-making.

'You've done a great job, Ellie. You've transformed the place,' said Sissy Kavanagh, who, together with her sister, Kitty, ran the small newsagent's along the street. 'You make the rest of us look dowdy.'

David Hannah and his wife, who ran the jeweller's down near the corner, were also impressed.

'You must have spent a fortune!'

'Not as much as you'd think,' she confided. 'I didn't have that type of money, just a small loan. But I decided to start afresh. Everything was cleared out and I expanded the shop's floor space a bit and redesigned my workroom. The fancy lighting makes a difference too.'

Some of the older shopowners said nothing as they inspected the place, for all of them were nervous of the huge construction project that was due to begin in a few weeks' time. Many feared that, like the other small businesses, they too would have to close down.

Harry Regan, who ran the shoe shop across the street, admitted he was also thinking of selling up.

'Couldn't you just do something similar to what I've done?'

'Ellie, girl, it's not worth it. I'm too old and none of my kids are interested in the business.' He shook his head. 'And don't tell me that when that fancy shopping gallery opens across the street there won't be an expensive shoe shop or two in there. No, it's better to take the money and go now, while I have the chance. The shop's been good to me.'

Ellie would be sad to see him close down, as he had been a good friend to her mother over the years.

'Seeing your shop, though, does my heart good,' he added, looking around him. 'It reinvigorates the street. Makes me remember what it was like when we all first moved in. Polished brass and glass and canopies – a bit of style, that's what the place always had.'

'It's such a lovely street,' agreed Ellie, 'I couldn't imagine the shop anywhere else.'

Chapter Nine

Regularly on her way to work Ellie stopped at Molly Ryan's flower stall on the corner of Harry Street and Grafton Street to buy fresh flowers for the shop. She'd known Molly since she was a little girl and enjoyed the chat as she considered two perfect long-stemmed cream lilies for the window.

'Going to rain,' remarked Molly. Plagued with rheumatism and, with the exception of a large green brolly, constantly exposed to the elements, the flower seller was always conscious of the weather. 'Downpour, maybe.'

Ellie looked up at the darkening sky and wished that she had brought an umbrella.

'How's the hat business?' she asked as Ellie paid her and she wrapped bunches of lilac in paper and lifted the lilies from their holder.

'Getting better. I think people are beginning to get to know where I am.'

'Remember Rome wasn't built in a day,' joked Molly. 'I'm

forty-five years here on this street corner and sure half of them don't even know my name.'

Ellie didn't envy the older woman as every morning she went to the early flower markets to buy her supplies for the day, before setting up her stall. The colours and scents of the huge array of seasonal blooms from all over the world were a major attraction in the busy shopping street and Molly was as good a businesswoman as you could meet.

'I'd better dash,' Ellie excused herself, keeping hold of her flowers.

She'd walked only a few yards when the heavens opened and the rain began to pour down, soaking her hair and shoes.

'Stand in under my umbrella and I'll walk you down the street,' offered a familiar voice.

She glanced up from under streeling hair, wondering why Neil Harrington was being such a Galahad.

'I'm going down this way anyway,' he responded as if reading her mind.

She relaxed, falling into step with him, realizing that he was one of those rather old-fashioned men who were naturally polite and helpful. He'd probably been a boy scout in his time and liked helping old ladies and damsels in distress. She wondered if he considered her a damsel in distress.

'Ellie!' He interrupted her thoughts, the umbrella above their heads. 'We're here.'

He had come to a standstill outside the shop. She stood there stupidly rummaging for her keys in her handbag while trying to manage the flowers.

'Here, let me.'

He was doing it again. Taking the flowers off her and holding the big black umbrella while she rooted! A packet of mints, a notepad, her wallet, two feathers. Phew! She had found her keys.

'Thank you,' she said, pushing the door open.

He kept standing there.

'Would you like to see the shop?' she offered, awkward. 'It's been all painted and done up.'

He glanced over her shoulder and around the small space.

'I'm sorry I missed your opening.'

'I didn't really expect you to come,' she blurted out without thinking.

'I was in court all day,' he explained. 'We ran late.'

'Oh.' She didn't know what to say. She found herself studying his watchstrap and the way dark hairs ran down lightly near his wrist.

'You could have a cup of coffee, tea, if you'd like,' she suggested, wondering why she was making such an eejit of herself, inviting him to sit down and lecture her on how foolish she'd been.

'I'm sorry, I have a meeting,' he said, stepping back towards the street. 'And I can't be late.'

He'd rebuffed her. He hadn't even bothered to look at all the work she'd carried out or noticed the hats or anything.

'You're still annoyed with me.'

He didn't answer for a minute.

'Obviously I had misread the situation about this property.'

'I just changed my mind, Neil. That's all.'

'A client is always free to do what they please,' he said coldly. 'Obviously Mr Casey was slightly put out we were unable to reach a suitable agreement, but that's business.'

An awkward silence loomed between them as he handed her the flowers.

'They're lovely, aren't they!' she prattled on. 'The shop needs flowers.'

'It all looks very pretty,' he said, before turning with his umbrella and disappearing in the rain.

Pretty! Ellie didn't know if he was being complimentary or

71

facetious or just polite. Why had she wanted him to say it looked great, to notice the work she'd done? He simply wasn't interested in the shop or her. He plainly considered she'd wasted his time. Anyway she didn't need his opinions. Guys like Neil Harrington were self-centred chauvinists who thought they were superior to everyone else and she wasn't going to waste another second of her precious time thinking of him.

Chapter Ten

Ellie was working late, stitching the band on a particularly difficult piece of fabric, when she noticed that the lights in the old dance hall had gone off and that it was suddenly silent. She had been getting used to the sounds of guitars and drums and saxophones from the bands that played in the hall. It had closed down years ago and would form the nucleus for the massive Casey Coleman development but in the meantime it was serving as a temporary concert venue and a rehearsal space for Dublin's legions of would-be U2 rock bands. She'd heard it was due to be demolished in a week or two. A few minutes later someone began knocking frantically on the shop door. Nervous, she got up from the stool and put down her work to peer outside. A stranger was banging on her freshly painted door. There wasn't another sinner in the street and she opened it only a fraction, keeping the new chain on the door.

'Sorry to disturb you, but I wondered if you might have a fuse.'

'A fuse?'

'Yeah,' he shouted through the door. 'We've blown the fuses across the road. Would you have a spare?'

She was sure that there was a box of new fuses somewhere. The lighting guy or the electrician had left them.

'I think I have some,' she said as she opened the door wider. 'I'll just check.'

Ellie could see longish hair and piercing blue eyes the same colour as the denim shirt he was wearing under his leather jacket. He didn't look too dangerous, she thought as she opened the door a fraction further, still leaving the chain on.

'Sorry to come hounding you like this at night, but I noticed your lights from across the street,' he explained. 'The lead guitar blew one of the big amps and I'm not sure what happened then. We can't find any fuses in the dark over there and the Centra up the street and the newsagent's have shut. The band were just rehearsing.'

'Band?'

'Yeah, Rothko.'

'Hold on and I'll just look for those fuses.' She tried to think where they were. Maybe near the fuse box at the back of the shop or where the torch and fire extinguisher were stored. A few seconds later she'd found the packet of fuses and took out three. Holding them in her hand, she realized that she would have to unlatch the door to pass them to him.

He sensed her apprehension.

'I hope I didn't scare you,' he apologized. 'I didn't mean to.'

'It's all right. Anyways here's a few fuses.'

'You're a life-saver, thanks. I'll drop you back some new ones tomorrow.'

'It's OK. Don't worry.' She blushed, realizing that one of the best-looking guys she'd ever spoken to was only inches from her.

He smiled at her as he dropped the fuses into his pocket. 'Thanks.'

A few minutes later the light and guitar sounds and drumming resumed as Ellie tried to concentrate on finishing the hat. Deciding to call it a night half an hour later, she shut up shop.

It was a lunchtime when she bumped into him next. She was queuing for a sandwich in O'Brien's and he was coming out of it, holding a caffè latte and a sandwich in one hand.

'Our saving grace.' He smiled, recognizing her.

'It's Ellie actually,' she informed him, hoping that he would somehow remember her name.

'Like above the shop,' he said with a twinkle in his eye, as she reddened. She was mortified.

'And I'm Rory, by the way, Rory Dunne.'

Introductions over and standing there in front of him she couldn't help but notice that he was much taller than her and had a very slight dimple in his right cheek. Stop it, she told herself.

'Just going to take a break, if you care to join me.'

'I have to wait for my sandwich.'

'Then I'll wait too.'

She cursed herself for ordering a messy tuna and onion on rye but it was too late to change her order and she would just have to eat it in front of him. She watched as the girl wrapped it and gave her change.

'Well, we can head back to the bowels of the old hall and the wail of two untuned guitars played by a bunch of desperadoes without a musical note in their souls, or take a walk up to the park.'

She laughed. 'The park please.'

They fell into step side by side, chatting easily as they crossed the busy road, and managed to find an empty park bench beside the lake to sit on.

'Always love those ducks,' grinned Rory. 'Talk a lot of sense, so they do.'

Ellie was amused, for she had come to the same conclusion long

75

ago that the ducks in St Stephen's Green knew far more about life and what matters than they quacked on.

She asked him about his band as she tried to eat her tuna sandwich in some kind of gracious way.

'I'm not in a band,' he protested. 'I'm their big bad manager.'

He sounded interesting, she thought.

'I used to sing till I was about fourteen but I literally woke up one morning and my voice was gone.'

'Gone?'

'Yep, I got height and hair and hormones overnight but my singing voice was kaput, truly awful and broken. There was my singing career down the tubes before it even got started. So I gathered myself together and since I could play a few notes on the old man's guitar I reckoned I'd find another way into the music business – I didn't realize Dublin was full to bursting with would-be Rory Gallaghers and Edges, so I gave that up too. Managing bands was the obvious and the last resort.'

She watched as he ate his sliced beef and mustard sandwich, praying that the tuna sandwich on her lap wouldn't fall all over the place as she discreetly tried to nibble it. 'And do you like it?'

'Some days the guys drive me crazy when they don't turn up, or forget where they are meant to be. They can be like a load of big babies that need serious handling, but most of the time it's great.

'What about you?' he quizzed, turning his gaze on her. 'How long have you been working in the hat shop?'

'The shop has been in the family for years. It was my mother's but she passed away a while ago and for some mad reason I decided to stay on and run it.'

'Good for you!'

'I'm not sure it was the wisest of decisions but I do love it.'

'We all have to take risks,' he said, fixing her with his blue eyes. 'That's what makes life interesting.'

Ellie swallowed hard, knowing that sitting here talking to an utter stranger over an al fresco lunch in the sunshine was risky.

'I'd better get back,' she apologized, standing up.

'Why don't you stay longer, chill out for the afternoon?'

'No, I can't,' she said, seriously tempted. 'I've someone collecting a hat at two thirty.'

'Well, I guess I'll hang out here with the ducks for another hour, but if you're free on Friday night the guys are doing a gig and you're welcome to come along.'

'Where?'

'Across the street. It'll probably be the last in good old McGonagle's,' he admitted as he tossed a crust of bread into the lake. 'Would you like to come?'

Walking back down Dawson Street a few minutes later with a smile plastered all over her face, Ellie could scarcely believe that she had accepted his invitation and was going to spend Friday night with Rory Dunne and Rothko.

Chapter Eleven

Ellie pulled on a pair of figure-hugging denim jeans, her black leather boots and a black T-shirt, dabbing expensive perfume on her pulse points. She was nervous about meeting Rory. It had been an age since she'd gone on a date. He seemed self-assured and easy to talk to, and the fact that he was five foot ten and good-looking and reminded her of Ewan McGregor was even better. She'd washed her hair and was glad that she had made the effort to chase home to the flat after work on Friday night to change.

Rory had said that he'd put her on the guest list and seeing the line of fans queuing along the street she walked past them and up to the door. They seemed a good-natured crowd out for a fun night, some wearing Rothko T-shirts. It reminded her of her student days when she had spent two years traipsing around after a guitar player called Steve, who had almost broken her heart. The last she'd heard of him he was married and working as a web designer in Cork.

Inside it was crowded and dark and she hadn't a clue where Rory might be. Hopefully he would find her, she thought as she surveyed the old dance hall. The patrons were for the most part male with long hair, cropped hair or dyed hair, dressed in leather and denim. A few females tottered around in killer heels, shaking their heads in time to the rhythm of the guitarist on stage as they greeted those around them. Ellie suddenly felt old and alone as she pushed towards the stage. She was mad not to be following her normal Friday night routine of drinks with Fergus and Mary-Claire and Kim.

'Hey, Ellie!' called Rory. 'I was looking for you. I told the guy on the door to give me a shout when you arrived.'

He was standing in front of her looking suitably dishevelled in a Rothko T-shirt and a pair of jeans. Ellie, surprised when he brushed his lips against hers, resisted the urge to kiss him back, blushing when she saw the answering grin on his face. He had got the picture – they liked each other.

'Come on and I'll get you a drink. The guys will be on in about twenty minutes. Jules is just the warm-up act.'

She followed him to the bar and sat beside him as he ordered two chilled beers. The band playing weren't bad and Rory filled her in about Rothko.

'The band's starting to get a few plays of this new album, get noticed. They've got a loyal fan base and they're building on it,' he boasted. 'I'll bring you to meet the guys backstage afterwards, OK?'

Rory introduced her to two other couples standing near them and a fantastic-looking girl with long blond hair almost to her waist.

'This is Jen. She's Sean the lead singer's lady.'

Ellie was left chatting with Jen while Rory ran backstage to check all was under control with the band. He reappeared at her side and slipped his arm round her waist.

Minutes later the crowd broke into a roar of welcome as the band strode on stage and plugged in their guitars. The sound reverberated round the hall as everyone went wild and surged forward.

Down low in her stomach Ellie could feel the bass guitar's notes resonate as Rothko launched into 'Cloud Chasing', the lead singer stepping forward, his dark hair swinging over his face as he began. The next hour and a half were great, the band different from others she'd seen. Ellie joined in with the surging mass around her, jumping up and down, heart pumping, sweating and calling for more until the band wound down and played their last song, 'Profusion'. She joined in the applause, for they were a great bunch of guys playing all their own songs.

A final encore of 'Dedicated' nearly brought the house down and Ellie had to grab hold of Rory's arm to avoid being pitched forward.

'Pretty good,' Rory announced proudly, as people congratulated him on the band's performance.

'They're amazing! Thanks for giving me the chance to see them play.'

'Always great to see a band when they are on the way up and just about to break through.'

As the crowd began to disperse, he pulled her along the edge of the stage and in through the stage door. The bouncer stepped back out of their way. Ellie was suddenly a little nervous as Rory gave her a reassuring squeeze of his fingers.

The backstage room was packed. Two of the band were drinking pints of beer while Sean and Ed, the lead guitarist, made do with spring water. Sean, stripped to the waist and with a towel flung over his shoulder, called Rory over immediately.

'I spotted Declan in the audience, he said he wants to talk to you later.'

'Sure, I'll sort it out. Don't worry. You did great – he'll have seen that tonight so it puts us in a way better position.'

Over the next hour Ellie chatted with a selection of wives, girlfriends, proud parents and a wild red-haired grandmother who kept telling her what a wonderful boy young Sean had been. They were a nice bunch of guys. Ed and Cian and Sean and the drummer Bren had been so welcoming to her that when Rory suggested she join them all in the Thai restaurant on George's Street for supper she agreed to go along. They got a table for twenty and Ellie tried to keep her composure when she was introduced to Declan O'Hagan, the guy from the record company, as Rory's new girlfriend.

She had a great laugh listening to stories of four skinny teenagers who drove their parents and neighbours crazy in the leafy suburbs of Rathfarnham playing loud music in the garage, and released their first single when they were still at school.

'It was bloody awful,' admitted Ed.

'Your aunt Mary bought forty copies and gave them to all the cousins and friends that Christmas,' Peggy Dockrell reminded him.

'Tell Rory we'll have to get Aunt Mary out on the road again!' joked Bren.

Afterwards they went on to the River Club and listened to a little jazz and soul till three o'clock, when she and Rory said their good-byes and took a taxi to her apartment in Hatch Street. She fumbled in her bag for the key and hoped that Rory wouldn't expect her to invite him in. It wasn't that she didn't fancy him, it was just that she didn't want to rush things.

'It's OK, El. I understand. I'm just the stranger from the park!' he joked, kissing the tip of her nose.

'I don't want you to be a stranger,' she whispered. 'I really don't.'

'Then let's solve that one,' he said.

Unperturbed, he pulled her towards him. His kissing was slow and deep and Ellie began to feel her resolve melt.

'Well, we're not strangers any more,' he teased, reaching to kiss her again.

Ellie wound her hands around his neck, up through the back of his hair. It would be so easy just to turn the key, invite him in, but she knew she wasn't ready yet to be that close to him.

She pulled away, staring at his face, the stubble on his chin, his blue eyes.

'You know you're beautiful, Ellie, different from the other girls I meet.' He traced her mouth slowly with his finger. 'There's no rush.'

She held her breath, waiting.

'I hope you will let me take you out again. Maybe next time on our own!'

'Yes, please,' she whispered, touching his face.

'I'll phone you tomorrow,' he promised, finally leaving.

A second later, standing inside the heavy front door, Ellie was tempted to run back out and grab him.

Chapter Twelve

Mo Brady was not a hat person, or a bag person, or a suit person or even a shoe person, but she was determined to do her level best to make the people of Dublin proud of their newly elected Lady Mayor. Looking at her own round face, square body and short, stumpy legs, she had to admit that she was built like an army tank rather than the city's glamorous first citizen, the Lady Mayor of Dublin. But one thing she did have was a big heart and the chain of office round her neck was worn with a constant pride in the honour of being chosen to serve the citizens of the town she loved so well. At times it hung heavy, for not only did the chain bestow the responsibility of her office and the duty to represent every man, woman and child in the huge catchment area of one of Europe's oldest cities but it also demanded that she dress and look the part, and attend more functions than she had ever dreamed humanly possible.

She stood in front of the long gilt mirror of the Lord Mayor's bedroom, accepting that her normal uniform of tracksuits, jeans, baggy T-shirts and fluffy woollen cardigans was a thing of the past.

Her old wardrobe was banished to the back of her cupboard, for now she would have to stuff her wide feet and fallen arches into high heels, buy some designer suits and dresses and a good heavy coat that would withstand all weathers, and a hat or two.

Mo still remembered standing outside the council's huge chambers, knowing that the vote of every single council member was important if she had any hope of being elected. She was the only female candidate and knew that to win the support of some of the council's old male stalwarts would be nigh impossible: they still held the view that women were meant to make huge pots of tea and hand round sandwiches instead of getting themselves involved in the rough and tumble of the city's politics. She had looked round the table at the circle of impassive faces, trying to guess which way some of them would jump. The party faithful would support Tom Leary. She could tell they considered him the front runner for the post of Dublin's new Lord Mayor, but she had the support of the smaller parties. Whether that was enough she couldn't tell.

She had held her breath, ready to go back inside to the fray as the votes were counted. Bill Byrne and Nuala Lawless, two other independent councillors, had whispered 'Good Luck!' as she took her seat and waited.

Mo cursed under her breath as, turning, she almost tumbled over the mountain of boxes on the floor. She would have blamed somebody else, only she knew that she had single-handedly packed them all herself. She guessed moving house and office all at the same time was enough to drive anyone a little crazy.

Joe and the kids had gone off to Morelli's for a bit of sustenance while she tried to sort everything out.

She sat down for a minute to take a breather, glad of the peace and quiet as she looked around the beautifully decorated Lord Mayor's quarters. With three bedrooms and private sitting room and kitchen, it was a world apart from the small terraced council house where she had spent her whole married life. From the moment she had stepped under the Mansion House's impressive glass-canopied entrance that bore the city coat of arms, through the blue door and into the hall with its portrait of Daniel O'Connell, Ireland's famous liberator, and the oak bar with its portraits of all her predecessors, Mo had realized how privileged she was to have been chosen to serve for the next year as Lady Mayor of Dublin. She still hadn't got used to the idea, that the city's councillors had actually put her forward for the post and elected her. She had won, and it was an honour she had never even dreamed of.

Joe and herself had been stunned by the news. After sitting up for hours night after night talking it over, they had made the momentous decision to move their family into the Mansion House on Dawson Street, right in the heart of the city.

'I want this job to be more than just an office, Joe. I want to be a mayor for the whole of Dublin and to have you and the kids be part of it.'

'Are you sure, Mo?' asked her husband of twenty years, who ran a small electrical contracting business.

'Of course I'm sure.'

'Mammy, are we really moving into the big Lord Mayor's house?' Lisa had screamed, so excited her face got red as she twisted her long brown hair.

'Do we have to change schools?' demanded sixteen-year-old Jessie.

'No, pet, you'll all still be staying in your old schools. Promise.'

'Can my friends still come and play in that big house?' worried thirteen-year-old Paul.

'Of course they can,' she reassured him, swooping her son into her arms.

That had been almost a month ago, a whirlwind month of playing politics, of filling in papers and permissions as she arranged for the Mansion House once more to become a family home, not just a place for official ceremonies and functions. The previous Lord Mayor, a retiring councillor, had handed over his chain of office at a ceremony in Dublin Castle and she had been sworn in as the city's new Lady Mayor. I must be mad, thought Mo as she surveyed the mess all around her. It was crazy to leave my home and neighbourhood.

The neighbourhood was where it had all started. She had never intended getting involved in local politics but had been dragged into it by default when a stolen car had driven into the estate at high speed and ploughed into a group of kids. They had made the simple mistake of playing rounders till after dusk on a summer's evening instead of sitting at home watching TV. She could still see the children in the road, injured, scattered like pins in a bowling alley, after three young fellahs not much older than themselves and high on alcohol and drugs had lost control of the speeding vehicle. Guards and ambulances and medics and journalists had all appeared and the estate was suddenly filled with strangers issuing statements about the tragic event. Little Robbie Breen, only ten years old, had died that night on the road, and young Tara Kenny had ended up having part of her leg amputated. Sometimes on summer evenings she imagined she could still hear the screams of the kids of Carney Close, her own daughter Lisa so shocked that she refused to walk past the spot on her own for a year and still had nightmares of standing outside the Kennys' house waiting for the ball to bounce as the sun went down. Her neighbour Mary Breen, overwhelmed with grief at her son's death, had landed in St Pat's with a breakdown two months after the trial. The journalists and Guards and do-gooders had by then all disappeared, leaving the people of the estate to fend for themselves once again.

Incensed, Mo had spoken out, determined something should be done for all the kids in the area. She had set about starting up the

Carney and Riverhill Kids' Project, turning the empty old shoe factory into a place filled with activities and fun for the young people of the estates to go to after school, at night, on weekends, and during the long summer holidays. There were discos and a cookery club, guitar lessons, outings, football and rounders, drama and a choir. The kids and parents had flocked to the place, many of the unemployed parents delighted to help out when they could.

It was the threat of its closure due to lack of council funding that had driven her to stand for the local council against the might of heavyweight Fianna Fail and Fine Gael party candidates. The estates backed her and her fight to keep the project open, and for the first time in twenty years Mo, an independent candidate, had managed to top the polls. Her victory had taken everyone by surprise and Mo Brady had suddenly found herself elected on to Dublin's City Council. Two months later the funding for the Kids' Project was renewed. It was a victory for the people of the estates.

'Mam, we're back!' interrupted Jessie. 'We got you a bag of chips.'

Mo grinned. There was nothing like a bag of chips from Morelli's, their local chipper.

'You OK, Mo?' She felt Joe's arm snake round her waist as they surveyed the huge rooms. 'We drove as fast as we could. They should still be warm.'

'Yeah, I'm grand,' she lied, trying not to give in to the tumultuous emotion she was feeling at leaving Carney Close and finding herself in the Mansion House serving as Lady Mayor.

Chapter Thirteen

Living in the Mansion House in the centre of the city had its advantages. There was lots of space and, although some areas smelled of dust and damp, for the most part they enjoyed large, gracious rooms with marble fireplaces, chandeliers and magnificent plasterwork ceilings. Mo loved the Lady Mayoress's room and the Blue Drawing Room with their calming pale blue curtains and antique furniture. Joe loved the fact that there was a bar on the premises with Guinness and Carlsberg on tap, even if it was reserved for functions. The Mansion House gardens, though small and over-looked, were well tended and planted with shrubs and roses to impress visitors and dignitaries, not for the benefit of a boisterous young family with a football-obsessed son. Thankfully the kids had St Stephen's Green on their doorstep and used the park as their back garden. At night the noise of traffic and the hum of the city kept Mo and her husband awake, but they soon got accustomed to the comfort and decadence of the enormous four-poster bed in the Mayor's bedroom.

For the first two days, overwhelmed by their surroundings, they had gone around speaking in hushed tones, afraid of the place, but then Paul had put on his CD player real loud when the staff had gone home and given them a blast of Thin Lizzy. They had begun to feel more comfortable as the kids shouted, 'The Bradys are back in town!'

She thanked God there were no neighbours to complain about them and bang on the wall. There was a huge catering kitchen in the basement to prepare food for functions and a serving station on the ground floor, but they all preferred the smaller galley kitchen where Joe cooked his usual chicken curries and Sunday fry-ups. Things didn't have to change that much.

'Good morning, Bernadette.' Mo tried to fix a pleasant smile on her face as her new secretary took out the engagements diary for the day and began to read through it. God in heaven, every hour of the day from ten o'clock onwards was taken up.

'You have the opening of the Ringsend Community Games, the cutting of the ribbon for the new flats on the South Circular Road, the welcome lunch for the American Librarians' Society, followed by a photoshoot for the *Examiner* to go with an interview about how much you enjoy your new position. But the journalist can't fit it in until tomorrow so I have scheduled him for 10.30 in the morning, before you visit Temple Street Children's Hospital.' Bernie drew a breath before running her skinny finger down the rest of the page. 'At four o'clock there are the Young Violinists' Awards in the School of Music and then you have that opening for a charity art show down in Temple Bar.'

Mo tried not to give in to a rising sense of panic. 'And after that?'

'There was an invitation to the opening of that new play in the Abbey, but the art show is bound to run a bit late and it might be too tight to get to the theatre and into your seats before the performance starts. So I felt it safer to decline.'

'Thank you,' Mo said, wondering how in heaven's name she was going to cope with going to so many events and meeting so many people. She was glad to have at least some spare time to spend with her husband and children after a few gruelling hours of being gracious and pleasant to all around her.

She looked at the list again: community games, a formal lunch, an art show. What the hell was she supposed to wear to all these functions? She possessed two trouser suits, one in black and one in beige, plus a host of skirts and separates but certainly not enough to take her through all these social occasions.

'Bernadette, you are going to have to clear the decks one day this week as I have to go shopping for a new wardrobe.'

Her secretary looked up from the diary. 'Clear the decks?'

'Yes, I have to go shopping, get a few new outfits, otherwise what am I going to wear to all these important shindigs?'

Bernie Conroy pursed her lips. In her twenty years as secretary to the Mayor, she had never once been asked for a day off to go on a shopping spree. It wasn't professional.

Mo could read the disapproval in her face. 'What did the others do?'

'Others?'

'Yes, my predecessors.'

Bernie reacted as if insulted, remembering a muddled range of men's suits and ties and tweed sports jackets and perfect black-tie evening suits and bow ties, all of course topped by the important chain of office.

'It didn't arise.'

'Of course it didn't,' laughed Mo. 'The situation didn't arise because with the exception of a few very organized ladies they were all men.'

The two of them stared at each other for an instant and Mo imagined she saw a glimmer of contempt in the other woman's face.

'Just see to it that next Saturday morning is kept free,' she said suddenly, turning and going back into her study. 'Excuse me, Bernadette, but I have a few calls to make before I leave for Ringsend.'

Back in her office she closed the door. Bernie Conroy was a wagon. Well, she hadn't got where she was without dealing with a few wagons on her way. Just because she didn't wear a pinstripe suit and do a macho strut around the place didn't give her staff the right to condescend to her. She was the Lady Mayor and if Bernie didn't like it she might well find herself being transferred out of the cosy surroundings of the Mansion House.

'Grafton Street, Brown Thomas, Kilkenny Design, the Stephen's Green Centre, and Arnotts.' Jessie had made a list of places to shop. Mo was conscious of the demands on her time and the need to be ready for an afternoon reception in Trinity College.

All her life Mo Brady had been used to bargain hunting, buying in the sales, making do, but now it was different: she was expected to look good, classic and expensive.

Joe and herself had talked long and hard about it.

'There is enough money in the bank account,' he'd told her firmly. 'So use it!'

Mo had never felt so guilty.

'Listen, we'll be saving on gas and electricity and the like,' he cajoled, kissing her before he set off for a job in Killiney, rewiring an old house.

'Mammy, will you hurry up,' called Jessie, leading her inside the doors of Brown Thomas and up the escalator to the second floor. Jessie had it all worked out. Her mother needed some basics: a black dress, some good shirts and a coat plus shoes and two knee-length skirts, one in beige and one black. Recognizing the Lady Mayor, the staff were discreet, and in less than two hours everything she sought

91

had been found, tried on and purchased. Then the two of them raced up to Nassau Street, to where the modern glass shopfront of Kilkenny Design displayed the best of Irish fashion and crafts and glass.

'Mammy, look here.'

Mo couldn't believe the exquisite clothes, exactly what she was looking for. A heather-coloured suit caught her eye, and a cream linen two-piece. They fitted. Staring at herself in the mirror, she wished she was one of those tall thin elegant women you see in magazines instead of being short and stocky – but in beautiful clothes like these she too felt attractive.

'You look gorgeous!' declared Jessie loyally, totally deserving of the vegetable lasagne and carrot cake and juice she'd have in the shop's café afterwards.

Walking back, Mo mentally checked she had everything she required. The small, black hand-finished leather bag she'd just discovered was another definite. Now all she needed was a hat.

Joe and herself had both spotted the hat shop literally round the corner from their new home. She'd try there first as it was so close and the hats in the window seemed very appealing. Jessie had abandoned her and gone off to meet her friends in the big music store. She supposed there was only so much a mother could ask a teenage girl to put up with.

The bell tinkled lightly as she stepped inside the hat shop. It had been done up recently, you could tell. It sparkled, the glass and mirrors gleaming, fresh paint, pots of violets and trailing lobelia round the door and fresh flowers adorning the counter. Why, it even smelled good.

'Hello, may I help you?' asked the young woman sitting on the stool behind the counter as she looked up under a fringe of dark hair.

'Actually, yes! I need to buy a hat.'

The girl stood up straight away and came over to her. 'Have you seen anything you like?'

'They're all lovely. It's just I'm not sure exactly what I want. For the moment I need a hat that will go with lots of things, be suitable for a number of different functions.'

The girl frowned. Most hats were purchased for a special occasion, so this was a rather unusual request.

'What kind of functions?'

'All kinds. You wouldn't believe the list of things I'm expected to do, and the places I have to visit . . .'

The young woman suddenly looked embarrassed.

'Oh, I'm sorry,' she apologized. 'I didn't recognize you at first. You're the new Mayor.'

'Yes,' laughed Mo. 'I'm your new neighbour.'

'It's an honour to meet you,' said Ellie, laughing, as they introduced themselves.

'Do you think you might have anything that would be suitable?'

Ellie looked around. Two of the hats on the stands were already sold and the pink and the oyster-coloured ones in the window were much too fancy and distinctive.

'I'm not sure I have anything in stock right now that would fit the bill for so many events,' she admitted. 'You are probably going to need something fairly classic and simple that will co-ordinate easily with your wardrobe.'

Mo looked at the beautiful hats and little feathered headpieces, all samples of this young woman's craft, and considered. She had never had anything made for her in her life. It seemed so extravagant and wasteful. And yet the demands of her position were such that to look good was essential.

'Would you be able to make something that would suit someone like me?' she asked bluntly. 'I'm hardly a clothes horse!'

'Of course,' replied the girl.

'Though I'm not even sure what I want,' the Mayor admitted.

Mo made no resistance as a number of styles were proffered, trying on each in turn and studying her reflection in the mirror.

'Shape and style are very important,' said the young hatmaker, helping to place another hat on her head. 'Nothing too tall as when you are small like myself you have to watch that the hat isn't emphasizing your lack of height. Here, let me show you. Try this one!'

'Oh, that's much better,' agreed Mo, studying the pale yellow hat that seemed to have an upward sweep.

'When you have a round face, a biggish hat with a brim or side-sweep usually works well. See how it balances the face and actually adds a little height.'

'I love the shape but I'd never wear this colour.'

'Then maybe we could make this style or a variation on it in one of the colours you do wear or you use for going to functions,' suggested the serious young woman.

Mo thought about it. She didn't want to spend a fortune she didn't have – but a hat made specifically for her, that would be something.

Before she knew it she was sitting in the chair to be measured, as Ellie Matthews took out her notepad and began to sketch her ideas for the Mayor's hat.

Chapter Fourteen

Ellie was busy finishing the details of the Mayor's cream and pale sand-coloured hat. For a small woman with broad features, a hat that would give her a lift and make her seem taller and slimmer was important, and its slightly upturned brim should work perfectly. As she fitted the final piece of satin trim on the inside, Ellie watched Harry Regan across the street as he began to shut up his shop.

She had a lump in her throat as she saw him stack the unsold boxes of shoes into the boot of his old Volvo Estate. Walking boots, fine Italian men's leather shoes, lace-ups and sandals, all unsold, would now be consigned to charity. He was such a nice man and would be missed. Her mother had always relied on Harry and he had helped her many times over the years. The time the pipes burst and the shop flooded, and when a mouse infestation had sent herself and her mother running out into the street, and only two years ago he had boarded up the shop window with a sheet of plywood after a break-in. It was hard to believe that today he was finally closing up and retiring.

At six o'clock everyone in the street gathered in Regan's Shoes to say farewell. Ellie sipped a glass of champagne as she admired the white-frosted sponge cake Sissy Kavanagh had made for Harry's retirement. Everyone was trying to be jolly as they wished him well.

'I might try fishing,' he joked, 'catch a few river trout down on the Shannon.'

'Dad's thinking of buying a riverside apartment down in Athlone, so he'll be near me and his grandchildren,' his daughter Sarah added. 'He won't know himself, not having to work all day in this place.'

Ellie knew from the look in Harry's eyes that there was no hobby on earth that could replace the enthusiasm he'd felt for running his own business.

'They made me an offer too,' confessed Scottie O'Loughlin, who owned the toy shop two doors down from Ellie. 'Obviously nothing like Harry's getting but they still want to buy me out lock, stock and barrel.'

'But what about the toy shop?' Sissy quizzed.

'I suppose they'd knock it down, get rid of the old and make way for the new. Put some fancy store or restaurant in its place,' he said, adjusting his gold-rimmed glasses. 'I'm a sitting duck. The kids nowadays only want those fancy computer games and DVDs and electronic gadgets. They don't want old-fashioned toys any more. I'm almost as extinct as those rubber dinosaurs I sell.'

'And will you sell up?' Ellie asked.

'No,' said Scottie emphatically. 'I certainly won't. I'm like one of those old pirates. I'd rather go down with my ship, fighting.'

'Good for you,' agreed those standing around him.

'No, I won't close up like Harry here. What would an old bachelor like me do with himself? I'd go barmy without having the shop to come in to every day.'

'Scottie, if you don't mind me saying . . . a bit of a paint job in those nice bright primary colours kids like would make a big differ-ence to the shop,' suggested Ria Roberts, who owned the women's fashion shop a few doors down from him.

96

'New shelves, and get rid of that big old counter that takes up half the shop and stops the kids seeing the toys,' advised Harry, who had joined the conversation.

'Scrap that bloody lino,' shouted Scottie, forgetting himself for a moment. Everyone burst out laughing.

'Doing it up a bit wouldn't have to cost that much,' Ellie confided.

'If you need anyone to give you a hand,' volunteered Harry, 'I'll be at a bit of a loose end once I hand over the keys of this place.'

'Dad!' protested Sarah, throwing her eyes to heaven.

'Those fish might have to wait a bit, love, while I help out an old friend.'

They all laughed, glad to see Harry wasn't going to turn his back on them totally. Scottie asked everyone to join him in a toast and they all raised their glasses as Harry said a few parting words and Sissy passed round the cake. When Harry locked up an hour later for the very last time they all stood out on the street and cheered him.

Thirty-six hours later the old dance hall, Regan's Italian shoe shop and the empty shop beside it had been boarded up and hidden behind high site hoardings.

Ellie couldn't get Rory out of her mind and had waited and waited for him to phone her. Nothing for the whole week, and just when she'd given up hope of ever hearing from him again she got a text saying he was missing her! Then he'd started texting her daily. Sending her lines and verses of songs. Ellie tried to keep up and remember who wrote them. He was witty and made her laugh and she hoped that they would see each other again. She checked the new message on her phone. *What about dinner in Eden on Saturday?* It was from him. *Yes, please*, she replied immediately before phoning Kim to tell her. Rory was the first guy in a long time to interest and excite her and Ellie couldn't wait to see him.

Chapter Fifteen

Ellie pushed through the crowded bar in the Clarence, relieved when she spotted Rory at a table in the corner, on his mobile, waiting for her. He looked even better than she remembered in an expensive black jacket and jeans. His eyes lit up when he saw her and Ellie was glad she'd made the effort to dress up too and was wearing an exquisite Kenzo wrap dress she'd bought in Tokyo. They automatically reached for each other and hugged.

'Let me get you a drink?' he offered.

Ellie ordered a glass of chilled white wine and they chatted easily. He was such good company. Although a few of his friends came over to talk to him she noticed he didn't invite them to sit down.

'Come on, let's get out of here,' he suggested. 'I'm starving.'

They walked through Temple Bar, which was already buzzing. Music blared from every doorway, rock, traditional, jazz and soul. The bars and restaurants were filling up, people already spilling out on to the streets with glasses and cigarettes in hand. Ellie was careful of her heels on the cobblestones in one of the city's oldest districts.

'This is the best place in the world to break new bands,' said Rory proudly as they turned into Meeting House Square. 'There's venues and a great dedication. That's what it's about. All the music scouts come here because the place has got an energy.'

He had booked at Eden, one of her favourite restaurants, and the waitress led them to a table overlooking the square. Ellie ordered a cocktail as they studied the menu. She still felt a little nervous of spending an evening alone with him.

However, once they had ordered and the waiter had opened a bottle of red wine she could feel herself beginning to relax and unwind. She was surprised at how Rory made her feel so completely at ease.

'This is my stomping ground,' he explained. 'I've an office nearby. Well, part of an office, I share it with two other guys, and my place is over near Custom House Quay.'

'Living in town or close to town is great,' she agreed. 'You only have to walk out the door and you've got everything.'

'I used to wait tables in the place down the road,' he laughed. 'They fired me when I dropped a tray of spaghetti in someone's lap. It wasn't pretty!'

'Was that while you were in college?'

'Never made it to college,' he admitted, 'too busy making a prat of myself trying to get a record deal with a bunch of useless eejits who thought they were the hottest band in town. The record companies ran a mile.'

'But that's changed now.'

'Yeah, with Rothko and one or two of the new acts I look after, I guess I'm beginning to build up the business. I try and get the best for them, promote and yet protect their talent.'

'They're a great band,' she agreed.

'What about you?' he asked, turning the tables on her as the waitress served their main courses. 'How did you get into all this feathers and bows and hat stuff?'

'I grew up with it. My mother was French. She trained as a milliner in Paris and served her apprenticeship with her sister. They worked with all the top designers. I suppose she would have stayed working with her except that she fell in love with an Irishman.'

'Your father?'

'Yes. Maman was so in love with him that she came to live in his city.'

'And they lived happily ever after?'

'Not quite!' she admitted. 'My dad got bored, unsettled. The marriage didn't last and they broke up when I was three. I don't really remember him. My mother stayed on here. She worked in Brown Thomas's and then began making hats for clients. I was quite small when she opened the hat shop. So it's what I've grown up with.'

'She sounds a remarkable woman.'

'She was. She died a few months ago and I still really miss her.'

'I'm sorry,' he said sympathetically. 'I didn't mean to make you feel sad.'

'I suppose it's good to talk about her, even if it does make me sad,' she admitted.

'What about you?' he asked a few seconds later, trying to rescue the conversation. 'You went to college and all that jazz, I bet!'

'Yep! Up the road to the College of Art! I studied fashion.'

'Hence the great style,' he teased.

'Then a stint in Paris. Not as grand as it seems as I was staying with my aunt and studying like crazy all day. After six months I got a job with a lunatic of a designer but I learned a lot from him. Then back here, working with Mum, and then I got a great offer from Hyland's and a chance to design and source fabrics for the fashion trade. It's strange but making hats . . . I guess it's in the blood.'

'Like music and madness.'

'Maybe,' she laughed.

They had a perfect meal, the conversation entertaining and fun as

Rory described the trials and tribulations and hairy existence of the music business. When they had finished neither of them wanted to part.

'The River Club and Lillie's are both close by,' he suggested, taking her hand as they walked along the boardwalk by the Liffey. The tide was full in, the lights of the city reflected on the water, the moon a dappled path along the dark river's way.

Rory stopped and pulled her into his arms, Ellie responding to his warm kisses. He tasted of wine and his skin smelled so good as she nuzzled against him.

'I've been wanting to do that all night,' he confessed, 'since the minute I saw you.'

She giggled, because the thought had equally crossed her mind. They walked slowly, talking and kissing all the time, crossing O'Connell Bridge, neither of them interested in clubbing. Rory hailed a taxi outside Trinity College. She gave the driver her address and leaned back against Rory's shoulder.

The driver let them off outside her door. Ellie pulled Rory into her arms as they stood on the steps saying goodnight.

'I don't want to let you go,' he admitted, candidly.

Ellie took a sharp breath. She had never met anyone like him, dated anyone like him, kissed or wanted anyone like him.

'But I don't want to push things, Ellie,' he said softly.

She considered. It had been so long since she had let anyone touch her or be close to her. He was charming and witty and made her smile and she found him so damned attractive it was unbelievable.

'There's good French brandy and whiskey and chocolate if you'd like to come in,' she said, knowing that she didn't want this perfect night to end either.

He kissed her again.

'You got me on the chocolate,' he teased as they walked up the stairs.

Chapter Sixteen

Mo Brady took a deep breath as she entered the splendour of Dublin's City Hall and welcomed guests to the Lord Mayor's Lunch. There was the Taoiseach and his ministers along with a mixture of TDs and ambassadors. Those who had contributed much to the city in terms of art and business, sport and science had also been invited. Mo, grateful for Joe's supportive squeeze of her hand, stepped in front of the cameras and smiled. Her speech, neatly printed out, was in her handbag. For once she didn't feel small and stout but stylish and confident as she turned round in her immaculate linen suit and tilted her head, showing off her Ellie Matthews cream-coloured hat with its fancy beige spiral. She felt great as she began welcoming everyone. Putting on the style sometimes was worth it!

The meal was a great success and the menu of Dublin Bay prawns, good Wicklow lamb and summer pudding was one of her favourites. Mo pushed the cream and ice cream to the side of her plate. She'd noticed after only a few weeks in office that she was putting on more weight. She cursed her slow metabolism and all the lunches, dinners and cocktail parties she was expected to attend. Exercise was needed, so she had built a walk twice round the park into her daily routine. Two hours later, standing on the steps of the hall, she breathed a sigh of relief as the last of the dignitaries said their goodbyes.

She had never entertained so much in her life. The Mansion House was constantly filled with strangers attending receptions, and herself and Joe often had to dress up to go out to some event or other. Joe and the kids were stars as far as she was concerned. After much discussion Wednesday nights had been declared family nights. No receptions or events were permitted and the kids would order in pizza and get a video.

'This is just like being back in Carney Close,' Lisa confided, snuggling up on the expensive damask-covered couch in her pyjamas as they watched *The Incredibles*.

Mo felt guilty thinking of all their neighbours and friends in the old estate, which now seemed a million miles away.

The next morning she couldn't disguise a grin as Bernadette laid out the daily papers for her. There it was in full colour: 'Mayor Mo puts on the Style! Dublin's Elegant New Mayor.'

'Is everything to your satisfaction,' asked Bernadette, 'or is there anything else?'

'Actually, there is something, Bernie. I want to organize a function for forty people in about two weeks' time. I will give you the invitation list with the names and addresses.'

'Very well, what will I list it under?'

'Carney Close.'

'Sorry, did you say Carney?'

'Yes,' she beamed. 'It's our old neighbourhood. It's high time I entertained some people I actually know.'

'But the Mayor's office should be—'

'Don't you fret about it, Bernadette, I promise that they are all good citizens of Dublin!'

She couldn't stop herself from baiting the sixty-year-old woman, who, with her neat perm and stuck-up attitude, seemed to question everything she did, and had no idea about the ramifications of family life under the gaze of the council staff.

The kids had given a huge cheer when she told them they were throwing a party in the Mansion House for their old neighbours.

'Plenty of Coca-Cola and crisps, Mammy,' warned Lisa. 'They mightn't like some of those fancy canopies you are always giving everyone.'

Mo herself was looking forward to a chance to sit down and unwind with her old friends without having to be all polite and Lady Mayorish, and this was the perfect house for a party.

Her car was waiting outside at four o'clock. After a whirlwind visit to a day care centre for Alzheimer's patients in the inner city she just about made it for the council meeting, telling driver Larry Flynn that she would phone him to collect her when she was finished.

There was a huge list of items to be covered, she noticed as she scanned the printed agenda. She sat in beside Richard Doyle, who represented the Green Party. He had a wad of notes and files with him. It looked as if it was going to be one of those marathon sessions. She took out her black folder and began to scribble notes. She voted for a grant to the children's playground in Sheriff Street, against the decision to extend paid parking in the inner city and for the compulsory purchase of a derelict Georgian house that could be restored and converted into flats or offices.

She listened to an interminable speech from Councillor Reynolds about the hazards of the City Council overextending themselves in terms of social housing, almost dozing off at the boring tones of his voice.

'Now we come to South Anne Street,' announced the chairman. 'There have been various hold-ups in this planned development in terms of renewing leases, completing property sales, etc. Casey Coleman Holdings, the developers, have applied for an extension to the plan. They have acquired more properties on the street and are hopeful that the remaining tenants and landlords will accept generous offers and vacate premises within the next twenty weeks so that work on the project can begin. There will be significant income for the council from this development.'

'I object to any extension of this development,' interrupted Richard. 'There is no need for it in what is already a heavily developed area of the city.'

'Hear! Hear!' added one or two voices.

Mo looked up. Richard caught her eye. That was the street where she'd bought her hat only recently. It was a lovely old street full of Dublin character.

'Are the sales on all these premises agreed?' She stood up to ask her question, noticing Councillor Des King's annoyance with her.

'Well, that is the problem,' he admitted tetchily. 'Some tenants and shopowners – only a few – have failed to close their agreements and are said to be reconsidering. This delay could put the whole project at risk.'

'Casey Coleman already have permission for a very large proportion of one side of the street,' she pointed out. 'Perhaps they should be satisfied with that. There is no guarantee the council will grant planning on their more recent acquisitions, is there?'

She could see one or two of her fellow councillors shifting uneasily.

'What about compulsories?' murmured Councillor King.

'The shopkeepers cannot be forced to sell,' Mo insisted. 'These are their premises. We have no right to interfere.'

'The development must go ahead.'

'Hold on a minute. The main development and rebuilding on the vacant site, yes, but I'm not so sure about the rest,' she insisted. 'It's a lovely old street, the type we should be trying to preserve.'

'It has no architectural merit,' Des lashed out.

'And I suppose the replacement will have?' responded Richard sarcastically.

'Richard is right. Why should the city lose another street to huge global retailers and the kind of bland copy-cat stores that are dotted all over the cities and towns of Ireland? That's all I'm saying.'

Richard gave her the thumbs-up when she sat down, and a load of her fellow councillors applauded. The chairman called for a motion to delay the vote until they received further information. Mo was delighted when the motion was carried.

Chapter Seventeen

Ellie smiled to herself as Kim and Fergus began the inquisition about the new guy in her life. The three of them had gone for something to eat after work at Café Bar Deli. The tables were still spread out under the Harry Clarke stained glass windows in the famous old Bewley's building.

'Listen, we've just gone out a few times,' she giggled as she ate her chicken Caesar salad. 'Give us a chance.'

'Then how come none of us have even laid eyes on this mystery man?' added Fergus. 'You are positively hiding him away from us.'

'No I'm not.' She laughed. 'It's just that Rory's out of town and back and forward to London a good bit at the moment. It's part of his job.'

'So what's he got?' joked Fergus, eating all the bread rolls on the table.

'Everything. He's interesting and charming, funny and great to be around. He makes me feel happy.'

'Can't compete with that,' shuddered Fergus.

'I promise when you meet him you'll like him. He's great.'

'You know that we're delighted you've met someone,' said Kim slowly. 'It's just that we don't want you to rush in – to get hurt.'

Ellie stared at the plate. There had been a fling last year with Mike McDonnell, one of the guys who worked with Kim. It had broken up by mutual agreement when he'd transferred to be a trader in New York. Neither of them had felt committed enough for a long-distance relationship, though they were still friends and emailed each other.

But she knew who they both meant. It had been a lifetime ago . . .

'He's nothing like Owen,' she insisted. Nothing. Owen Cross had been one of her lecturers in college. In her final year, after a class trip to the Burren, they had started to see each other. Ellie considered him not just a guy she was in love with but also a mentor. She was working on her end-of-year projects and her thesis when his wife had returned from a six-month sabbatical in Stockholm. She'd had no idea he was married and felt humiliated and used.

She never wanted to see him again. She wanted to quit college, walk away from it, forget her projects and everything. It was only her mother and Kim who had made her finally see sense, telling her that she had done nothing wrong. Somehow she had got through those awful final weeks and banished Owen from her life, escaping to Paris once she got her degree.

'Rory's different.' She smiled. 'He makes me feel good.'

'Then bring him along to Ryan's on Friday night for a pint after work,' suggested Fergus, 'and we'll all get a chance to meet him.'

'I'll see if he's free but he goes to a lot of gigs to check out new acts or be with his bands,' she explained.

'Do you get to go with him?'

'Sometimes.' She laughed. 'Or we'll meet up afterwards.'

Ellie was nervous about whether Rory would be accepted by her small group of very close friends and also about whether he would think they were all too ordinary and not interesting enough. She loved Fergus and Kim but compared to Rory's crazy friends they were a pretty tame crowd.

They had arranged to meet up after work on Friday when Rory cancelled out, citing a meeting at RTE. Secretly Ellie was almost relieved.

She was sitting in Ryan's on Friday night drinking a glass of red wine in an old jumper and jeans, her hair tied in pigtails, when Rory walked in. She couldn't believe it and jumped up and called him over.

'My meeting at RTE finished early.' He grinned. 'So I thought I'd surprise you.'

'Well, you did,' she said, kissing him and introducing him to everyone. She watched open-mouthed as he single-handedly schmoozed them all. He had Fergus confessing about the band he was in when he was thirteen and their performances of Duran Duran classics, and Kim discussing her ancient record collection, and even Mary-Claire was batting her eyelashes at him. All she prayed for was that no one would sing.

However, snug in the corner of Ryan's just before closing time Fergus broke into an awful rendition of 'Purple Rain', which attracted the whole bar's attention. Everyone was laughing and clapping and jeering him.

Rory handled it manfully and bought Fergus another pint of lager to console him on the obvious disintegration of his singing potential.

'You know, with the right training when I was young enough I could have made it!' claimed Fergus. 'It was just the old man wanted me to be an accountant or a doctor.'

'Thanks,' she said to Rory afterwards as they made their way back to her place.

'I like them,' he teased, pulling her into his arms. 'I really do.'

Chapter Eighteen

The sturdy figure of Dublin's Lady Mayor walked up and down South Anne Street, noting the construction site on one side and the shops, some of which were boarded up, on the other. She could see why so many of the street's traders were tempted to sell, fearing their shops would go bankrupt once the large-scale development opened.

The empty fruit and vegetable shop brought back memories of her father's greengrocer's store in Phibsboro with its trays of polished Granny Smiths and fresh oranges from Israel. Her father had been forced to close down when a huge supermarket opened only five hundred yards away. They'd moved to Crumlin, to a new estate filled with young families. Danny Sullivan had never said much, but in hindsight Mo supposed that losing the shop must have broken his heart.

For the rest of his working life he had been an employee, a wages clerk, and at fifty-eight he had found himself at home, no longer the wage earner but dependent on social welfare. His pride and hope had dwindled away. Mo could still remember his fierce loyalty to the ordinary working man and his lack of resentment about all that had happened to him. A wonderful father, he'd encouraged all of them to go out and embrace the world. In his own gentle way he had given each of them more than any millionaire could have given his children.

Mo took a breath. There was a big sale in the expensive boutique with its knitted twinsets and tweed skirts. Were they closing down too? She would go and talk to them.

'I've a huge rent review, costs are soaring and God knows what will happen when those big shops open,' Ria Roberts said angrily, shaking her immaculately coiffed grey hair.

Looking around at the shelves of expensive cashmere and lambswool and the rails of exquisite skirts and jackets, Mo disagreed.

'But you have such an elegant shop here,' she remonstrated, 'with a loyal clientele, I'm sure. Don't give up your hard-earned custom so easy.'

It was the same story everywhere – the jeweller's, the small Italian restaurant, the print and art shop. Every single small trader was worried about their livelihood and their ability to withstand the tidal wave of the forthcoming galleria, with its massive retail outlets, restaurants and hotel.

Mo stood outside the windows of the toy shop. Its freshly painted red and yellow shopfront was attractive and welcoming, as was the display of wooden toys and kites in the window.

'I was about to throw in the towel and give up,' Scottie O'Loughlin admitted, 'but young Ellie down the street told me kids still want proper toys, not just cheap plastic rubbish but good stuff. No matter how many videos and computer games they have, kids still want to play.'

'I reckon she was right,' laughed Mo.

'She did a great job on her own shop so I suppose that gave me a bit of encouragement to get rid of all the junk and old stock and smarten my place up. Make it nicer for the kids.'

'It's just what a toy shop should be,' said Mo admiringly, looking up at the hand-painted mobiles over her head and the wooden aeroplanes that bobbed from the ceiling.

'The property company weren't too happy about me not going ahead with the sale but I told them I wanted to stay put and I wasn't budging for anything. Kids and toys are my life!'

Mo looked around the shop with its well-displayed toys on low shelves and found herself buying a wooden kite with a jaunty red and blue tail for Lisa and a big green crocodile to put on her desk.

Shops like this certainly mustn't be allowed to disappear. Surely the city manager could see the sense in providing all kinds of shops for customers to enjoy?

The small black cat greeted Mo as she opened the door of the hat shop and rubbed itself against her legs. The young milliner had done a marvellous job in making her shop such an enticing treat for customers and passers-by.

Ellie Matthews put aside the feathered trim she was working on.

'Lovely hat!'

'It's for a christening,' confided Ellie. 'It makes me feel good, making a hat for a mother with a new baby.'

'Your hats make everyone feel good,' laughed Mo. 'I love mine.'

'That's such a kind thing to say, Mo, thank you. And your hat was a great success.'

'The media aren't used to seeing me dressed up and looking smart!'

Mo was tempted to try on the fuchsia-pink hat on the stand but steeled herself to resist. She couldn't have all her mayoral salary going on clothes and style.

'The reason I'm here today is to talk to you about the shop and the street.'

'My shop!'

'Yes, you have done a remarkable job – but it would be such a shame to see any more of the other shops and businesses round here closing down.'

'They're scared,' confided Ellie. 'Frightened they'll lose their trade. Some of them reckon it's better to get out now while the going is good and there is an offer on the table.'

'You didn't think that!'

'Oh, I most certainly did, but when it came to it I couldn't bear the thought of closing up my mother's business. She had worked too hard all her life running it, and it wasn't up to me to just go and sell it off to the highest bidder. I have to see if I can make a success of it myself.'

'But you have already turned it round, it's such a lovely shop.'

'Thank you,' Ellie said, accepting the compliment.

'Mr O'Loughlin told me you encouraged him to continue trading.'

'I'm not sure about that. But I have loved that shop ever since I was a little girl and I'd hate to see it close. Scottie thought he couldn't compete with all the latest toys. He didn't realize there is a big market for classic old-style things that kids love, boats and trains and arks and doll's houses. They never go out of fashion.'

'And kites,' joked Mo, lifting up the one she had bought.

'Yeah, see what I mean? Good toys are irresistible.'

'What about the other traders?' urged Mo. 'What do they want?'

'I'm not sure, Lady Mayor, but I suppose we all just want to save our street.'

'Save our street, SOS. That's a thought!' grinned Mo. 'Perhaps if you all got together . . .'

'We have talked,' admitted Ellie. 'We are not opposed to this new galleria, it's just we want to stay and trade here too.'

113

'Then set up a proper meeting,' she advised. 'And I'll try and get as many councillors along to support you as possible. No one can stop the development, but we can ensure that it doesn't get any bigger and that the street manages to retain a sense of identity and individuality.'

Walking back to the Mansion House, Mo smiled to herself. She was certainly doing her best to look after all the citizens of this great city.

Mo sucked in her tummy and pulled on her new linen skirt. Perfect. She'd had her hair blow-dried and her nails done. Funny, she was more nervous about tonight than about any other function she'd attended.

'You look a million dollars,' assured Jessie, 'and don't worry, the party's going to be great!'

Her daughter looked beautiful in a figure-hugging denim skirt and pink string top, her long dark hair hanging straight round her shoulders. Mo blinked, wondering when had her little girl grown up.

'And you look amazing, Jessie. I'm so proud of you.'

Joe was whistling as he fixed his tie, a sign he was happy. Wearing the new grey suit he'd bought and with the touch of silver in his hair, he looked very distinguished, Mo thought, as he went downstairs to the hall.

The party in the Mansion House on Dawson Street was a great night! Lisa and Jessie gave everyone tours of the house, the Blue Room and the Oak Room while Joe stood at the front door to welcome each new arrival.

'It's only gorgeous,' said Mary Clarke enviously. 'Must be wonderful living in a palace like this.'

'You lucky woman, and you don't even have to clean it yourself,' joked her friend Lorraine Ryan.

'I'm only here because you lot got me elected,' she admitted, looking round at their faces, seeing years of hard work and struggle reflected in their eyes. 'I'll never forget it for all of you.'

'Well, we elected the best woman for the job,' responded Paddy Hayes, 'and gave Dublin one of its finest mayors.'

There was wine and beer and Guinness and the barman kept the drink flowing all night. Carmel and Seamus, the two cooks, had done her proud with tasty chicken and beef dishes and a huge range of desserts. Afterwards they sat around talking and chatting till all hours, Paul and the rest of the kids disappearing upstairs. Spotting the piano, Paddy Hayes rolled up his sleeves and began to play, like he always did. It was almost two o'clock when Joe and herself finally said goodbye to the last of the partygoers and made their way to bed.

As she watched her husband undress, carefully putting his clothes away, Mo knew that without his support and belief she would never have got to where she was. Fortune had smiled on her the day she had met him at Byrne's Cash and Carry when he'd offered to help take the groceries out to the family car. She'd loved him ever since.

'Thanks, Joe.'

'Thanks?'

'Thanks for making tonight such a good night.'

'Wasn't it grand, having all the old crowd here to our place,' he joked, sitting on the edge of their bed as he took his socks off.

'I couldn't do it without you,' she said, serious, reaching for him. 'Tonight and all the nights, and all the dinners, the whole bloody lot.'

'And I wouldn't do it, any of it, without you,' responded Joe Brady, taking the Lady Mayor in his strong arms.

115

Chapter Nineteen

Claire Connolly stood at the lower end of Andrews Street and waited for her cash to appear. There must be something wrong with this ATM, she thought as she waited, ignoring the irate-looking businessman behind her who was standing much too close for comfort. She peered at the yellow message on the screen. *Insufficient Funds*.

She blushed, then grabbed the stupid card and rammed it back into her purse. She tried to look nonchalant and pretend she had simply been checking the balance on her account as the man pushed in front of her. From yards away she could see the wads of notes he extracted from the machine. She stood for a second considering what to do. She had planned to while away the lunch hour in Zara and Marks and Spencer's and treat herself to a lovely O'Brien's Cajun chicken and salad wrap and a bottle of fresh orange juice, but now a small cheese roll and a bottle of water seemed a more likely option. How had she spent so much money in a month? She stood in the centre of the busy street feeling totally dejected. She'd grab her roll

116

and head back to the office; there was no point moping around looking at things she couldn't afford. Besides, she could make herself a
cup of tea in the kitchenette and skip the Ballygowan.

Back at her desk she worked out that she had a grand total of
eighty-two euros to do her for the next week. Pay her bus fare,
lunches and going out. Well, obviously that was out of the question.
She grabbed a calculator off Derek McCoy's desk so that she could
tot up outstanding debts and forthcoming bills, trying not to give in
to the growing sense of panic now churning in her stomach as she
realized that she was stony broke. She had no savings, no little stack
of money squirrelled away anywhere for a rainy day. The money
sitting forlornly in her purse was all she had. She felt like throwing
herself across the mock-beech desktop and bawling her eyes out but
she was aware of the trickle of other staff back to the office after the
lunchbreak.

Working in Murphy and Byrne's, the insurance brokers, was
meant to have been a stopgap job until she got her modelling career
started.

'I'm just filling in,' she had cheerfully told the middle-aged
women and serious-looking men she worked with. She had
absolutely no intention of ending up like Sheila Sweeney or Derek
McCoy or any of the other staff in the busy claims department.

Things were serious on the financial front, but at least she was in
great shape after nearly six weeks on the Atkins diet. Her hair was
glossy and trimmed, the colour perfect, her skin flawless from drinking gallons of water, and six months ago she had managed to get
herself on the books of Elaine's, one of the best model agencies in
Dublin. She had got work on an advertisement for one of the big
supermarkets, playing a girl about town flirting with the young
cashier, and she had modelled at a big charity fashion show in the
Four Seasons Hotel – but otherwise the phone had stayed quiet.

She'd phone the office discreetly to enquire about something else,

117

for she didn't want them to forget about her. Taking out a yellow Post-it, she made herself a list of things to do. Money was needed urgently for her next payday was miles away.

'Nice lunch?' asked Sheila, returning to the adjoining desk.

'Mmm,' Claire lied.

'Anything big to look forward to this weekend?'

Sheila was married with two kids, teenage tearaways by all accounts, and had worked in Murphy and Byrne's since she was sixteen. She'd moved up the ranks from lowly filing assistant to the lofty heights of Serious Claims Assessor. She had a soft spot for toffees and caramels and kept a packet in the top drawer of her desk, chewing them as she crunched numbers and scribbled in pencil on the big files on her desk.

'No plans yet!' shrugged Claire, unable to mask her disappointment at the thought of being confined to the airless dump that had described itself as a three-bedroomed modern apartment along the canal. 'Bit of a walk, see a friend or two, maybe go out for a bite.'

'Oh, how I envy you young ones,' smiled Sheila. 'Kevin and I have to take ten youngsters bowling and for a pizza afterwards. It's Tara's birthday. Then we promised we'd have a try at fixing up this decking Kevin bought for the back garden. It'll take us hours, and you know we'll end up sitting on the patio with it half done having a beer.'

Claire looked at the round, relaxed face and for once envied her.

Cop on to yourself, she warned as she went to the bathroom later, you'll be getting jealous of Derek McCoy next.

The next night she sat on the couch watching her flatmates getting ready to go out.

'Come on, Claire! We're going to Q Bar!'

Claire admitted she was tempted but considering the very slim bulge in her purse she decided she had better stay home.

'No, thanks! I was on to the agency yesterday and I'm up for a commercial next week so got to stay clear of pubs and bars.'

'Oh, that's great, Claire.' Her best friend, Fiona, who always encouraged her in her modelling career, gave her a big hug.

Claire felt momentarily guilty about the lie as she listened to her friends clunk down the hall and stairs in their high heels and laugh and giggle as they went out on the usual Saturday-night razzle.

Claire curled up on the couch and ate two bowls of cornflakes and made a honey sandwich, flicking on the remote control and skipping over *Who Wants to Be a Millionaire* and the usual weekend game shows. Everyone was trying to win something, she thought grimly as she watched two families fight it out in full view of the nation. They all needed money. She sighed. She hadn't lied to Fiona about phoning Elaine's. She'd phoned the office on Baggot Street, only to be told that Lainey and four of her girls were off in Barbados on a shoot, the agency owner acting as a chaperone for two schoolgirl models. Claire, at twenty-two, suddenly felt she was ancient. The secretary ran through the listings, telling her there might have been a possibility of a commercial but unfortunately the advertising director was set on girls who had massive mouths and teeth and piercings. Claire thought of her soft, full lips and perfectly formed post-braces teeth and piercing-free face and body as Angie put the phone down on her.

She had to consider her options. She could take on another job in the hope that it would pay more. Or double jobbing. Maybe she could do restaurant or bar work after office hours or at the weekends, but then when would she have the chance to go out? It was a right conundrum. This was just a temporary hitch – OK, so it had been building for a while – but she knew there must be some way round it. She was young and fit and bright and ready to work. The other options were she could take her money and go out and buy a load of Lotto tickets and get down on her knees and pray, or she could phone

119

her uncle Mick, the gambler of the family, for a tip on the horses and put the whole lot on it. She licked the honey from her fingertips. There must be some other way, she thought, there's got to be. Then she saw it. The paper flung on the couch, near her slippers, with the advertisement for the Dublin Horse Show.

She'd visited the show once or twice when she was a kid, sick with excitement driving up from Kilkenny. There was the showjumping, the Aga Khan Trophy, the horses, the ponies, the stalls, the fashion, the crowds of visitors cramming into the Royal Dublin Society's Annual Horse Show in Ballsbridge. But it was Ladies' Day, with a huge prize for the winner of the Best-Dressed Lady competition, that caught her attention. She fell on the page, devoured it. They were looking for style, finesse, looks, class. She could do it. For heaven's sake, she was a model! The first prize was a ten-thousand-euro diamond, with vouchers for the runners-up. She couldn't believe it, imagine getting your hands on that much money! Claire grinned from ear to ear. This was something she could do – even on a budget. She was going to go to the Horse Show and try to win the Ladies' Day competition!

Chapter Twenty

Putting on her dark glasses and a haughty demeanour, Claire sashayed through the designer department of Brown Thomas. She passed through the busy make-up stands, spraying herself with a little Chanel before she took the elevator upstairs. Designer after designer and their season's style imprinted themselves on her memory as she made a mental note of what looked right and what did not. The prices were exorbitant but she was determined to do it in her own fashion. Making squiggly marks in the small shopping jotter, she noted details on the styles that looked best, tiny features, trims, etc. The right dress or suit, shoes, bag, hosiery, make-up were all essential for the winner of the Ladies' Day Prize at the RDS, she decided as she researched back issues of the newspapers in the National Library in Kildare Street. A hat was definitely needed if she wanted to make a favourable impression with the judges. It looked hopeless given that her credit limit was totally maxed out, but Claire was not about to give up on what she now considered a good bet.

She had a wardrobe and a case full of clothes at home. OK, so some was rubbish and too trendy – the judges definitely didn't go for trendy – but a few pieces were bought at considerable cost in the sales, when their original designer bank-loan prices were slashed. Claire's eyes were well able to spot a classic bargain.

There must be something suitable in the wardrobe of Canal Quay and it would be just a matter of dressing it up.

While Fiona and Bridget lost themselves in *Coronation Street*, a repeat episode of *Friends* and the latest *CSI*, Claire calmly took out the entire contents of her wardrobe and spread it across the bed. Anything denim or corduroy immediately returned to its place on the rail. There was the retro sixties-style St Laurent she'd picked up last year in Paris. No, too different. An expensive cream and beige pinstripe suit, no. The red silk dress that she'd worn to her cousin Betsy's wedding two years ago was too skimpy and definitely not suitable. She had got her Louise Kennedy pale blue linen suit at a bargain price because someone had smeared make-up all over the neck of the jacket. After a special-care dry cleaning it had come up perfect and was a real possibility. There remained a frilly sexy full-skirted summer dress that made her waist look tiny, a strappy pink fitted dress with a short skirt that drove men crazy and, of course, her simple black linen dress with its square neck and neat bodice and a skirt that came to just above her knees. She collapsed on the bed to consider, retrieving her notebook from the recesses of her bag.

'Hey, Claire! We're going to get a takeaway. Do you want something too?'

Claire thought of Little China's delicious sweet-and-sour chicken balls and their tasty chicken, spring onion and water chestnut dish. Her stomach groaned. She'd made do with only a scrambled egg on toast when she'd got in from the office.

'Will I order you a curry?' asked Fiona, stepping into the room.

'I haven't any change,' she fibbed.

Fiona said nothing for a minute. 'Tell me what you want and I'll get it, OK?'

Claire didn't know how it was that she had ended up with the most generous-hearted friend and flatmate in the whole of Dublin.

'Listen, the minute I get some money I'll pay you back, all right?'

Her humour picked up and she decided once she'd eaten she'd consult the girls about her wardrobe possibilities, have a try-on and see what they thought would be best.

'The black.' It was unanimous. It looked expensive. It felt expensive and it exuded classic style. No one had ever won in plain black so she would have to dress it up. A bag, a belt, a jacket, shoes but most definitely a hat was now needed. She ranged through the possibilities – pink, pale blue, white, red and lemon. These were her likely colour options. Shoes most definitely classic black. Her much-loved Jimmy Choos were taken from their box. Tapered heel, sexy little straps and the most delicious pointed toes. No wonder she felt like Cinderella as she slipped them on to her feet. They had been a surprise present from her parents for her twenty-first and along with her gold chain and silver locket and the string of pearls she had inherited from her grandmother they were her most prized possessions. Now she just had to find the rest.

'You OK?' asked Sheila at work.

Claire pulled herself up. She had been daydreaming of winning the first prize at Ladies' Day at the horse show.

'It must be love,' beamed her colleague, passing her a file on a massive case involving sausages and food poisoning with a group of nuns claiming against the food company. Yuk.

Claire blazed. Sheila was always trying to find out if she had a boyfriend or was dating someone. She had no intention of telling Sheila that men seemed to keep away from her for some bizarre reason. They might flirt with her, dance with her, even ask her back to their flats but usually that was as far as it went. There were no long intimate phone calls, or romantic gestures, or requests to see her again. It hurt like hell but she'd read in one of the magazines that it was something experienced by most models and one only had to follow the lives of supermodels like Naomi Campbell in the press to see that it was true.

'Just a bit tired,' she said. 'Too many late nights!'

Studying her dress and shoes, she had to decide how to accessorize them. The handbags she'd seen were an outrageous price, and as for a hat her spirits had plummeted when she'd read the price tags hidden inside their brims. She'd look for a second-hand one in one of the thrift shops, that's what she'd do.

Saturday morning she got up early and spent hours trailing through the market in Cow's Lane, Temple Bar and a succession of Vincent de Paul and Oxfam shops. Claire had been about to give up when, rooting through a box of berets and tweed caps and a straw boater, she'd found it! A classic elegant black hat that was a perfect fit.

'Would you like a mirror, dear?' asked the grey-haired lady in the purple skirt and Hush Puppy shoes.

Claire's eyes widened as she recognized the discreet 1950s label. The hat was exactly what she had been searching for.

'It's lovely,' she murmured, 'but I'm not sure . . . and anyway it's a bit too pricey at thirty euro.'

The volunteer studied the hat, considering it rather plain and old-fashioned herself. 'I could let you have a bit of a discount,' she offered. 'Five euro off.'

'I only have twenty,' Claire said, holding her breath.

'That'll do.'

Claire paid for it quickly and watched the lady wrap it in a super-market bag, hoping she wouldn't damage it. Everything was coming together – but she couldn't just wear black or she'd look like she was in mourning. What would she put with it?

She was walking back uptown when she turned into South Anne Street. She resisted the temptation to visit the deli near the corner and kept walking. It was a pity so many of the shops on the little street had closed down; the area was about to be redeveloped, she guessed. The greengrocer's and the lovely shoe shop where she'd taken her Jimmy Choos for the delicate replacement of their tiny leather heel tips were gone.

She slowed down, noticing the hat shop in the middle of the street. Funny, she hadn't spotted it before. She'd have a look: you never knew, you might get an idea, she thought, gazing in the window. It had all been painted up and was now a pretty cream colour, flowerpots round the tiled porch, the window a feast of tantalizing colour. The hats were gorgeous. Bright blue, pink and mauve, creamy white in the shape of a lily. She gasped in admiration. If she had a hat like any of these she'd be bound to win. There were no price tags to be seen, just the curly signature of the designer over the shop door. The black hat in its plastic bag in her hand suddenly seemed totally dreary and drab as she stood looking at the wonderful confections displayed. She had to go inside. She just had to.

Chapter Twenty-one

Ellie smiled; she had just spent half an hour chatting to Rory. They had returned from a night away in Galway, where they had stayed in the new fancy Philip Treacy-designed hotel. Rory had driven down and been so attentive. At lunch they'd eaten oysters out in Clarinbridge with an agent and composer friends of his and later they'd toured the city. Rory wanted to see some hot new young rock band who were playing in King's and he had persuaded her to join him. It was the longest time they had spent together and Ellie had really enjoyed herself. He was fun to be with and Ellie guessed she would have to learn to accept that once he was around musicians he got so involved that he would always be part of a crowd.

This weekend, she'd told him, was going to be different as she was cooking a great meal for the two of them with plenty of wine and the time to relax and be together without bands or deals or anyone else. She wanted Rory to herself.

She watched in the mirror as the girl with the long legs picked up the delicate dragonfly-wing turquoise hat she'd finished two days ago. It was exquisite and picked up the green in her eyes and the fleck of copper in her hair.

'It suits you.' She smiled.

'Yes,' replied the customer, giving a wobbly sigh. 'But I . . . I can't afford it.'

Ellie frowned. She hadn't even put a price tag on the hat yet. She was puzzled. The girl gently removed the hat and put it back on the stand.

'Everything, everything here is so beautiful! Amazing! Did you design them?'

'Yes,' Ellie said proudly. 'It's my shop.'

She studied the girl. She was young, tall and much too thin, like those models. She had huge eyes and perfect pale skin and beautiful lips.

'I'm going to the horse show next week and I need something for it.'

Ellie stopped smiling. She had eight hats to be ready in the next few days for the horse show plus a wedding headdress and a mother of the bride. She couldn't take anything else on, she just couldn't.

'I love all these hats, they're beautiful, but I couldn't afford them. I'm broke,' confessed the young customer, who suddenly looked vulnerable and rather tearful.

Ellie was taken aback, for the girl was immaculately groomed in an expensive pair of tan leather mules, a crisp white shirt and a beautifully cut pair of beige trousers with a leather belt that emphasized her slim figure. She was used to customers getting emotional over the purchase of a hat for a wedding or even a funeral, but breaking down without warning like this was unexpected to say the least.

'I've got a dress and shoes but it's not enough, not enough at all!' wailed the girl, tears springing into her eyes.

Ellie was surprised. This wasn't one of those Dublin 4 types or a

127

southsider like she appeared, for her accent had a soft Kilkenny lilt to it.

'It's just hopeless. I bought this and I thought maybe I could do something with it! Cost me twenty euros,' she admitted, lips trembling as she pulled a hat from a plastic bag.

Ellie studied the simple black cartwheel worked in fine mesh and crafted and balanced perfectly. Most definitely French: it shouted classic Parisian style. At least fifty years old. She wondered where the customer had bought it.

'It's a beautiful hat.' She smiled encouragingly. '*Parfait*.'

'I got it in the Oxfam shop in Aungier Street. The lady wanted thirty for it but I managed to bargain her down.'

Ellie sympathized. She remembered her own student days, fighting fiercely at market stalls and boutiques for much-desired designs. Money had never been plentiful where she was concerned.

'I know it's beautifully made,' admitted the girl. 'It's just that it's too plain for what I want it for. I need to dress it up as I'm wearing it with a very simple black dress.'

Ellie considered the problem. 'We could put a ribbon on it – I have a huge selection of colours – or a flower perhaps?'

The girl shook her head. 'No! No! That won't do at all. I have to be noticed, stand out. That wouldn't be suitable at all.'

The two young women stared at each other. Ellie could read the desperation in her client's eyes, the search for something unique and beautiful, a quest that guided her constantly every day when she sat down to work.

'Could you do a drawing of the black dress you intend to wear with this hat, to give me some idea of what you want?' she suggested.

The dress was, as she had expected, a perfect example of simplicity with its narrow fitted bodice and fuller skirt.

'Have you a belt?'

'No.'

'Perhaps something on the hat and a trim on the waistline and a bag would work well.'

'Oh yes, that sounds divine, but what kind of trim and how expensive would it be?'

Ellie considered. An idea was tingling in the back of her mind.

'Please can you wait a few minutes while I look in the back of my storeroom? I might have some of the turquoise left.'

She left the girl sitting reading a magazine while she raced through her basket. She found the organza immediately, but there was something else. There were five white daisies, her mother must have made them, beautifully stitched and glued, perfect petals ready to trim a straw sunhat, but their bright shapes against the classic black . . . Perhaps it would work.

'Here we are.' She smiled, wrapping the turquoise loosely round the black. It looked well and set off the colour in the customer's eyes but there was definitely not enough for a belt.

'It's beautiful but . . .'

'That's what I was thinking,' agreed Ellie. 'Pass me the hat again.' She very loosely laid the daisies round the crown. The white and green and hint of yellow already made a splash against the dark material.

'Oh, I do like them,' smiled the girl.

Ellie frowned. The daisies emphasized the girl's youth and were summery but they weren't quite right as they gave the impression of a sunhat. 'Excuse me a minute.' With her scissors she separated two, three daisies and gently taking a pin off her blouse she positioned the flowers right on the brim of the hat so they came down over the girl's face and hair and eyes. The effect was startling.

The girl looked up . . . holding her breath as if frightened the image in the mirror would disappear.

'Oh my God,' she whispered. 'It's just perfect.'

Ellie could feel the rush of joy at seeing a creation come together.

'Yes, daisies all round the brim! I will have to measure and decide how many more to make, play around with placing so they are uniformly matched and perhaps spray them with a little stiffening.'

'Oh, I can't believe it,' laughed the girl, her eyes shining.

'If you had the dress we could stitch one, maybe two, right on the cinch of your waistband and for a purse if we put a few together . . . perhaps with plain material underneath and a little strap?'

The girl almost hugged her. 'I can't believe it . . . I'm going to have a wonderful outfit.'

Ellie smiled to herself, feeling like the fairy godmother telling Cinderella that she was going to the ball.

'But . . .' the girl hesitated, 'how much is all this going to cost?'

Ellie totted up the materials in her head, plus there would be a few hours' work. She would make no profit but the customer would be happy, and return again hopefully.

'Fifty euro,' she said softly.

The girl's smile lit up her face. She was actually quite beautiful.

'I will have enough,' she said.

The arrangements were made and Claire Connolly filled in the order book, paying a deposit of twenty and promising to drop the dress in during Monday lunchtime.

Ellie put the book away, delighted, for she knew she could make the hat show off Claire's bone structure and emphasize her willowy proportions. With all the orders due around the same time she would have to work right up till the weekend, she thought as she scribbled down a long shopping list for her romantic dinner.

Chapter Twenty-two

Dublin basked in summer sunshine for the week of the Dublin Horse Show. Gardens and flower beds and window boxes were bursting with roses and geraniums and pink fuchsia as the city enjoyed the warm temperatures. Claire, nervous with anticipation, woke early on the morning of Ladies' Day, and after a quick cup of coffee and some toast showered and blow-dried her hair. All week she'd been preparing for the best-dressed lady competition and she'd given herself a full facial with a cleansing peel and a nourishing face mask at the weekend. Her hands and nails had been buffed and French-polished to perfection and Fiona had helped her apply a lovely light golden fake tan to her limbs and torso, which gave her a sun-kissed glow. Her hair was glossy and conditioned and as she applied her mascara and dark eyeliner she realized her eyes looked huge.

She thought about calling in sick to Murphy and Byrne's but just supposing she did win and her photograph was plastered all over the papers in the morning, how would she explain that to her bosses? So instead she had taken a day's holiday and confided in Sheila what she was doing.

'Oh, you're entering the Ladies' Day competition at the horse show, that's wonderful!' beamed Sheila kindly. 'I used to love going along and seeing the style when I was younger. A beautiful girl like yourself will be totally at home there, and knock the judge sideways!'

Claire grinned, glad of the older woman's enthusiasm and promises to say a prayer for her and to get Derek to say one too.

She dressed slowly, almost catching her breath with surprise when she lifted the hat out of its box and put it on her head, her eyes peeping out from under the large daisy brim. What with her little black dress and her daisy bag on her wrist, she looked just the way she'd hoped.

'Wow!' said Fiona and Bridget when they saw her. 'You look stunning. Like a film star.'

Claire felt a bit jittery and anxious, as if she was going to an audition. She had intended getting the bus but Fiona had insisted on driving her right to her destination.

'Bridget and I are doing promotions out in Blackrock at two o'clock. The least we can do is give you a bit of support when you go in to register, though we won't be able to stay for the judging.'

Claire was eternally grateful to her friends for adjusting their busy schedules to suit her.

The traffic out of town was heavy and it seemed like the world and his wife were making their way to the Royal Dublin Society's showgrounds in Ballsbridge for the annual Dublin Horse Show. Every hotel and guesthouse and B&B in the city and suburbs would be booked out, the restaurants packed as horse lovers, show–jumping teams and visitors crowded into the city for the week.

'God, it's mad,' declared Fiona, pulling out in front of a van driver in her bright red car. Undaunted, she managed to whiz up in the wrong lane and find a minute parking spot meant to be reserved for customers of one of the nearby restaurants.

'I'll be gone before the lunch-hour crowd,' promised an unrepentant Fiona as they strolled across the Merrion Road.

Claire stood at the entrance and decided to purchase a family ticket. 'We're sisters,' she said, smiling at the disbelieving steward as he took in the blonde, brunette and redhead in front of him.

The showgrounds were already crowded, the sign for the car park 'Full' as they walked across the grass. The inside halls were busy selling everything from conservatories to horse blankets, ice creams to foot baths. It never ceased to amaze Claire that such a huge range of products was to be found at the show.

'Come on, this way,' she signalled to her friends.

Outside it was already hot. The tannoy called out, 'A perfect round,' as the noise of horses' hooves and the chatter of the crowd filled the air. She had forgotten how wonderful it was, that scent of grass and hay and horses that overwhelmed the senses as soon as one stepped on to the grassy lawns and fenced areas of the Royal Dublin Society's grounds.

The Moët & Chandon-sponsored Ladies' Day competition was being held under a bright blue and white awning, with everyone queuing to register their entry. Claire straightened her back and joined the rest of the women and girls in the line. Her eyes roved the crowd. She mentally said a prayer of thanks that she had worn a hat. Hats were definitely the flavour of the day . . . Some were hideous, some fun, some just simple sunhats, but there was no doubt that they added to the sense of occasion. She also breathed a sigh of relief that she had not worn pink as almost half the women present had kitted themselves out in various shades from salmon to raspberry. After the recent warm weather, the colours combined with their sunburn to give a weird strawberry-like effect. There was an older woman and her friend in expensive cream and beige suits with co-ordinating handbags, shoes and gloves, their hair immaculately done.

'We enter every year,' they laughed, 'just so our husbands have to pay for a new outfit and the day out. Beats sitting at home and watching it on the television!'

Claire suddenly felt guilty and pulled out her mobile to dial the number for home, hearing it ring five times before her mother answered.

'Where are you, Claire?'

'I'm at the RDS, Mum,' she shouted over the noise. 'Just thought I'd let you know!'

It was about eight years since she'd been to the show with her parents, entering the novice riders and pony events, her hair plaited, wearing jodhpurs and riding gear. It seemed like a million years ago.

'Are you in one of the events?' her mother asked excitedly.

'No, no. Well, not that sort, Mum! It's the Ladies' Day thing.'

She could almost hear the harrumph of indignation from her mother's end of the call, imagining Cora Connolly standing there in her old faded jeans and Wellington boots and a T-shirt, just in from the stables or the paddocks.

'Just thought I'd let you know in case it's on the telly.'

'Are you all right, love?' asked her mother. 'We haven't seen you for ages.'

'I'm fine, Mum, just been busy, that's all. Listen, tell Dad I said hello. I've got to go now,' she said, killing the signal.

She slipped the phone back inside the daisy bag with its black handles. Ellie Matthews had done a wonderful job.

She filled in the form, listing her occupation as model. She was hardly going to put boring old insurance clerk. Then she was given a number and approximate time to come back and meet the judges. Two o'clock – she had ages to wait. She stood around taking in the opposition. There were a whole load of debby types in flowery mini-dresses and wrapover skirts showing off cleavage and belly buttons and sexy sun-tanned legs, chatting on about villas in Tuscany and apartments in Puerto Banus. They certainly didn't need to win the money, she thought enviously.

A few girls she recognized from the Irish modelling circuit, eyes shaded discreetly behind dark glasses, clad in top-to-toe designer gear that they had borrowed from exclusive boutiques with the promise of mentioning the designer if they won. Then there were the amateurs. Mothers, daughters, grandmothers, wearing their very best outfit, who'd come along simply for the fun of it. Claire considered them. Some had made their own clothes; some were young designers, college students trying to get a bit of attention; others were wearing chain-store-bought outfits, trying to keep out of the way of people wearing something similar to themselves. There was a magnificent pure white linen coat and skirt worn by a tall girl with black hair cut tight into her head. It was most definitely an original, and the plump girl with the frizzy hair and hopeful look standing beside her was obviously the designer. There was a leopard-skin jumpsuit worn by a blonde with tawny eyes and massive high heels, who clung on to an older man with a navy blazer and a co-ordinating leopard-print bow tie like there was no tomorrow. There were young girls in Laura Ashley dresses, all sprigged cotton and lawn with frills and bows. Their mothers looked like Stepford wives in neat linen pastel suits and highlighted trim hair, minding toddlers and buggies as they edged up the queue.

'Hey, did you register yet?' enquired Bridget.

'Yes. I got my number and time,' admitted Claire, joining her friends back out in the sunshine.

'Let's get an ice cream and chill out for a while,' suggested Fiona.

They found a small metal table and some chairs under a parasol. Bridget was dispatched to buy the refreshments. Fiona grinned as she caught the approving glances of members of the opposite sex who passed by their table en route to the ice cream stand.

'Told you, you look stunning.'

'Do you really think so?' asked Claire nervously.

'You look like Audrey Hepburn in *Breakfast at Tiffany's*, or one of those amazing French films we had to go and see when we were in college.'

Claire squeezed her friend's hand warmly and suddenly wished that Fiona could stay to give her moral support later when she needed it.

'Lots of luck!' they both screamed at her when they had to leave for work.

Claire took a deep breath as they disappeared into the crowds. Suddenly she felt very alone and wished she could just run out of the place with them. Still, she hadn't come this far to turn back now. She walked up towards the competition area. There was still ages to wait. She'd get some water and a roll, and maybe have a stroll around the place.

With nearly an hour to kill she decided to go and watch the jumping. Pushing her way into the wooden stands, she was calmed by the cantering circles of the horses and the fluid movements of their riders as they followed the jumping course. She'd always loved horses and soon got engrossed in the battle between riders. Suddenly realizing the time, she jumped up and made a run for the ladies' cloakroom to quickly freshen up before making her way to the Moët & Chandon stand.

There was still a queue, so obviously everything was running late. A peroxide blonde wearing a bright red silk top, a slit skirt and high heels was ahead of her. A petite Italian-looking woman in a beautiful pale pearl-coloured Chanel suit and matching bag spoke in broken English to admire her 'magnificent hat'. Claire watched as other women emerged from the judge's area, hoping to glean some information about what was going on. She giggled as a hefty six-footer emerged from the doorway dressed as a nun and gave a thumbs-down to a load of his mates who were falling around the place laughing.

'Must have been a bet, you think,' joked the dainty Italian beside her.

Claire noted a pretty blonde young mother in a straw hat and a floaty pale pink dress emerge with a little girl of about five dressed in the exact match of her mother's outfit. Even their hats were the same. The little girl, who was waving to everyone, looked so cute. Claire wouldn't have allowed a dress near her at that age. She had spent most of her time in dirty denim shorts and a green T-shirt that her dad told her matched her eyes.

The Italian disappeared and then, trying to control herself, Claire stepped forward. The judges asked her to turn round. There were two women and two men. One had his own television show, and she knew that Tara O'Neill was the chief fashion buyer for one of the bigger chain stores in Ireland. Pretend it's a modelling job, she told herself as she walked forward.

'I see you're a model.'

'Just starting.' She smiled and told them about the advertisement she'd been in and mentioned she was signed to 'The Agency'.

'Did one of the designers lend you the clothes?' quizzed Tara.

'No,' she replied, affronted. 'The dress and shoes, hat and bag are all my own.'

'Even the hat?'

'I bought the hat – it's French – in an Oxfam shop. Ellie Matthews, the milliner in South Anne Street, helped me to pull the outfit together by redesigning it.'

'With the daisies and the bag?' The intense man with the glasses was scribbling on the pad in front of him.

'Yes, Ellie's wonderful and so is her shop. Do you know it?'

137

He shook his head.

'It is just such a sweet shop and she has some great ideas.'

She could see them all writing and fell silent.

'Miss Connolly, we would like to see you back here at four o'clock if possible.'

If possible? Of course it was possible!

Claire felt like hugging them. Being called back meant she was being shortlisted for the final ten in the Best-Dressed Ladies competition. Claire wanted to jump up and down with excitement.

She stood around, not knowing what to do. If she walked round the busy exhibition area she risked having a kid bump into her with a big ice cream cone or a drink in its hand. Anyway she felt tired, wound up. If she went back to watch the showjumping, she reckoned she might begin to feel like a rider in a jump-off, all anxious and excited. Instead she opted for the gardening hall, with its huge floral displays and plants.

Many of the flowers had been cut from gardens this morning. Some stood in solid well-watered pots, the air heavy with the scent of old roses and blowzy hydrangeas and sweet peas. She wandered around, admiring them and the cheerful gardeners who spent so much time and energy growing them. She explored the kitchen garden section, with its herbs and tomatoes and home-grown lettuces and cabbages and celery and courgettes, which reminded her of her mother's endeavours back in Kilkenny.

She found a bench alongside an elderly couple who were arguing over the merits of peas and beans. Claire closed her eyes in the warm summer sunshine.

She almost jumped when a photographer asked if he could take her photograph.

'Noel Foley,' he introduced himself. 'I'm with the *Times*.'

She agreed, smiling as he positioned her against a tumbling display of blooms, scribbling down her name on his jotter and wishing her luck in the competition. Claire grinned to herself, suddenly feeling more relaxed and confident. Winning was the reason she had come here; now it was time to do her best.

Back at the Ladies' Day Stand the queue had dissolved and been replaced by a huge number of curious onlookers and two camera crews. When she arrived and gave her name she was immediately served with a glass of chilled champagne.

She walked around, taking in the shiny first prize of a ten-thousand-euro diamond, crates of champagne, vouchers for Brown Thomas, and a load of other delicious freebies. But it was the diamond she was after. She just had to remain composed for the next twenty minutes, she reminded herself. Be professional. Stand straight. Be elegant. The tall girl in the white suit appeared. Then she spotted the small Italian woman whom she had met earlier. And of course one of the debs had the photographers in a tizzy with her floaty turquoise blue dress with its shoestring straps and a wrap-around skirt that caught on the breeze. There was a woman old enough to be her grandmother in a magnificent lace top and skirt in soft mauve, wearing a muted purple hat over her grey hair. The mother and daughter in pretty pink had made it through, as had one of Ireland's well-known models in a sailor-suit-inspired outfit in navy and white. Claire noticed the judges over in a corner talking in a huddle as she grabbed hold of another glass of champagne. The sun beat down on them and she felt hot and nervous as the time went on. Everyone suddenly came to attention when the chat show host stepped forward to make the announcement. Claire felt her mouth go dry and her legs shake as he said her name.

Chapter Twenty-three

Claire found herself pushing through the crowds, accepting their congratulations and pats on the back as the cameras and photographers surged forward towards the winner. She didn't know what to do or where to go as a strange mixture of disappointment and delight overwhelmed her. The onlookers were beginning to disperse as the event ended.

Claire stood near the bandstand trying to collect herself, surveying Caviston's busy al fresco seafood dining area and all the people thronging the Ring Bar and Bistro as she then made her way down past the Pembroke Boxes and Saddlery.

Glancing upwards at the old Clock Tower, she headed towards the main grandstand and pavilion, where the horses waited or were warmed up in the nearby rings. The crowds were silent in the main enclosure as the jumping continued. She hadn't the heart for another competition and quickening her pace she fled towards the stables. The smell of horse dung and straw and sweat and leather greeted her like an old friend as she walked across the cobbled yards. Some of the stalls were already empty, the young riders with their horses in horseboxes on their way home to the far-flung counties of Ireland. Others displayed fancy rosettes and ribbons tied to their gates, where the horses whinnied and neighed.

She was drawn to this place and found herself stroking a beautiful bay mare, who stared at her quizzically and sniffed at her hat.

She felt like a little kid again, ready to cry. It was so bloody stupid. Fiona and Bridget had both texted her for news and she was deliberately ignoring them. She should have known that the cute five-year-old in the pink dress with her blond mother would win it. They were a PR person's dream, especially when the mother had announced she was about to open a children's clothes shop out of town stocking her own designs.

Claire felt like screaming. She had got second place. The runner-up, winning a voucher for five hundred euros and a crate of champagne. She should be delighted. Happy. She shouldn't have drunk so much of that bloody free champagne. It just made her maudlin and stupid and weepy. She couldn't go around disgracing herself. She sniffed and pulled a tissue from her bag.

'Hey! You'd better watch your fancy shoes in the muck,' warned a voice.

She looked up. 'Don't worry. I'm used to horse-shit. I've been around horses and dung all my life,' she muttered, wishing this do-gooder would go away and leave her alone in her misery.

'Are you OK?' he asked.

She said nothing for a moment, trying to compose herself.

'I used to enter the pony classes here when I was younger,' she sniffed.

'Did you then!' He sounded surprised.

Claire looked up at him from under her brim of white daisies.

'Ever win?'

'No!' She burst out laughing, giggling like a fool. 'I only ever came second, runner-up. Same as today.'

141

He looked at her as if she was cracked.

'That's what I got too,' he said kindly.

'You?'

'Second in the jump-off.'

'Then we're a pair,' sighed Claire.

'I'm Andrew Ryan,' he said, introducing himself.

From under the daisy hat Claire could see he wasn't at all like the usual wimps she met around town. He was at least four inches taller than her even in her heels. Standing there in a load of horse straw and muck in his jodhpurs and open-neck blue check shirt, with his sandy hair and blue eyes, he actually was drop dead gorgeous.

'I see you already met Chloë,' he said, patting the horse. 'She's a great lady. Tomorrow I'm riding her brother Dandy. He's there across the yard if you want to see him.'

'Yes, please,' she agreed, curious.

'Here, let me give you a hand,' offered Andrew, reaching to lift her up with a whoosh over a steaming pile of horse-shit.

The Jimmy Choos were definitely not made for slippery cobbles and she would have tripped except that he managed to steady her.

Dandy was a gorgeous big horse with luminous dark brown eyes and he nudged against her, snuffling her bare skin in a way that made her laugh.

'Back off, boy,' warned Andrew, teasing her.

He made her laugh too and even helped her clean her Jimmy's before they left the stables.

'Don't want you destroying those fancy shoes of yours with all this dung.'

Claire, in her daisy hat, couldn't help getting a fit of the giggles at the absurdity of it all.

'You're not from the city, are you?' he asked later as he escorted her to the bar.

She was about to joke and deny her culchie roots, but seeing the serious look in his eye and guessing he was a nice guy she told him the truth.

'No, actually I'm from Kilkenny. My folks have a farm there.'

'Same neck of the woods as myself then,' he said, passing her a glass of chilled white wine. 'I live in Carlow.'

She had another two drinks, Andrew confessing that daisies had always been his favourite flower while she told him about her temporary job in an insurance office and confided her hopes of being a model as they shared plates of tasty fish and chips. After three hours of talking he excused himself, saying he had to get back to the horses, Claire marking it down as one of the most unusual brush-offs she'd ever had. She'd really fancied him but he obviously wasn't interested. Clutching her daisy bag and hat she made her way on to the Merrion Road. There was no sign of a bus and throwing caution to the winds Claire hailed a passing cab.

'Congratulations. You did brilliant, Claire,' yelled her flatmates when she got home. Fiona opened a bottle of wine as she collapsed on the couch, kicked off her shoes and replayed all that had happened.

'Claire, you looked amazing and coming second is brilliant!'

'Let's face it, no one stood a chance against cutesy mother and daughter,' argued Fiona.

'They shouldn't have been allowed in the competition!' insisted Bridget loyally.

'And think of all that champagne you've won! Maybe you could trade some of it in or sell it. And then you've got those lovely Brown Thomas vouchers to spend and a gold bracelet and the weekend away in Killarney.'

Claire took another sip of her wine. The girls were right: when she heard them list off all she'd won it sounded fabulous. She began to recount her day again, blow by blow, including meeting the dishy Andrew Ryan and how charming he'd been. Perhaps it had been a bit of a triumph after all.

Chapter Twenty-four

Ellie had raced home from work on Saturday to tidy the apartment, organize dinner and have a shower and wash her hair before Rory arrived. She felt all domesticated and romantic. As she tossed the marinated chicken and set the candles on the table the phone rang. She grabbed her mobile. It was Rory.

'Ellie. Sorry but I'm not going to be able to make dinner at your place.'

'Where are you?' she blurted out, all concerned.

'I'm in Manchester,' he said apologetically.

'Manchester!'

'Well, Manchester airport, actually. I've just arrived. The guys have been asked to play in a big open-air gig, Rock in the Park, next Thursday. One of the other bands dropped out so they're standing in for them. I said I'd come over and suss out the scene.'

She could hear laughing and joking already in the background.

'Why didn't you tell me earlier? You could have let me know,' she argued, annoyed with him.

'It just happened so fast and I . . .'

She knew what he was going to say. He hadn't thought about her. He'd forgotten! She swallowed hard. There was no point losing her cool with him. He wasn't even in the country.

'No problem,' she lied. 'It was only supper and a DVD.'

'No harm done then,' he joked. 'Listen, I'll see you when I get back, OK?'

'When are you back?' It had slipped out before she knew it and she inwardly cursed herself for sounding so needy.

'A few days. Maybe a week. Hey, Ellie, have a good weekend.'

She stared at the phone for fifteen minutes, not moving, waiting to see if he would call her back.

The table was set, candles, white linen, flowers, the lot. What a waste, and she had gone to so much trouble with the food. She was wearing the Deborah Veale dress she'd recently bought and had already opened a bottle of wine. What a crap Saturday night. Maybe she should just eat and go to bed, curl up under her duvet and never come back out. She was tempted – and then she thought about who might share her feast, her fingers already calling up Fergus's number.

It took her only a few moments to discern that he had not eaten yet and his dinner intentions involved a microwaveable ready meal of lamb hotpot, which had been sitting in his fridge for far too long.

'I've got free food,' she bribed, 'and wine.'

It took all of fifteen minutes for Fergus to arrive and sit with linen napkin on his lap as she served him prawns tossed in Pernod, a spicy chicken and rice pilaf, and a white chocolate tiramisu.

'That Rory guy must be gone mad,' he declared stoutly as he complimented every element of the meal. 'Missing this on a Saturday night.'

Ellie flung the cushion at him.

'I mean missing being with you.'

Ellie pulled her feet up under her on the couch near Fergus and sipped the red wine.

'It's just he's away so much and I'm never sure when I'll get to see him . . .' She began to talk about the pros and cons of her relationship with Rory.

'Are we going to sit here all night and mope about this guy?' asked Fergus.

Ellie could have strangled him. 'No! You go out and enjoy yourself,' she shouted. 'There's no one stopping you. I'm sorry I spoiled your plans.'

'Ellie,' he remonstrated, catching hold of her, 'you're crazy. I had no big plans for tonight, though there's late night opera on in the square. I was going to wander down later to see it. Why don't you come too?'

Ellie had intended wallowing in self-pity but now the thought of sitting alone in the apartment didn't seem so appealing.

'Come on,' he coaxed her. 'If we hurry we can get there before the fat lady sings!'

She grabbed her turquoise wrap and, after making sure every last candle was out, the two of them ran for the bus to get them downtown.

Temple Bar was busy and they managed to chase up to Meeting House Square just as the huge stage lights went on in the open-air concert arena. The place was absolutely packed and they squeezed into two seats near the back. Ellie held her breath as the soprano in her bejewelled figure-hugging dress stepped forward on to the stage, her voice filling the night air with the opening aria from *La Bohème*. The rapt audience followed her every nuance as she sang. Fergus, a huge opera fan, sat forward in his seat, his red hair standing on end as he concentrated.

147

'Thanks,' whispered Ellie, squeezing his fingers as she let the music and the voice carry her.

It was an exquisite performance, emotional and soaring, the audience bursting into huge applause as Paola O'Reilly bowed. Then came Richard Patterson. The Irish tenor's massive stage presence and voice filled the square, broken only by the sound of an overhead plane, as he sang of love and loss and the madness that ensued. They later duetted, and Paola finished by singing from the last act of *Carmen*. The crowd rose to their feet in appreciation as the performance ended. Ellie pulled her wrap around her. The night was slightly chilly and she snuggled up to Fergus as they left their seats and joined the throng of people leaving the square.

'Good evening, Miss Matthews,' said Neil Harrington as he moved past them. He was with a tall, striking dark-haired girl, his arm round her shoulders.

'Wasn't it magnificent!' enthused the girl. 'We could have been in Verona or Milan.'

'Yes,' laughed Ellie, glad to be out in the open air under a starry sky with people who had shared the same experience and had been touched by the performance.

Fergus, in a post-opera daze and his tie-dyed T-shirt and tatty jeans, nodded in agreement as she introduced him.

'Come on, Rachel,' urged Neil, 'we don't want to be late meeting the others.'

The girl seemed nice and it was clear Neil was mad about her, for Ellie couldn't help but notice the protective way he looked at her.

'I hope that you and your boyfriend enjoyed the night,' he said politely, head bent whispering to the girl as they moved away.

Ellie smiled. She didn't bother enlightening him. Anyway Fergus was better than a hundred boyfriends to her mind.

'You OK?' she asked, grabbing his hand.

'Yeah.' He grinned. Opera always overwhelmed him. 'What about you?'

'Not a bother,' she lied. 'What about a glass of wine and the rest of that tiramisu back at my place?' she offered, as they walked towards Dame Street.

Chapter Twenty-five

Claire settled back into Murphy and Byrne's, presenting a delighted Sheila with a bottle of champagne from the crate in her living room.

'You and Kevin enjoy it.'

Sheila Sweeney thought what a nice girl that young one really was, even if she didn't eat a pick and needed serious feeding up to put a bit of weight on her.

Someone had put her daisy hat photo up on the staff noticeboard, and everyone who passed her desk congratulated her. Even grumpy old Arthur Roberts, one of the senior executives, had stopped to express his good wishes and to mourn the fact that she hadn't mentioned the company name when she gave them her details. Claire had said nothing. Honestly, as if she was going to tell anyone where she worked!

'Thanks,' she said, putting her head down to concentrate on the reams of figures she was meant to be inputting into the computer.

'Claire, your modelling agency is on the phone for you,' Sheila announced about an hour later, so loud that half the office heard and were glued to their desks with curiosity.

'Just phoning to say I loved the photo,' purred Elaine. 'Front page of the *Irish Times*, well done. It couldn't be better. Fought off a lot of hot competition from the other agencies and a few big names too, so I heard.'

'Thanks.'

'Anyway, there's a chance of a new spring water ad coming up. You'll have to meet the casting director but he's keen.'

'That's great,' gushed Claire, not believing that all this was happening.

'I'll be back in touch with the details.'

She sat at her computer feeling stunned. For the first time the agency had actually phoned her. She still couldn't believe it. She felt like kissing Derek, who was sitting behind her totting up a list of figures.

Things only got better when on Wednesday the switch put through a call from a Mr Andrew Ryan.

Claire was genuinely surprised as she had given up hope of ever seeing him again.

'Andrew!' she exclaimed, wondering how he'd found her. She had long ago stopped giving guys her phone number unless they really asked for it. She'd heard far too many 'I'll phone you's and then spent days waiting for calls that never came.

'Actually I called every insurance company in Dublin,' he admitted, 'trying to find where you worked.'

'Oh, I see,' she said, accidentally deleting a week's revenue figures from the spreadsheet as she imagined him tracking her down.

'I should have got your number when we met. I went out after you to get it but you'd gone. I couldn't remember exactly where you lived and thought it best to try work.'

She loved even the sound of his voice.

'I tried lots of offices – I think the girls on the switch thought I was some kind of lunatic stalker.'

'It's good to hear from you.' She tried to sound calm.

'Anyway, one of the reasons I'm phoning is that I'm going down to Carlow on Friday night and I thought I might check and see if you had any plans or if you were going home this weekend,' he said. 'Of course you might have plans already, be doing something else . . .'

'No. I'm not,' she said, smiling, forgetting to play it cool. 'I'm not doing anything this weekend.'

She hoped she didn't sound too eager, too desperate.

'I could collect you at your flat if you like. Also there's a bit of a do – a barbecue in the local rugby club on Saturday night – and I was wondering if you might be interested in going with me.'

She didn't know what to say.

'Claire?'

A barbecue with Andrew and she hadn't been home for an age. She could go up to Brown Thomas after work and get one or two things for her parents and brother and sister with her vouchers and surprise them.

'A weekend down home would be wonderful, Andrew.'

'And the club?'

It had been so long since she had been on a proper date she had almost forgotten.

'That would be wonderful too.' She smiled, giving him her address and mobile number. 'What time will you pick me up?'

Claire stared at the computer screen, hitting letters without thinking.

'Is that him?' whispered Sheila, her double chin wobbling. 'The boyfriend?'

'Yes,' grinned Claire. 'I rather think it might be.'

Chapter Twenty-six

The apartment in Hatch Street was spick and span. Fresh white bed-linen, clean towels, and bright summer flowers in vases and jugs in each room, and every piece of glass she possessed handwashed before Yvette's eagle eye could spot a speck of dust. While Ellie looked forward to the visit of her mother's sister, she was also a little nervous about her aunt's reaction to the changes she had made to her home and the shop since her mother's death.

'Don't worry,' Kim assured her. 'She's coming to see how you are, and how you are doing, not to check on the business.'

Ellie wanted to believe that, but she knew that a perceptive woman like her aunt would be keen to see the shop and discover how her niece was surviving in the world of millinery.

Yvette Renchard was pleased to see her young niece, kissing her twice, French fashion, as they greeted each other. Ellie noticed that despite the journey her aunt looked as elegant as ever in an immaculate Chanel suit with a pale blue cotton shirt underneath, her short grey hair accentuating her eyes and bone structure. She helped her aunt to carry her bag and the simple brown leather valise upstairs, Yvette praising the sun-filled apartment with its welcoming display of tall blue delphiniums and baby's breath on the sideboard.

'How are you, Elise *chérie, vraiment?*' she asked, patting the cushions on the couch beside her as she settled down for a cup of coffee. 'You must miss Madeleine terribly.'

Ellie realized how good it was to have someone to talk to about her mother, someone who was not afraid to mention Madeleine's name.

'I do get sad and lonely without her,' she admitted, holding her aunt's hand, 'but I have the shop and my friends and so many people I care about here in Dublin.'

'Then that is a good thing,' her aunt reassured her. 'Your *maman* would not want you to be maudlin or too sad to enjoy your life. You are a beautiful young woman with the world as your lobster.'

Ellie smiled to herself. Although her aunt spoke almost perfect English, she did tend to get sayings mixed up.

'What would you like to do, Yvette,' she asked. 'Would you like to rest after your journey?'

'Rest?' protested her aunt. 'I am an old woman. I will have all the time in the world to rest. No! I did not come to Dublin to rest but to spend time with my sweet girl. Perhaps we could go to the church and have a Mass, say prayers for your mother, then take a little stroll around the city.'

Ellie had forgotten what a devout Catholic her mother's older sister was, and readily agreed to walk to the nearby church on St Stephen's Green for Sunday Mass.

The weather was glorious as they strolled to the church. Afterwards she knew her aunt would suggest they pass by the shop. She had brought her keys along so Yvette could sate her curiosity and see the changes she had implemented.

'*C'est très joli!*' her aunt congratulated her, standing enraptured before the brightly painted shopfront, tears filling her eyes when she saw the name change over the door.

Inside she touched the newly painted shelves and the counter, admiring the colour scheme and the simple layout.

'*Ma chère*, it is exquisite. I will steal you back to Paris, *immédiatement*!'

Ellie was so pleased that she liked the décor and explained what she had tried to do, to maintain her mother's style but to also put her own imprint on it.

'Well, you have succeeded!'

Then her aunt turned her attention to her work, studying the hats on display in the window, on the hatstands in the shop and on the blocks in the back.

'You have a lot of work,' she praised. 'And I understand why! You have all your mother's *classique* training, but you also have the *je ne sais quoi*. That is the little piece of your soul that goes into every hat you make. Of course you are young and fresh, full of ideas.'

Ellie laughed despite herself as Yvette, her glasses halfway down her nose, peered closely at every stitch.

'What is this?'

'It's a two-tone sinamay. Simple but with a twist. I've run a bit of antique ribbon through the edges, to create this sort of twirl effect between the colours. It's for a charity event to raise funds for the National Maternity Hospital.'

'A kind heart for a good cause,' remarked her aunt, patting her hand. 'And this *bonne bouche*?'

The pink and red disc with a feather cut and shaped like a paint-brush across the centre had been commissioned by an artist with a studio in Baggot Street. Janna Rowan's summer exhibition was opening in the Hallward Gallery in a few days' time.

155

'She wanted something to get her noticed!'

'Well, you tell her she succeeded,' giggled Yvette. 'And this?'

Ellie could see her aunt's delight as she examined the gold spun-silk topper with its whorls of Irish cream linen.

'It's to co-ordinate with a beautiful linen dress and jacket that the client got made for her wedding. It's very intricate but I managed to get some offcuts and shape them, then I sprayed them with a little stiffener.'

'The gold and the cream is delicious and the Celtic influence with the pattern of the Irish linen, *merveilleux*!'

'Do you really like them?' Ellie could not believe the reaction of such an accomplished hatmaker to her work.

'Elise, *tais-toi*! In all my years have I ever lied to you? No, I am always honest, which as you know has caused me problems. These hats of yours are so pretty and stylish and each in its own way contains your *joie de vivre*, which is as it should be. Madeleine's business has changed, it is refreshed. You are young with the new ideas and your own designs. A born milliner!'

Ellie felt an overwhelming sense of pride as her aunt definitely did not give praise lightly.

'Now I have seen the shop I can rest easy,' Yvette admitted. 'It is a great success and I am so proud of you, *ma petite* Elise.'

Ellie hugged her aunt and was enveloped in a cloud of perfume.

'So let us go for lunch!' suggested Yvette.

They got a table in Fitzers café on Dawson Street, her aunt remarking on all the changes in the area as they ate.

'Years ago when we were young, women wore hats, they dressed up, took care of themselves coming into town, going to work, going out, socializing. Good coats to keep them warm and hats to keep their heads warm also and protect their hairstyles and hide those bad hair days. They walked, took the tram, the metro, the bus. Then it all

156

changed. They wore leggings and tracksuits and those awful head-bands and jogged or took their cars everywhere. Now it is come full circle again, I think. Style is back. Women want to look good again.'

Ellie loved listening to her aunt's thoughts on style and fashion.

'Look around us. This town is full now that Catholic Ireland has decided to go shopping on a Sunday!' Yvette said wryly. 'At least the small businesses do not have to open on the holy day! That is for the big stores and boutiques.'

'The small businesses are finding it hard,' explained Ellie, out-lining what was happening in their own street, and how so many shops were closing down. 'We are having a meeting next week about it.'

'They must hold tight, your little shopkeepers,' insisted Yvette, spearing a juicy prawn on her fork. '*Naturellement* the galerias and the large department stores bring thousands of people to shop every day but there is still enough bread to go round for everyone. I promise. Just look at Paris. We have the best shopping in the world, huge stores, but many of our finest shops are small, exquisite and individual.'

Afterwards they strolled along by Trinity College and down to Merrion Square, where artists were bargaining and selling their paintings from the display on the park railings. On a sunny day they always attracted a huge crowd. Back at home her aunt rested for a little while before Ellie cooked a simple chicken and vegetable dish for the two of them. They sat up till late talking about family holidays in the Renchard house in Provence, and the good times they'd both shared with her mother.

The next three days passed far too quickly as Yvette expressed a wish to visit her sister's grave in Wicklow and they managed to get tickets for the new Marina Carr play in the Abbey Theatre. Ellie persuaded

Rory to join them for supper, though he couldn't make it to the theatre as he was going on to a music gig in Whelan's.

He was chatty and charming and very polite to her aunt, ordering her an aperitif and asking about her shop in Paris and the state of the French economy. For once he had put on a shirt. OK, so it was black, but at least he had made an effort to impress her relative.

Ellie smiled as he tried to give her aunt a rundown of the Irish music industry and the top bands over their wild salmon served with baby new potatoes. She could see he was charming Yvette just the way he charmed all the women who crossed his path.

After the play Ellie and Yvette went back to the flat to drink coffee and enjoy a Baileys nightcap before they went to bed.

'Ellie, I hope you don't think that I am being intrusive but this young man in your life, is he important?'

'We are seeing each other.' She hesitated. 'But not for very long.'

'Do you love him?'

'I'm not sure,' she admitted, wondering if Rory was the type to fall in love with.

'Then I hope he is good to you,' said her aunt, staring at her intently. 'He is not a professional, his career is perhaps erratic, and he is a little *dangereux*. But love is important, always remember that. Your mother knew it, she followed her heart!'

Ellie waited for a lecture about the mistake her mother had made in running off with her father and was surprised when her aunt said the opposite.

'Your mother, she fell in love with her Irishman and followed him here. She truly loved your father. Of course you know that. Despite everything I don't think she ever stopped loving him. Perhaps she hoped that some day Philip would come back to her. She was *désolée* – devastated, is that the word? – when she heard he'd passed away.'

'I remember,' said Ellie softly. 'Uncle Pat phoned to tell us about his heart attack.'

'Madeleine never hesitated in the matters of the heart,' continued her aunt. 'And look at what she got in return, a beautiful daughter, so like herself, a business which gave her immense pleasure, along with an income and a life I would say well lived, and she was spared the awful indignities of old age.'

'Thank you,' whispered Ellie, moved by her aunt's truth and honesty.

'I on the other hand have my business. I am a wonderful success, so they tell me. I worked so hard I turned my nose up at all the young men who might have made a good match, and even the old men if truth be told. I had no time for romance and love. Then I discovered I'd left it too late – so here I am with only Monique's two big hulking boys and you, my dear, to enjoy. The fine things of life are all very well but it is nice to have someone to share them with.'

Ellie had never imagined Yvette having any regrets. Now she realized how solitary her life must be at times.

'I think that you are a lot like your mother. But promise me you will not make the same mistakes as your proud old aunt,' she joked.

'I'll try,' said Ellie, hugging her.

Ellie was surprised at how sad she was to see her aunt return to Paris.

'Promise me you will come in the autumn, when you are not so busy,' urged Yvette. 'The apartment is huge and you are welcome to bring some friends or even that charming boyfriend of yours.'

Ellie promised, imagining Rory and herself walking hand in hand along the Left Bank or exploring the Musée d'Orsay as the autumn leaves fell.

Chapter Twenty-seven

The meeting of the South Anne Street traders took place after the shops and businesses had closed on Friday evening. Reverend Lewis, the rector of St Anne's Church, was an affable and easygoing host, making them all feel welcome as they streamed in and helped themselves to tea and coffee. Damien Quinn, who owned the deli, provided sandwiches for everyone. Ellie was delighted to see that Mo Brady and a few of their local councillors were present.

'Work has already begun on the development of the galleria and hotel on our street,' announced Frank Farrell, first to speak, his face serious. Farrell Antiques was a long-standing family firm and one of the oldest on the street. 'Some of these buildings have been vacant for years and from looking at the plans and the photomontages, this new scheme could be a big improvement. However, what does concern and worry us is that Casey Coleman Holdings are now seeking to extend their scheme. They seem to be trying to buy up the shops adjacent to their site, and to attain as many properties on the opposite side of the street from the new galleria as possible.

There are even rumours that they intend to open a large retail store across from the galleria. They are looking for planning extensions, and all kinds of permissions. Changes on this scale would have huge ramifications for those of us still trading.'

'The thing is,' said Scottie O'Loughlin, getting to his feet, 'most of us here tonight want to stay on in the street. We are not interested in relocating, or retiring and closing down. These are our businesses that we have worked hard to build up over the years. We need to let the City Council, Casey Coleman Holdings, the planning depart-ment, the government, landlords, whoever it is that matters, know that we are not going anywhere. We are staying.'

He got huge applause and support. Ellie smiled, knowing that at least they were all united in wanting the same thing.

'We need to show the council and the planning people that we object to what they are doing,' Damien Quinn added. 'That we should be involved and consulted about what is going on in the street where we own our properties. Most of us owned our properties long before Casey Coleman Holdings arrived.'

'Hear, hear!'

'But we've already written and objected, phoned, done everything we can,' said Kitty Kavanagh. 'All to no avail.'

'Maybe we should protest?' suggested Gary Murphy from the art and print shop. 'It might get us noticed.'

'We could march on the Dail,' suggested Leo from the Italian restaurant.

'Please may I say a few words,' interrupted Mo Brady. 'I don't know if you realize how many marches there are on the Dail every month. Unless you have a crowd of thousands that will stop traffic and bring the city to a standstill, there is absolutely no point in a march. I can tell you that.'

They could all sense the disappointment in the room, as there was no way a few shopkeepers could rally such massive support.

161

'What about if we staged a protest directly outside the Dail and government buildings?'

'There are protests almost every day,' Mo added. 'Obviously some get more notice and news coverage than others. If you want to save your street, you need to do something different, something newsworthy.'

'We could close up our shops for a day,' suggested Kitty Kavanagh, 'in protest.'

'But sure, what good will that do?' asked Scottie O'Loughlin. 'People won't care if we close for a day or go on strike.'

'We need to bring more people into the street, not send them away,' argued Ellie.

'We need to attract crowds if we want to save our street. Let them know why we want to keep businesses like ours open.'

'The street is closed off to traffic already during opening hours, so maybe we should use that? Think of all the pedestrians who are on our street every day, passing through to get to Grafton Street,' urged Damien.

'What can we do?' A rumble of questions went up around the room.

'We can show them what we do,' said Gary. 'I spend my day framing pictures, posters, photographs. I already have some displayed outside the door, but I could put my table outside too. Talk to anyone who's interested about some of the beautiful prints and pieces we have and how I work.'

'People are always interested in antiques,' mused Frank Farrell. 'Finding out how old things are, if they are antique and of course if they are valuable.'

'Like that programme on the TV,' joked Sissy Kavanagh. 'Kitty and I love it.'

'I suppose I'd be prepared to sit at a table outside the shop for a day and people could bring their pieces for me to look at, no valuation charge for getting my expert opinion.'

'And I could demonstrate how to trim a summer hat,' offered Ellie.

'Well, this certainly sounds a bit different,' applauded Mo. 'Think of the crowds and the publicity it would get!'

'I have those kites you put together and those lovely new blue sail-boats that need a bit of work,' joked Scottie, getting into the swing of things. 'And a few of those free bubble-blowers should go down a treat with the kids.'

'We could demonstrate how to make proper pasta. Make a perfect pizza, give some free samples,' offered Leo and his wife Andrea.

Nearly everyone on the street agreed that they had something they could do.

'Will we be closing for the day?' asked Noel Hanratty, who ran the small jeweller's.

'Yes,' said Frank firmly.

'So we have to close up and have no sales?'

'Better no sales and goodwill for a day than closed up for good,' said Scottie seriously. 'We have to give this a shot.'

Noel had no intention of putting his precious stones and valuable diamonds on display but did agree to show how to clean and polish jewellery and advise on redesigning old, outdated pieces.

Councillor Richard Doyle took the floor. 'I promise, along with my colleagues here, to raise your concerns about these important issues with the council.'

They agreed that their South Anne Street Day would be held on a busy August Saturday. Newspapers and TV and radio programmes would be informed of the traders' attempt to highlight what small businesses like theirs did to keep the streets of the city alive.

'What will we do if it rains?' asked Sissy.

163

'We need sunshine and blue skies,' insisted Frank as they began to talk about hiring tables and maybe some parasols.

'We shall all pray for clement weather,' added the Revd Lewis as the meeting broke up.

Chapter Twenty-eight

Just like the song, Ellie didn't like Mondays. First and foremost because Rory had only told her last night, while they were at a party, that he would be away in England for the next few weeks.

'The lads are playing double dates in London, Manchester, Liverpool, Birmingham and Newcastle. If they are going to get noticed and pick up some publicity,' he predicted confidently, 'England is the place to be.'

'I'm going to miss you,' she said shyly, wondering if he would miss her too.

'Listen, Ellie, when the band go on tour, I do too,' he explained. 'You have to understand that. Next year, if we get lucky and get some gigs in the States, we could be gone for six or seven months. That's just the way it works.'

She hadn't meant to put pressure on him and cuddled up in his arms for a fond farewell.

'Hey, beautiful, we'll have fun when I get back,' he promised, stroking her hair.

Ellie said nothing, knowing that if she was going to have any sort of relationship with Rory she must get used to his way of living and learn to accept it.

Reaching the shop, she noticed in dismay that the last remaining buildings opposite had been demolished over the weekend. Only their narrow redbrick façades had been left standing as the serious building work began. Overnight dust and debris had blown everywhere. All her lovely paintwork, the front step and the windows were covered in a dirty layer of dust.

Ria Roberts was standing in the street, shaking her head.

'Look at the state of the place,' she whispered. 'How can I open?'

Scottie O'Loughlin had left his toy shop and marched up to the site to look for the foreman.

'You keep out of the way,' she warned Minouche, the black cat, as she got out the mop and bucket of water and began to wash the outside step of the shop, 'or you'll bring dust everywhere on your paws.'

Rinsing out the bucket, she decided to wipe the paintwork round the door and then do the windows. Her mother had never tolerated dirt or mess and she wasn't about to start. She'd clean up the place quickly before the town got busy.

Ellie got the stool and her cloth and a bucket of clean water and stretched as high as she could to wash the windows. The dust was everywhere, she thought, annoyed, as she sloshed the water around. She wished she had a higher stool or a chair to stand on or was a little bit taller herself: it was a much harder job than she had imagined. Minouche sat on the step and stared at her balefully, avoiding the drips of water.

'Cleaning again, I see, Miss Matthews.'

Ellie froze. Why did he always catch her at her worst!

Neil Harrington was standing a foot away from her as Ellie

perched like an eejit trying to manage the bucket and cloth and water and not wobble on the narrow stool.

'Unfortunately I am trying to clean up the mess that your clients made when they demolished the shop across the way,' she replied sarcastically. 'The dust is everywhere.'

'I'm sure it was not intentional,' he replied pleasantly, 'and that they will do their best to rectify the situation.'

'Well, I hope they do,' she said as the stool gave an alarming tilt.

He caught her neatly and steadied her, his hands around her waist.

'Got you!'

He certainly had got her. He was clasping her firmly in his large hands, his fingers on her bare skin.

'Ellie, please come down off there before you fall!' he said, taking hold of the water bucket as she flung the cloth into it, the water sloshing everywhere, the stool wobbling again. Neil almost tripped over the cat, who'd jumped for cover. As she suspected, he'd got splashes of dirty water on his good suit and white shirt.

'If you could just pass me up the dry polishing cloth,' she asked sweetly, 'that would be very useful.'

'So you are staying up there?'

'Yes. I'll finish it off.' She hoped he wasn't going to stand there watching her as the window was smeared in places and still wet.

'If you'll excuse me,' he said, 'I have an appointment.'

She watched open-mouthed as he turned and walked three doors up from her to Ria's shop.

'I hope that you are not trying to browbeat poor Ria into signing one of your contracts!' Ellie called. 'Because that wouldn't be fair.'

He looked offended. 'I have a meeting with Mrs Roberts,' he said firmly, 'but the matter that we are discussing is none of your business.'

Well, that was her put in her place, thought Ellie, as she tried to tackle the window.

167

*

Just before lunchtime a team of window cleaners appeared in the street and went from shop to shop cleaning up, compliments of Casey Coleman Holdings.

The shop was quiet, windows sparkling, when one of her mother's regular customers appeared wanting to order a classic navy felt hat for the winter without any trims. Beatrice O'Reilly, or Lady Bea as she was better known, was a large and forthright woman adored by children and dogs, given to wearing navy or red, who lived in a shabby old country house in Kildare and ran a kennels. Ellie remembered going to visit her a few times with her mother to see the puppies and play with the 'hounds' as she called them.

'Binky, my spaniel, ate my last one,' she'd confided, 'and I have to have something good to wear to funerals and to church, especially if I don't make it to the hairdresser's.'

Ellie had nodded in agreement, trying to keep a serious face, for Lady Beatrice had been a loyal customer for years and had been taken aback when she'd seen the changes in the shop.

'You have done wonders, my dear,' she said, looking around her, 'but thank heaven it's still got the same atmosphere it always had. Poor Madeleine would be pleased.'

Ellie had shown her the felt colour choices in navy, promising to have the hat ready in less than two weeks.

'I'll be back up to Dublin then as I have an appointment with a chiropodist. I'll call in and collect it afterwards.'

Ellie smiled and walked her to the door, her good humour restored. Did other milliners have clients whose dogs ate their creations and who regaled them with stories of their bunions and corns?

Chapter Twenty-nine

Rosemary Harrington stared out of the tall window of the morning room in her Georgian home on Merrion Square, and prayed that the rain would hold off and the sun would shine for the annual fund-raising garden party for Holles Street Maternity Hospital. She had been on the committee for ten years and she still quaked at the memory of the sudden deluge one summer when guests had to run for cover under the trees as food and wine, chairs and tables were abandoned. She studied the sky above and agreed with the meteor-ologist on Sky News, who had predicted perfect weather.

'Thank God,' she said to herself, and turned her attention to the long to-do list she had to get through to ensure the smooth running of one of the hospital's main fund-raisers.

'Everything OK?' interrupted her youngest son, searching for his briefcase after a hasty breakfast of coffee and toast.

'Yes, everything seems to be fine, but promise me that you will be there on time.'

'Do I have to come?'

She arched her eyebrows as she gazed at him, sensing his discomfort.

'Neil, it's all I ask of you, once every summer to support the hospital where I worked and where you and your brother and sister were born.'

'I know,' he apologized, 'it's just that I thought I might do something different this evening.'

'Like what?' Rosemary knew her son too well, and guessed that he was just trying to avoid one of her favourite shindigs.

'Maybe a swim out in the Forty Foot or a walk! I need some fresh air.'

'We will be dining and listening to music and perhaps even dancing al fresco,' she reminded him, 'so there will be plenty of fresh air.'

'Then I'll be there.' Defeated, he gave in, giving her a quick hug before he left for the office.

Rosemary watched his tall loping figure disappear through the door, thinking he was getting more like his late father every day. She still daydreamed of Sean walking through the door and embracing her, nuzzling his lips into her neck, making her put aside whatever she was doing to concentrate on him and hear about his day.

She refused to get sentimental today of all days and tried to focus her mind on the catering and entertainment lists, hoping that nothing had been overlooked. She put on her shoes, grabbed her handbag and leather Filofax and set off for the park, ready to go through the checklist one more time with Yvonne Callery and Beth Donnelly, her fellow committee members. Afterwards she had an appointment for a cut and blow-dry in the hairdresser's. But first there were a hundred things to do before tonight's event.

Merrion Square looked wonderful, Rosemary thought, as she began to greet guests as they arrived for the garden party. Chinese lanterns gaily swung between the trees, and the wooden trestle tables and chairs were set with gay pink and turquoise tablecloths. The large barbecue area was well organized, with long serving tables for the salads and breads and arrays of chicken and steak and hamburgers. The wine bar was under a stripy awning and there was a small group of stands and stalls, one showing the hospital's good work, one for the raffle with the prizes displayed, and one with a luscious variety of ice creams. Rosemary allowed herself a smile, for it all looked wonderful. Everything was going swimmingly.

By eight o'clock the buzz was beginning to build up. The still summer's evening was filled with the sounds of the jazz quartet playing on the terrace above the lawn, the air scented with the appetizing aroma of chicken and steaks grilling on the large barbecues. The stalls were busy and their loyal supporters had sure turned on the glamour for the evening, with silks and satins and chiffon in a rainbow of colours. Rosemary watched photographers from the daily newspapers and *Image* and *Tatler* magazines vie for pictures of the pretty young things and their beaux. Fingers crossed, they might make the covers or social columns tomorrow.

'Rosemary, may I interrupt you?'

She turned. It was Jo-Jo Hennessy, her old schoolfriend, who had surprised them all by becoming one of Ireland's foremost magazine publishing magnates. They hugged each other wildly, clinking their champagne glasses.

'Cheers, Ro! You've done a great job. Sean would be proud of you!'

'He's weather-watching for me,' she smiled.

Jo-Jo nodded in agreement as she gestured for Heather Lannigan, their fashion photographer, to join them.

'Can I get a photo for the magazine?' she asked.

'Oh Jo-Jo, there's no need . . .'

'Our readers will be interested in seeing a bit of real style, I assure you.'

'Perhaps the two of you together?' suggested Heather, who was more stunning-looking herself in her figure-hugging jeans and trademark black T-shirt than most of the women she was asked to photograph.

'Of course,' they said, trying to look suitably relaxed.

'Perfect,' grinned Heather.

'I have to check on a few things, Jo-Jo, but what about a G&T in a while?' said Rosemary.

'Sounds perfect,' agreed Jo-Jo. 'I'm off to rescue poor Charlie, he's stuck with that awful government man he's trying to get a department raise from. Don't think it will do any good myself but I suppose there's no harm in trying.'

Rosemary glanced over. Charlie Hennessy was deep in serious conversation with a bespectacled civil service type. Dr Hennessy, one of the country's top paediatricians, would do anything to fund-raise for Holles Street's overstretched neonatal department. Rosemary hoped that this evening's fun would help swell the coffers of a few of the hospital departments, including his.

She did a quick scout round, greeting friends, pointing new-comers in the right direction for food and drinks and welcoming the Minister for Health, who would not be giving a speech. The annual garden party was a fun event, not a party political propaganda tool, and the minister for once was a guest like everyone else.

The stall displaying the tempting array of goods for the charity auction was busy and Rosemary gave a silent prayer of thanks for the generosity of all their sponsors and donors, who had as usual come up trumps. She glanced around, hoping to catch sight of her son. Neil was bound to be here somewhere, for she had spotted a group of his friends at one of the tables near where the champagne was being served.

'Don't fret, Mum, I'm here,' he said, suddenly appearing at her side in a cream linen jacket.

'Oh Neil, I knew you wouldn't let us down.'

'Can I get you a drink?'

'A gin and tonic would go down well!' She laughed, finally beginning to relax, as she watched him make his way up to the bar. She said a few polite hellos to people, as supporters of the hospital strolled through the iron gates and into the gardens. She reckoned half the medics in Dublin were here, all ready to donate to a very worthy cause.

'It's going very well,' grinned Neil a few minutes later, passing her a drink. 'Even more people than last year.'

'It's the good weather, people like being out in their finery on a beautiful evening like this.'

'Well done anyway,' he said, clinking her glass.

'Who did you come with?' she asked.

'Les and Ryan and Barbara and Oisin are all here somewhere.'

Always with the same crowd, she thought. Rosemary tried to disguise her motherly concerns for her son. There were plenty of eligible young women here this evening, if her son would only have a care to look around him.

'Do you need me to do anything?'

'No, I think everything is in hand at the moment. Yvonne and Beth and the committee have done a great job but at least I know you are here if needed, Neil. So thanks.'

'Then I'll go and say hello to a few people.'

'Jo-Jo and Charlie are around.'

'Then I'll go and say hello to them.'

Rosemary Harrington watched him disappear in the crowd as she joined the minister and his wife, introducing them to a few people. She pasted a polite smile on her face as Gayle Leonard, in a figure-hugging pink chiffon dress and high heels, interrupted them.

'Hello, Mrs H, nice to see you again. I'm just looking for Neil.'

'He's somewhere over beyond the bandstand, Gayle, with some friends.'

'You look lovely, Mrs H.'

'So do you, dear, pink is your colour.'

Gayle had been an on-off dalliance in her son's life over the past few months. The glamorous twenty-nine-year-old was a regular feature in the gossip columns with her corkscrew blond hair and tan and pert little face. There were romances with rugby players, actors, a well-known ageing journalist and lately her son. Rosemary couldn't see what attracted Neil to such a little minx, but given the possibility that she might yet end up her daughter-in-law she had diplomatically held her tongue and welcomed Gayle to her home and dinner table.

'A friend of my son's,' she said, briefly introducing the young woman to the group she was with. The minister raised his eyebrow as she tottered over the grass, spiking the ground with her heels as she set off in search of Neil.

Ellie couldn't believe it. She had spent three quarters of an hour trying to ease a beautiful champagne-coloured straw that she had decorated with gilded feathers back into shape after discovering Minouche had made a bed on it in the back of the shop.

'*Tais-toi!* You bold little thing!' she remonstrated as she locked up.

The woman who was collecting it in the morning would have a fit if she knew the little black cat had curled up in it and fallen asleep.

It was a glorious evening and she had time to race home and change before attending the charity garden party in Merrion Square. She normally had no interest in this kind of fund-raiser, but Yvonne Callery, the woman on the committee, had been most persuasive and she had found herself donating a pretty cream hat she had designed to the charity.

'It will be good publicity,' Yvonne had sworn.

In return she had received an invite to attend the fund-raiser. Kim had cried off as she had to work overtime on a special project, so Ellie had decided to go alone. She needn't stay too long; besides, it would be nice to see the park all lit up with a jazz band playing.

Ellie jumped in the shower and afterwards pulled on a pale lilac dress with shoe-string straps and a sweet little kick in the skirt, the waist highlighted with a narrow black band. She pulled her hair off her face with a black ribbon and slipped into her comfy black sling-backs with a low heel, suitable for walking and partying. After a quick spray of perfume she grabbed her dark glasses and a wrap and pulled open the door of the flat.

Dublin on a summer's evening like this was magical and she couldn't help but wish that Rory had been able to accompany her. Still, no point moping, she would enjoy herself anyway.

As she approached Merrion Square the rhythm of the saxophone lured her towards the gardens, and she joined the merry throng sipping champagne in the glow of the evening sunlight.

'Ellie, welcome!' cooed Yvonne, bustling over. 'I'm so glad that you could make it. Your gift of a wonderful hat is much appreciated.'

'Well, it's all in a good cause.'

'Come and let me introduce you to a few people.'

Ellie smiled politely during the whirlwind round of introductions, wishing that she could be bright and witty as she desperately struggled to catch names and remember faces. Her mother would have loved an evening like this, while Ellie was shy and awkward sometimes in such a large group of strangers. She did her best to make polite conversation and when Yvonne drifted off found herself wandering round the garden, sipping a second glass of chilled champagne as she admired the park after hours.

*

Rosemary could feel the tension ease from her shoulders as her adrenalin levels began to flatten out. It was a perfect summer's evening party, better even than she had planned. She said a silent prayer of thanks and, with a purposeful look on her face as if she had to fetch something important, detached herself from the rest of the party and meandered over to a quieter area of the park, enjoying the tranquillity and the muffled noise of laughter and chatting.

One of the guests had had a similar idea and was just soaking it all in. They nodded at each other, Rosemary admiring the pretty dark-haired young lady in the stylish dress who'd had the good sense not to wear high heels.

'Good shoes!' she laughed.

'And they are comfortable too.' Ellie grinned, her dark eyes sparkling.

'Enjoying the party?'

'Yes, thank you. It's wonderful and the square, it looks so beautiful.'

They found themselves sitting on a bench together.

'I met my husband in this park,' confessed Rosemary to the young stranger.

'How lovely and romantic!'

'Well, I'm still not sure about that.' She laughed. 'I was studying to be a midwife in the hospital across the road, part of my nursing training. I'd just done a long shift and delivered three babies and I came out here to the sunshine and sat down on a bench to rest. I don't know what happened but I dozed off. I fell asleep in the August sunshine. He spotted me from his window. He was studying for his law finals and came over to wake me. It was so embarrassing – I was red as a lobster. A bad case of sunburn, my nose peeled for a month and my legs were such agony I could barely walk the next day. Matron almost killed me!'

'What about the young man?' Ellie couldn't help but be curious about the tall, immaculately dressed woman beside her.

'Sean always said he fell in love with me that instant, sunburn and all!'

'How wonderful to have someone fall in love with you like that.' Ellie sighed wistfully.

'We had thirty-eight good years together and three children, all grown up now. A lifetime of happiness together and there isn't a day goes by that I don't think of him and how lucky I was to meet him.'

'And you still come to this square.'

'I live close by, and the hospital . . . Well, I concentrate some of my efforts on fund-raising for it. It keeps me busy.'

'Yvonne on the committee invited me along,' admitted the young woman. 'I'm Ellie Matthews, the milliner who donated the hat.'

'I'm Rosemary Harrington, the committee head, and I know that loads of people have been eyeing your beautiful creation on the stand.'

'That's nice of you to say.' Ellie wondered was she any connection to Neil?

'True, honest. Anyway, I'd better get back to the fray. Mo Brady, the Lady Mayor, is supposed to be making a late appearance after a council meeting. She's saying a few words about a new donor scheme we are starting. I'd better be there to welcome her!'

'Enjoy the rest of the evening!'

'You too.' Rosemary got up. 'Go mingle, there are lots of young people here.'

Mingling was something her mother or her aunt Yvette would tell her to do, she thought wryly. Still, the music was good and the jazz band were certainly getting the crowd going. Some were already up dancing on this perfect summer's evening.

Chapter Thirty

The sounds of the city stilled as night fell. The party crowd was cocooned in the heady atmosphere of the old Georgian square where Oscar Wilde had once strolled and many a government minister had walked off the stress and tensions of official duties. Ellie was delighted to see that Mo Brady had arrived. The Lady Mayor was wearing a softly draped taupe jacket and trousers set off with a peacock-blue scarf, her hair highlighted as she stepped up to the microphone to huge applause.

'Isn't she a tonic!' remarked the elderly man in the navy blazer beside her, as Mo congratulated all the committee on their efforts and outlined a new scheme for donors whereby contributions could be offset against tax liabilities when the rebuilding of the old hospital wing got under way. She then called on James Sherry, the well-known auctioneer, to come up and start the charity auction. There was a holiday to South Africa, a weekend for six in Rome, golf games, skiing lessons, weekends away, luxury spa days . . . Ellie cringed when she realized that instead of being in a raffle her hat was among the many items that were to go under the hammer. John Rocha glass, two paintings, a case of vintage wine, a Mary Gregory coat, a Paul Costelloe jacket, golf in Mount Juliet, a weekend in London – it was an impressive list.

Mo kept up a running commentary as the bidding began, encouraging people to give generously to such a good cause.

'Now something very special, from someone very special,' she enthused. 'A delicious hat from my favourite milliner, Ellie Matthews, who is standing over there.'

Ellie resisted the temptation to flee and tried to smile. Inside she was mortified and desperately regretting her decision to come along and disgrace herself.

'What am I bid for this beautiful creation by one of the country's new up-and-coming designers, ladies and gentlemen?' boomed the auctioneer.

Ellie wished that the grass would open up and swallow her as a sudden silence descended on the band area. This was excruciating, one hundred times worse than any torture or humiliation she could have dreamed of.

'Come on, ladies and gentlemen,' he continued. 'Think of the beautiful young ladies in our company who would do anything to wear such a fine hat to their next outing, a wedding or christening perhaps.'

Utter silence.

'Two hundred euro.'

Ellie almost collapsed with relief at the masculine voice coming from somewhere behind her.

'Three hundred.' This from a middle-aged man who was standing with a glass of wine in his hand over near the minister.

'Four hundred,' the first voice insisted again.

'Five hundred euro,' interrupted a plump woman sitting down near the front of the bandstand.

'Six hundred,' continued the first voice.

Ellie couldn't believe it. Three people wanted to buy her hat. Relief washed over her and the shaking in her knees steadied.

'Seven hundred,' countered the other bidder.

'Eight hundred,' laughed the woman, not wanting to be outdone.

'Nine hundred euro,' said the first voice.

'Nine hundred and fifty,' called the older man, determinedly.

'One thousand euro.'

'All done? Then going . . . going . . . gone,' declared the auctioneer. 'Sold to Mr Harrington.'

The crowd spontaneously burst out clapping as the bidding ended and the hat was finally sold.

'We thank him for his generous contribution to the hospital's fund.'

Ellie couldn't believe it. Had she heard right? She turned round, mortified.

'Miss Matthews! Ellie!'

She recognized the voice. Neil Harrington was standing right beside her.

'Thank you,' she said. 'It was very kind of you to bid, and to pay that much . . .'

'It's for a good cause.' He laughed, putting his hand on her shoulder as they stood back out of the way of the auction.

He looked different in an open-necked shirt and a light jacket. Younger, more relaxed. She blushed, remembering the last time they'd met when she'd almost thrown the bucket of water over him.

'The suit dry-cleaned perfectly,' he told her, as if reading her mind.

'I'm sorry, Neil. I took my bad temper out on you.'

'Anyway,' he teased, 'windows aside, the hat business is going well?'

She wondered was he trying to pump information out of her or simply being polite? She just couldn't tell.

'Yes.' She smiled. 'It's hard work but I love it.'

'Well, it suits you. You look even more charming than usual,' he said, eyeing her up and down.

'Neil!' she warned.

'What I mean is, on a balmy night like this with music and wine, well, it couldn't be better.'

She laughed despite herself.

'Let me get you a drink,' he offered. 'More champagne?'

'No, thanks.'

He looked crestfallen.

'But a glass of white wine would be lovely, please.'

'The tent is over this way,' he said, taking her elbow as they fell into step together.

As she sipped her wine and stopped to watch the quartet perform, Ellie expressed her surprise.

'I wasn't expecting to meet you here.'

'I was invited,' he assured her.

'And you being a jazz aficionado!'

'I grew up with it. My father played clarinet and a little sax. On a night like this it comes into its own.'

Ellie had to agree with him, as they sat down to listen to the music and the songs of Miles Davis, Ella Fitzgerald, Peggy Lee and Dizzy Gillespie filled the air. His expression was intense, she saw as she secretly watched him.

When the band took a break they joined the queue for food under the striped awning, the barbecue smoke filling the air. The steaks, sausages and burgers all smelled delicious.

Ellie helped herself to sizzling pieces of tender chicken sprinkled

181

with herbs, a baked potato and a delicious green salad as Neil held her wine glass. They joined a throng of his friends squashed on a long trestle table.

'Hey, Neil, go get me some more food!'

'Les, you already had a huge steak and a burger,' he chided.

Ellie squeezed in beside him as he tucked into a steak and all the trimmings.

'This is great,' she said, realizing that she was enjoying herself far more than she had planned and was finding Neil and his friends better company than she'd expected.

Neil was the perfect gentleman, keeping her wine glass topped up and insisting on fetching her a big bowl of strawberries and cream for dessert. It was getting darker, the moon overhead, as the Chinese lanterns swinging from the trees lit up the pathways.

'Neil, where have you been?' interrupted a peeved voice. 'I've searched the place for you.'

'I've been here with the guys, Gayle. Where were you?'

'Some of the photographers wanted to get a few shots for the mags and weekend papers. What could I do?'

Ellie felt uncomfortable, unsure what to do as the blond girl fixed her eyes on her and where she was sitting. The girl looked put out but there was certainly no space on the bench beside Ellie and most of Neil's friends seemed suddenly to have become very interested in the food on their plates. An awkward few minutes crawled by until Les stood up.

'Here, princess, you can take my spot. I'm going up to get some more strawberries.'

His seat was at the far end of the table and no one offered to move down to accommodate her.

Neil made a perfunctory introduction.

'Gayle, this is Ellie, she's a business acquaintance of mine.' Ellie nodded towards the girl, who seemed slightly mollified by his description of her.

'Here, let me move down and then you two can sit together,' she offered, for she had no intention of playing pig in the middle between two lovebirds.

'Thanks,' smiled the blonde as she took her place beside Neil.

Out of the corner of her eye, Ellie watched as Gayle flirted with him. Who would have thought it? Neil Harrington was such a ladies' man. Fortunately Ryan and Barbara were good company and Ellie relaxed and enjoyed the banter between the friends. Barbara, a buyer for Brown Thomas, gleefully discussed the latest design trends for autumn from Paris and Milan, which would hit the store over the next few weeks.

'Most of the stuff is to die for but some is just pure awful but we know it will sell.'

She watched as Gayle and Neil got up to dance.

'She sure can move,' sighed Barbara. 'Drives them all crazy!'

'Come on, ladies, your turn to dance in the moonlight!' offered Ryan, jumping to his feet. Barbara excused herself and Ellie found herself almost lifted off the ground as he pulled her up. Ryan might be large but he was nimble and could sure pound to the beat as the music got faster and faster and he swung her round and round. Ellie laughed aloud as he got crazier and crazier. She was out of breath as Ryan went in search of water and the tempo slowed.

She had just sat down when Neil asked her to dance. Things were a little less frantic as people slipped up to the bar and off to sit in the moonlight, and Ellie to her surprise found herself agreeing to dance with him. There was no sign or mention of Gayle and she relaxed as he slipped his arm round her waist.

'Enjoying yourself?'

'Oh yes. It's been a perfect night.'

'I'm glad.'

'Your friends are very nice,' she found herself saying.

'You seem surprised that I have friends,' he mocked.

'A little,' she admitted. 'I thought that work was all you thought about.'

'I'm sorry if you were insulted by the way I introduced you to Gayle . . .'

'No, not at all! Anyway it's true. We are business acquaintances.'

'It's just that it makes things less complicated for someone like her.'

The dance area began to fill up again and he drew her closer into his arms, her cheek against his shoulder. He smelled good, a mixture of expensive aftershave, male sweat and the fresh air. Surprised, Ellie found it hard to resist the temptation to touch his skin with her lips or fingertips as they moved together. The night air was so warm and heavy it made her almost drowsy as the blues music filled the park.

'You look lovely,' he said, slowly moving a tendril of hair that was tumbling across her face. 'Beautiful.'

She didn't know what to say, what to make of him. Twenty minutes ago he had been dancing with his sexy girlfriend and now he was trying to sweet-talk her. She should never have had two glasses of champagne and got so wrapped up in that woman's romantic love story. They were only business acquaintances and that was a good thing for them both to remember.

'I think I had better get going,' she said suddenly, breaking the spell and pulling apart from him. 'I have work tomorrow.'

'Saturday?'

'My shop opens on Saturdays.'

'We're thinking of going to Leeson Street in a while. You are welcome to join us.'

'I'm sorry, Neil, but I have to go.'

184

'Stay,' he pleaded, gripping her wrist and pulling her closer to him.

'I can't.'

'Then let me walk you home?' he offered, reaching for her hand, his fingers clasping hers.

Ellie felt torn, all mixed up. What was she doing? Tempting and all as his offer was, she'd met him with a girlfriend, Rachel, and now there was this Gayle. And she already had a boyfriend. It was just too complicated. Ellie shook her head vehemently.

'No, thanks, Neil,' she said, disentangling herself. 'I like walking and I live only a few minutes away – I'll be fine. You stay and enjoy yourself.'

She bade a hasty goodnight to his friends, noticing as she made her way towards the park entrance that Gayle had detached herself from one of the government ministers and was back wrapped in Neil's arms, dancing cheek to cheek with him, sporting the hat he'd bought in the auction. Neil must have given it to her.

Expensive tastes, she thought, lightly tossing her wrap round her shoulder as she left the confines of Merrion Square, trying her best to put Neil Harrington out of her mind as she made her way back home.

Chapter Thirty-one

Constance O'Kelly sat in the corner of the kitchen in her house on Cross Avenue and almost wept. Today was the anniversary of the day her life had ended, the day Shay had told her he was packing up his things and moving out. At first she had thought he'd gone mad, had a bump on the head or was suffering from male menopause or midlife crisis or whatever those American experts liked to call it. Maybe it was stress? Working too hard. God knows, he rarely took a break and worked night and day in the busy quantity surveying business he had built up. There were always new jobs to tender for, and he constantly ignored her requests to take some time off to spend with his family.

For the previous six months he had seemed exhausted, distracted, locking himself away in the study late at night, cancelling their annual trip on the Shannon and pleading he had to meet clients in Frankfurt. He had even been rude to their friends, saying that Rob and Kevin and even his oldest friend, Tadhg, were turning into a shower of bores only interested in playing golf and talking about their kids. Constance had blushed as she had just spent an hour on the phone talking about Sally and her boyfriend Chris to Tadhg's wife Catriona.

For weeks he had turned his back to her in bed or pretended to be asleep when she lay down beside him. Chilling thoughts of some serious illness or mysterious complaint nagged at her as she studied his long thin face and wary eyes. Then out of the blue he had told her he was leaving the house, moving somewhere else, that he didn't want to live with her any more.

At first she had said nothing, too shocked to take it all in – then she had begged, begged him to sit down, talk to her, tell her about whatever it was that had driven this wedge between them.

'We can fix it,' she pleaded, 'whatever is wrong we can fix it. We've been together for thirty years, raised three children – you don't just go and throw away a marriage like ours for no good reason!' she argued.

'It's over, Constance,' he'd said, refusing even to go through the motions of rescuing their sinking marriage. 'I'm moving out. There's absolutely no point me staying as we have nothing to say to each other.'

She had watched flabbergasted as he took his shirts and trousers from the wardrobe and folded them neatly into the suitcase, before turning his attention to his drawer filled with socks she'd freshly laundered and matched and his boxer shorts. Funny, she had noticed a change lately: the ditching of his traditional white Y-fronts for navy blue and checks and patterned boxers. She had read in a magazine that this was one of the biggest warnings of infidelity but had stupidly imagined that in Shay's case it was to do with personal comfort rather than his desire to attract a younger member of the opposite sex.

Shay had at first tried to imply that their marriage break-up was due to the gradual disintegration of their relationship and the fact they had grown apart and were bored with each other. She had screamed and nagged and howled at him until he had finally

187

admitted, two weeks after he left, that there was someone else.

Another woman. Constance felt like he had taken out a knife and stabbed her. She had never dreamed that her reliable, strait-laced husband Shay was capable of infidelity.

The younger member of the opposite sex was called Anne-Marie and Shay had met her at the bridge classes they had both started last autumn, in an attempt to discover a hobby of mutual interest. She had dropped out after only four visits, bored out of her brain as she struggled to remember about bidding and aces and clubs. Working out what card to lead with had given her a headache. Shay had continued learning to play and, needing a partner, had discovered Anne-Marie, who had fitted the bill perfectly. Sometimes when Constance pictured Anne-Marie, visions appeared in her head of being led away in handcuffs for what she had planned to do to the other woman!

Three hundred and sixty-five days, twelve months, a year had passed since it had happened and, despite what her friends and neighbours and family said, it hadn't got any easier. The hardest part, she found, was the loneliness of sitting in at night with only the TV for company. She went to the odd dinner party, cinema or theatre visit but for the most part she was left to her own devices, which after thirty years of marriage took some getting used to. Their elder boy, Brendan, was married to Miriam and lived down in Meath. A busy GP, he did his best to keep in touch but since the arrival of little Max, he had barely a minute to himself. Their younger son, Jack, was off in New Zealand, working in an Irish bar, and showed no sign of wanting to return home, and Sally and Chris had moved in together after only six months.

Her mothering skills almost obsolete, she now had to learn to accept her new role as a discarded wife. Her twenty-five-year-old daughter had just announced her engagement and forthcoming marriage to Chris.

'I know it's hard for you, Mum, with Chris and me deciding to get married when you and Dad's marriage has just fallen apart,' Sally had confided. 'But you know how much we love each other. Now that we have made up our minds we don't see the point of hanging around for years. We just want to get married straight away.'

'Of course you do, pet,' Constance had agreed, opening a bottle of champagne. 'You and Chris are the perfect couple. It's only natural you want to get married. I'm so excited for you. Chris will be a wonderful husband. You know I couldn't be happier for you both!'

'I know,' beamed Sally, hugging her. 'It's so exciting organizing a wedding and everything is going to be such fun!'

The wedding was to be in September. Constance had studied the rough guest list that Sally had drawn up, and even a very quick perusal had showed at least two hundred names.

'It's quite a big list!'

'Well, Chris is from a big family. His mum is one of six and his dad has five brothers and two sisters, and of course they are all married and have loads of cousins. Then there's our lot, my work friends, a few of the guys I was in college with and my schoolfriends. Mum, I don't know how I can shorten it.'

Constance's heart sank. The thought of organizing a big fancy wedding at this particular time of her own life filled her with dread. She had always imagined Sally's wedding as one of the most joyous occasions of parenthood, herself and Shay the proud mother and father of the bride. She had never envisaged an alternative scenario. And what about paying for this wedding?

Would Shay pay for it, or would he expect her also to contribute towards it? At the moment they were at daggers drawn, trying to reach agreement on some sane form of maintenance payments. She thanked heaven that at least there was no mortgage on their big five-bedroomed detached home.

'We had always planned to sell the house once the kids were grown and buy something smaller,' Shay argued, forgetting to mention the part of the plan that involved buying a small low-maintenance exclusive townhouse in their own area and a spectacular holiday home in the south of Spain.

'You know, I can't afford to keep renting,' he complained, 'and I'm too old to take on a new mortgage.'

She had bitten her tongue and refused to retort that age hadn't stopped him taking on a new woman.

'If we sell the house and divide up the proceeds fairly, there will be enough for both of us to purchase a property outright.'

She had dug her heels in and refused to budge. What was it the lawyers always said? Possession was nine-tenths of the law.

'Did you discuss this with your father?' Constance asked Sally.

'Yes, Mum, of course. Daddy wants me to have the wedding I want. The one we always planned.'

'Well, I'm glad to hear that. Glad he's paying.'

'Of course he's paying,' replied Sally, tumbling out a mess of wedding brochures and magazines from her brown shoulder bag. Constance searched for her glasses. Sally, their only daughter, had always been her father's pet. From an early age she'd had her doting dad wrapped round her finger, so if Shay had agreed to pay for Sally to have an expensive wedding, well then, an expensive wedding was what he was going to get. She would make damn sure of it!

Chapter Thirty-two

The organization of a daughter's wedding had certainly helped take her mind off her other problems as there was so much to be booked and arranged.

The wedding would take place in their local church with a reception afterwards in an antique-filled Georgian mansion, Kildevin House, about an hour and a half from Dublin. Then there were the flowers, the cars and, most important of all, the dress. Constance was impressed when Sally made an appointment with Marcus Foley, one of Ireland's most expensive dress designers.

'You will come along with me, Mummy?'

'Of course, darling, I wouldn't miss it for the world.'

Constance sat in the cream leather chair of the Molesworth Street shop-cum-studio as Sally had a second fitting for the dress she would walk up the aisle in. She looked stunning, so young and vivacious. The smooth cream satin followed the slim curves of her figure and accentuated her glowing skin and long neck and curling blond hair.

'Sally, you look so beautiful,' she cried, overcome with emotion.

'Most of the mothers cry,' assured Marcus, passing her the tissue box.

Sally twirled slowly round, looking at herself in the long mirrors.

'I just can't wait for Chris and Dad to see me in this dress.'

Constance was momentarily stunned. So far all she had been thinking of was Sally and Chris's day; now she realized that, as the father of the bride, Shay would have to be involved in a little more than just bankrolling the wedding.

'Chris will think you even more adorable than ever and your father will be proud as punch, I know that.'

Marcus wanted to shorten the sleeve a fraction, have a little more lace detailing on the back panel.

'People will see it as you walk up and back down the aisle after the ceremony,' he advised, scribbling in his notepad and pinning the sleeve.

Sally and herself agreed to return in two weeks to collect the dress. Constance's heart gave a lurch when she saw the bill, relieved that Shay was the one paying.

Afterwards they had walked over to Avoca for lunch. Both of them ignored the temptations of the menu and desserts and opted for chicken salad and a glass of wine.

'Mum, I don't know what I'd do without you helping me,' confessed Sally. 'I'd never get it all organized.'

'That's what mothers are for,' Constance said, laughing, so pleased that the bond between herself and Sally was so strong and that they had such a close relationship.

'Mum, have you got your outfit for the wedding?'

'Don't worry, Sal, once we have you fixed up I'll go and look for something for myself.'

'It's just that since Dad left you haven't hardly bought a stitch.'

Constance had no intention of enlightening her daughter to the fact that her precious father was reluctant to give her a euro more than he had to. She was managing to pay the bills and save a bit for a wedding present for Sally but the likelihood of his forking out for an expensive outfit for his ex-wife to wear was slim.

'Don't worry, I won't let you down.'

They were sipping their frothy cappuccinos when Sally broached the subject of the invitation list.

'Mum, there's no way of getting round this so it's better I say it out straight to you.'

Constance looked up. Sally seemed serious, hesitant even. What could it possibly be?

'Dad wants to bring Anne-Marie to the wedding.'

Constance felt like she had been punched in the stomach.

'When did your father tell you this?'

'He called round to the flat last night. Chris and I . . . we tried to talk him out of it, Mum, but he wouldn't listen.'

'I can't believe it,' she gasped. 'Your father wants to humiliate and embarrass me on your big day. The most important day of his daughter's life! What kind of man is he?'

'He says Anne-Marie is his new partner. They live together, share everything, and that she is entitled to be there for his daughter's wedding.'

'That pig of a man! I can't believe he would even think of such a thing. Has he no sensitivity?'

Sally looked uncomfortable. 'He's set on it, Mum. He says if Anne-Marie can't go he's not coming!'

'Not coming to your wedding? I don't believe it!' she blurted out. 'Your father has to walk you up the aisle. Are you telling me he's prepared to give up that privilege for that little . . . I wouldn't let myself down by saying the word.'

'Mum, he's serious. He really is.'

'Will he still pay for the wedding?'

'He says he will pay for it but he won't come.' Sally's eyes filled with tears. 'I love both of you and I want both of you to be at my wedding. I couldn't bear it if one of you wouldn't come.'

Constance felt so angry she could have throttled Shay if he had been in the vicinity. She was furious that her husband would even consider holding them to ransom like this just to satisfy his whim of introducing his new lover to their close family and friends.

'He can't do this to me,' she said forcefully. 'It's your wedding day, Sally, and your father can't just go and ruin it for us.'

'It's only a day!'

'A big day!'

'That's what Chris says,' whispered Sally. 'A day to bury the hatchet, forget the past.'

Constance knew that there was absolutely no chance of burying the hatchet unless it involved sticking it into her husband's skull.

'Over my dead body is your father bringing his girlfriend to your wedding.'

'I understand how hard it is for you, Mum,' said Sally, 'being left on your own, but it's just that Dad . . . well, you know how stubborn he is.'

'Like a mountain goat! You tell your father to take a running jump along with that girlfriend of his,' said Constance sarcastically as they gathered their things together and paid the bill.

Back at home in Blackrock, Constance O'Kelly had collapsed into bed, overwhelmed. She knew she shouldn't let the mention of Shay or Anne-Marie reduce her to this stupid quivering mess of a woman, but she couldn't help herself. She had never imagined herself alone in this house, scrimping and scraping to pay the electricity and the gas bill. She didn't know what she was going to do next month when the insurance on her car was due for renewal. Shay had paid all the bills year in year out but now she had to do it herself.

194

'You're daft, Constance,' advised her friend Helen Kilmartin, 'rattling around in this big house with the boys gone and Sally getting married.'

'I know, but it holds far too many memories. Why should I agree to sell it just so that Shay and his fancy woman can get their hands on some money?'

'Selling it would sort out your finances too.'

'Helen, this is my home,' she retaliated. 'I'll not let Shay and his girlfriend drive me out of it.'

'Forget that pair,' urged her best friend. 'If you sell the house, do it for you! Think of the extra money you would have. The security you'd have, the savings.'

Constance knew that a large family home on Cross Avenue with a generous garden would fetch a premium price. Over the past few years Shay had fended off approaches from a number of Dublin's top auctioneering firms. But the thought of selling and moving out was too scary. She couldn't do it. How could she bear losing the home she had lovingly created and kept for the past twenty-five years?

Despite what Shay said, she had made economies. It had almost choked her the day she had to give notice to Annie Finnegan, their home help, after years of loyal service to the family, but there was no way Constance could justify the cost of someone coming in to clean the house and do the ironing and laundry now that she lived alone. She had also dropped the expensive gym membership that she rarely used – besides, the very thought of facing the ladies' dressing room and meeting people who would be curious about her business made her shake.

'You can't hide away and pretend this isn't happening,' cautioned Helen. 'You have to go out and face people.'

Constance didn't want to face anyone. As far as she was concerned, if Shay had dropped dead or been killed in an accident she would have had all the sympathy in the world from her neighbours and acquaintances and distant family. The fact that he had run off with another woman was a severe embarrassment. Everyone was reluctant even to mention her husband's name. God blast him, she thought to herself – he couldn't even do the decent thing and die!

Her best friend had proved a tower of strength over the past year and had helped her keep her sanity.

'You are not going to let Shay think that you are utterly hopeless and can't manage on your own, Constance. It's high time you showed him that you are your own woman, not some stupid cast-off.'

Constance had washed her hair and blow-dried it with the utmost care, put on her good beige suit and a black top and a comfortable pair of black court shoes, ready for the trip to town to get a wedding outfit. She studied herself in the mirror: she looked and felt like a sensible middle-aged woman. Running into the church in Clarendon Street she had just caught the end of Mass and lit a candle to St Teresa to give her the strength to stand alone, like so many other women.

Helen was waiting for her outside Brown Thomas's with a determined expression on her face.

'Will we go for a coffee?' Constance suggested.

'No,' insisted her friend, 'it's much better to start now while the changing rooms aren't busy and the assistants can give us their time.'

'Perhaps we should look somewhere else first?'

'No, we're starting at the top – Louise Kennedy, Paul Costelloe, John Rocha . . .'

Constance's heart gave a lurch as she followed Helen on to the designer floor of Dublin's most exclusive fashion shop. She had always considered herself a good dresser but the sophisticated and expensive clothes all around her seemed made for catwalk models, not for ordinary women.

'What do you think?'

196

'I think they are just beautiful . . . but not for someone like me.'

'They are especially for someone like you,' contradicted Helen, lifting four items off the rails and passing them to her. 'Now go and try them on.'

In the privacy of the changing room she leaned against the mirror and tried to compose herself. She must be gone mad.

'Have you got the cream on yet?' ordered her friend.

'In a minute,' she said as she eased the cream suit trousers up over her thighs and hips, amazed at the beautiful cut and fit. Carefully she lifted the silk jacket off the padded hanger and pulled it on. It felt good, every seam and hem perfect.

'Hey, that looks good, Constance. It makes you look taller and slimmer.'

'You don't think the cream makes me look too drawn?'

'No.'

'I like it but I'm not sure about wearing a suit . . . well, trousers!'

'It looks amazing but you're right, something that will show off your legs and a bit of flesh would be even better.'

'Helen!'

'Well, you know what I mean!'

After sifting through the rails they decided that black, though classic, was not suitable for the mother of the bride, pink was too girlie and the more exotic designers were just not her.

The Louise Kennedy designs were simple but stunning. A black linen dress with a white band and a neat co-ordinating white fitted jacket; a champagne satin coat worn over a sleeveless cream and champagne dress with a low neck and a skirt that skimmed above her knees; but her favourite was a stunning jade silk boxy jacket and dress.

Standing observing herself, Constance suddenly felt attractive and young and light-hearted.

'Wow!' Helen complimented her. 'You look wonderful.'

'Do you think so?'

'You know so – it's just your colour and shape and perfect for the wedding. Why don't you bring Sally in to see it on you? I'm sure the girl will hold it for you if you ask.'

'It costs a fortune,' she worried.

Helen raised her eyebrow, daring her to say one word more.

'You're right. I'll organize to meet Sally tomorrow.'

Sauntering round the store, Constance admitted to feeling more relaxed than she had in a long time and agreed after a little persuasion to lunch in Bang.

'Now that it looks like you've got the outfit for the wedding, we have to think about the rest,' cajoled Helen, sipping her chilled wine. 'Have you ever thought about highlights? They would give your hair a bit of a lift.'

Constance could see her reflection in the mirror behind Helen. Her hair had been practically the same light brown colour since she got married, except for the odd layering or light fringe. Maybe she'd been stuck in a time warp?

'And you'll need shoes and a bag, and a hat!'

'A hat?'

She hadn't thought about it, but a hat – that would be lovely! As she sat sipping her wine and eating her tossed chicken salad, Constance O'Kelly realized that for the first time in a very long while she was feeling happy.

Chapter Thirty-three

Constance spotted the little hat shop on the corner immediately. The shop had utterly changed. The classic powder-grey and blue paint-work had been replaced by a bright cream colour. The floor was now sanded wood and the heavy mahogany furniture had disappeared. She supposed everything changed, the old giving way to the new. It was fresh and bright, with a striped sun canopy, two lavender plants at the door, sprays of scented stock in a modern glass vase on the counter.

The few hats on display held the attention within the simple elegance of the room, their colours reflectcd in the mirrors on the wall.

Sally had thoroughly approved her choice of wedding outfit, complimenting her madly and insisting that she must accessorize it with a hat. Constance's own mother had always been a firm believer in the merits of a perfect piece of millinery to set off an outfit. It was just the thought of the expense and the whole rigmarole of it that made her hesitate.

'I'm not sure, pet . . .'

'Mum, it's your day too,' argued her daughter, blue eyes flashing. 'I want you to look beautiful and enjoy it all as much as I do.'

Constance suddenly felt such a rotten killjoy. It would be wrong of her to dampen Sally's high spirits and enthusiasm.

'You're absolutely right, darling – a hat is essential.'

The pretty young woman who sat behind the counter hand-sewing the edging of a ribbon to a hat welcomed them.

'Oh Mum, look at this one. Isn't it simply divine?' enthused Sally, popping the daisy-covered straw on to her own blond head.

Constance looked around her. Perhaps the shop was like so many others, catering only for the younger clientele, no longer interested in dealing with women of a certain age. She struggled to mask her disappointment.

'It's beautiful, Sally, just beautiful.'

'Yes, but I'm not the one that needs a hat. You are!'

'Can I help?' offered the girl.

'Yes, we're looking for something for my mother,' explained Sally. 'I'm getting married in a few weeks and she has got a gorgeous outfit for the wedding but needs a hat to go with it.' She produced the Brown Thomas bag with a flourish.

'Congratulations on your wedding,' smiled Ellie, taking a peek, 'and I'm sure we can find or make something that will be perfect with this. The colour is exquisite.'

Constance tried on one or two hats, lifting them carefully on to her head and tilting her neck from side to side. The larger-brimmed ones did nothing for her but the smaller, neater ones made her feel sophisticated and polished.

'A taller crown might work well,' suggested the young woman, handing her a yellow one off the stand. 'Don't mind the colour or the little details of all these because I can make exactly what you want.' She passed Constance a white cartwheel hat with a simple black ribbon trim. 'It's just we need to decide what shape suits you and what you feel good in.'

'I love this,' admitted Constance, 'but I think it is a wee bit too young for me!'

A topper, a Mont Blanc, and a large down-brim in bright pink with a purple satin trim were all rejected straight away. A fun feather mix in various tones also did nothing for the older woman.

'No, not right at all,' agreed Ellie, moving them aside.

A double crown in sand and black was much too heavy and made Constance look shorter and dumpier.

'Try this one,' suggested Ellie.

It was a two-tone concertina topper that suited most women, as it was not too wide or overwhelming. Constance settled it gently on her hair.

'I don't like these colours but the shape is good and I like the way the band wraps over on it.'

Ellie could see that the style would work and put the hat to one side.

Next there was an aubergine-coloured up-brim.

'It's certainly stylish but I just don't think it's me,' admitted Constance, studying it in the mirrors from every angle. 'Maybe it shows off too much of my face and it's not balanced properly.'

'That one is too big for you,' laughed Ellie, passing her a red sinamay disc with a bold decorative black feather, which looked stunning on.

'I'd never be brave enough to wear this,' Constance admitted ruefully, 'but it is lovely.'

The orange sidesweep with its taller crown, slightly upturned brim, contrast cream band and festoon of feathers that Ellie lifted from the window looked the part and Ellie could tell the client was happy the minute she sat it on her head.

'Oh, this is gorgeous. It's not too big or too small.' Constance burst

201

out laughing. 'I must sound like I'm Goldilocks testing out beds and chairs! But this one fits perfectly and is just that bit different. I do like it!'

'So do I,' agreed Ellie. 'It really suits you. It's elegant and fashionable without being over the top. Let me see what other versions I have of it. I have it in black with leather flowers somewhere, and a pure white version. I'll get them for you to see.'

Constance tried them all on. 'I do love this shape and style,' she enthused.

'Yes, the taller crown and slightly shorter brim with even a slight upturn or sweep works well,' mused Ellie, taking in the customer's square face.

'I really like this one,' admitted Constance, putting the orange back on again and staring at herself from all angles in the shop mirrors. 'But it's the wrong colour.'

'We could either try to match the colour of your suit or provide a contrast,' offered the hatmaker, 'or we could just pick up a tint of it, a certain hue.'

'Mum, go and try your new suit on,' urged Sally.

Although she had dropped almost a stone and a half with the stress of Shay walking out on her, Constance wasn't sure about parading around the small shop showing off her slimmer figure.

'It would help if I could see you in it,' said the hatmaker.

Constance disappeared into the changing room.

'We could pick up the jade and try and match it exactly,' suggested Ellie when she emerged. 'I would probably have to dye the colour for you. Or we can go for a total contrast, perhaps bring out another colour and blend or mix them with trims and bands or two tones, whatever style you like. Perhaps if we took another shade and then brought in elements from this and combined the two it would look even nicer. The suit and hat not just the one block of colour.'

'What other shades were you thinking of?'

'Mmmm,' Ellie hesitated. 'We could go for cream or white, or a warm reddish tone might work well.' She held her colour samples against the material. 'I quite like the reds.'

'I never wear red,' admitted Constance.

'Well, I don't mean a red red,' laughed Ellie, 'but something spicy and warm. A terracotta or a cinnamon, even a deep dusky pinkish red might work.'

'This is wonderful,' murmured the middle-aged woman, touching the cinnamon, 'but maybe the cream would be safer.'

Ellie raised her brow. 'Do you want to play safe?' she asked slowly. She had already picked up on the fact that Constance was going through a rather messy marriage break-up.

'No.'

'Then I suggest a band or flower or even a swirl of fabric,' she offered. 'Here, let me show you what I mean.'

Quick as a wink the girl had taken a pad from below the counter and sketched exactly what she was trying to explain to them.

'I could do it like this . . . or this way if you'd prefer to use something else.'

Constance was astonished that the girl had not only sketched a hat or two but also managed a simple ink and coloured-pencil version of the outfit she had bought.

'It's just perfect,' laughed Sally. 'I love your drawing. It's like something out of *Vogue*.'

'I studied fashion design,' admitted Ellie.

'If I look anywhere near as good as that design of yours I'll be thrilled,' confided Constance, who was beginning to feel a frisson of excitement at the thought of the wedding and her role as mother of the bride.

'I'm glad you like them, but which would you prefer?' asked the young hatmaker.

Constance stared at the drawings. 'I'm just not sure,' she admitted.

203

At the moment her brain was like fudge and she found it impossible to decide on anything, what to wear, what to buy in the supermarket, what video to rent from the local store, even when to buy petrol for her car. It was as if every capable atom in her body had gone on strike and left her a wobbly jelly who had no idea what she wanted.

'What if I make the hat in cinnamon and put a weave and trim of jade through it?' said Ellie firmly. 'If you don't like it we can go back to the plain colour, which is lovely anyway.'

'Is it a lot of extra work for you?' worried Constance.

'No, because I want to get it right,' she said, taking down the details in her order book.

'I am an old customer,' admitted Constance. 'I bought a hat for my brother's wedding here and a headpiece for a big corporate do I had to go to with my husband. That was a few years ago—'

'I've taken it over fairly recently,' Ellie interrupted. 'My mother Madeleine used to be the proprietor.'

'The French lady. How is she?'

'Sadly, my mother died a few months ago.'

Constance felt such a fool for putting her foot in it.

'Well, the shop is lovely. Your mother would most definitely approve.'

'Thank you for being so kind.' Ellie smiled.

Constance felt a guilty lump in her throat as she chatted away to this dark-haired petite beauty in front of her who had no mother to attend her wedding, or even to see the changes she had made to the business. She was a silly woman to be so wrapped up in her own miseries when she had the wedding and Sally's new life with Chris to look forward to.

Paying the deposit, she agreed to come for a fitting the following week.

Walking back up Grafton Street, she linked arms with her daughter, stopping to buy two enormous bunches of the pink-scented stock for Sally and herself from the flower seller on the corner.

Chapter Thirty-four

As the long hot August evenings passed, Ellie decided it was high time she repaid the generosity of her friends and invited a few of them to dinner.

Madeleine Matthews had ensured that her daughter was well versed in the culinary arts and was able to create a classically simple dish using the best fresh ingredients available. Dinner for ten would be perfect, as they would sit comfortably around the cream-painted antique dining table that had been in the family for years. If the evening was warm she would open the French doors and serve chilled Martinis and cold beer on the small terrace outside the conservatory that had been added to the second-floor apartment of the Georgian building. Yes, a simple menu was best: a little salad with something from the charcuterie in town, fish baked with wine and herbs served with roasted vegetables and some lovely new organic potatoes, then her favourite dessert, *tarte aux fraises*, served with vanilla ice cream. A cheese board and some good wines should help to say a big thank you to all those she cared about.

Ellie designed the quirky illustrated invitations and asked Rory if he would like to join them.

'Of course, beautiful,' he whispered. 'I can just imagine you with your apron on slaving over a hot stove and still looking sexy!'

The shop was hectic. Theatre designer Bill Braddock was collecting hats and headpieces for a show that was previewing in the Peacock Theatre a few days later, and more orders were coming in than she could single-handedly cope with. But at five o'clock on Saturday evening she determinedly turned the lock on the door and headed back home through the Green, resisting the temptation to sit on a park bench and chill out, reminding herself that she had dinner guests coming.

'Oh, your place always looks so beautiful,' gushed Mary-Claire, handing her a bunch of big white daisies and a bottle of chilled chardonnay. 'I just love it.'

Her new boyfriend, Sam, was quiet and went round the room looking at Ellie's photos and few pieces of art as she fetched them a drink.

'Love the bronze snail – it's very different,' he said.

'I made it when I was fifteen.'

The doorbell rang loudly and she hared down the stairs two at a time to greet Fergus and Polo. Fergus almost lifted her off her feet.

'Put me down, you big brute, or there'll be no dinner for you!'

'Hey, El, don't turn away a starving man!' he pleaded. 'I've had nothing since breakfast except for coffee and wine gums. I didn't have time for lunch.'

Upstairs they all relaxed and chatted, the French doors open and the conservatory giving them a view of the rooftops and a few trees that grew in the laneway. The white-painted wicker chairs were padded with an array of embroidered cushions and her plants were in full flower. Polo had brought some expensive bath and shower gels and a bottle of Fleury, while Fergus had simply produced a bag of dolly mixtures, her secret favourite sweets.

The girls arrived in a flurry of noise and squeals, Kim and Laura collapsing into the couch and demanding Martinis after the climb upstairs to the flat.

'I told you to take off your heels,' she chided, laughing.

'Women always have to suffer for beauty,' joked Kim. 'What would the boys think if we arrived in a pair of sandals with these skirts!'

'Doesn't bear thinking about,' winked Fergus, topping up Ellie's glass.

The last to arrive were Aoife and Jonathan, who were always late for everything. They muttered their apologies as they passed her a sinfully big box of luxury praline chocolates.

'You are forgiven,' murmured Ellie, before dashing off to check on the oven. Everything was going to plan and from the buzz of conversation she could tell her guests were enjoying themselves. The only problem was Rory. Where was he? She couldn't delay the meal too much longer or it would be ruined. She would settle herself with another Martini before worrying any more about him.

'Hey, El, is there any chance of some grub?' pleaded Fergus over an hour and a half later, coming into the narrow galley kitchen to join her. 'I'm starving, I've eaten nearly every little bowl of nuts and crispy things you have outside.'

'I was hoping Rory would be here by now, but you're right. Let's eat! He can catch up when he comes.'

Pushing her annoyance aside, Ellie lit the candles and served the starters as Polo passed round the wine.

'Here's looking at you, kid!' He smiled, the others joining in. Ellie listened as Fergus launched into the latest piece of office gossip about his new boss and got the conversation rolling.

207

The meal had gone splendidly, the fish perfect, everyone complimenting the cook and saying how delicious it all was. Surreptitiously,
while she was in and out of the kitchen, she had tried to contact Rory
on his mobile about four times but there had been no reply. She was
furious with him. The *tarte* had been demolished, the men at the
table demanding second helpings. She was just about to serve the
cheese and coffee when she heard the doorbell ring. The others
looked up expectantly.

'It must be Rory.' She excused herself and ran downstairs to let
him in.

'Hey, babes,' he said, leaning forward to hug her.

'You're late, we've almost finished dinner. What happened, where
were you?'

'I had to see a man about a record,' he apologized profusely. 'And
the meeting went on a bit longer than planned.'

'You've been drinking.' She could smell the alcohol on his breath.

'And so have you,' he said, placing his lips on hers.

'The others are all upstairs waiting – I delayed as long as I could.
Why the hell didn't you phone or text me?' she demanded.

'Sssh!' he whispered, leaning against her, pulling her into his
arms.

Rory went round kissing and hugging the others like they were all
long-lost friends, sitting in between Laura and Fergus and helping
himself to a glass of red wine.

'Do you want some food?' she offered. Perhaps it would sober him
up a bit.

'If there's any left!' He shrugged, throwing her that bad-boy smile
of his.

She ran to the kitchen and popped the small portion of the baked
fish that had escaped Fergus's ravenous appetite into the microwave
along with two potatoes. It wouldn't taste half as good as earlier

but food was food and that was what Rory needed at this stage.

She flicked on the kettle for the coffee and opened the box of pralines.

Although she had been gone only a few minutes, Rory, Fergus and Polo seemed embroiled in some kind of a row.

'The bosses and their companies are scumbags. Everybody makes money and cuts off their pound of flesh as they bleed the recording artists dry!'

'I don't think that's always the case,' reasoned Polo. 'They invest millions in some of those groups.'

'They create and clone artists and bands, and want to bloody own them body and soul. If the band object, they are ruined! Because Mr Record Company well knows another poor sucker of a band will be along in a minute or two.'

'Your fish is ready,' she interrupted, putting the plate down in front of him, 'and you should really eat it while it's hot.'

She hoped the conversation wasn't going to be unpleasant and glanced at Kim to see if she could rescue the situation, as Kim always had something to say.

'El, how's your street protest thing coming along?'

'We're getting there. We got permission from the corporation. We hope to get a big turnout for our SOS Day.'

'SOS?' queried Aoife.

'Save Our Street Day. All the shops will be shut. But there will be loads going on. Everyone is doing or giving away something. It'll be fun. I'm trimming hats and showing how to make a few simple headpieces.'

'That sounds great,' teased Laura. 'I must drop down to see you.'

'The more the merrier,' invited Ellie. 'We're hoping to get as much press and news coverage as possible.'

'I must make sure Mags sends a photographer,' promised Aoife, who worked as a sub-editor for the *Irish Times*'s *Weekend* magazine.

'Thanks, Aoife.'

Ellie passed round the coffee and chocolates, bursting out laughing when Fergus bagged about five for himself. Up one end of the table the talk continued about the merits of small businesses in towns and cities. Rory ignored the coffee and went for more wine.

'It won't make a shitload of difference what you do,' he pronounced. 'Big business and the government only care about profits. They'll play you along, then eat you up and spit you out.'

'I don't believe that,' said Ellie adamantly, furious that he was embarrassing her guests.

She watched him refill his glass. Fergus diplomatically removed the wine bottle from the table and put it on the sideboard.

'Hey, Ellie, I didn't see you in your sexy apron,' teased Rory, 'but maybe later!'

Ellie could feel her cheeks blaze and hoped the others hadn't overheard. She wasn't surprised when Aoife and Jonathan announced about fifteen minutes later that they had to leave.

'We'd better hit the road,' Jonathan apologized. 'I'm driving to Clonmel early in the morning to see my parents. It's their anniversary and we're taking them to lunch.'

'We had a lovely time,' said Aoife, 'and the food was great.'

As the others left over the next hour they were all equally complimentary about her culinary efforts as she walked them to the door.

'See you tomorrow, Ellie.' Fergus hugged her as he and Polo flagged down a taxi. 'It was a great night.'

'I'm sorry about Rory,' she said.

'We didn't come to see Rory,' he reminded her kindly, kissing her forehead.

Rory stayed sitting at the table finishing his wine as she cleared up.

'Hey, babes,' he cajoled. 'Sit down beside me and have another glass of this marvellous red.'

She was tempted to continue with the tidying but instead she left the empty crystal glasses on the table and sat down beside him, saying nothing when he reached forward and tried to kiss her.

'Hey, Ellie. Don't be so uptight.'

She had no intention of getting into a row with him and ruining such a perfect night.

'I'm tired.'

'And I'm not,' he grinned. 'Don't be such a prig.'

Ellie couldn't believe him. He'd behaved like an absolute pig, insulted her and her friends and then expected her to roll into bed with him.

'Rory, I'm calling you a taxi,' she said.

'I don't need a taxi,' he protested. 'I'm fine where I am.'

'No,' she insisted, grabbing his jacket. 'You're going home.'

On Sunday morning as she washed the dinner plates and tidied her small kitchen, Ellie reflected on the night before. She was mad at Rory but glad she'd made the effort for her friends.

It was lovely outside and once she'd cleared up she itched to put on her trainers and get some fresh air. She was making a pot of coffee when Rory arrived, looking far the worse for wear. Hair dirty, eyes behind his dark shades. She decided not to scold him and instead put two slices of bread in the toaster and poured him a glass of orange juice.

'Don't know if you noticed but it's a beautiful day.' She smiled, passing him the marmalade.

'Yeah, so I see.' He grimaced, scrunching his eyes against the sunlight.

She sat across the table from him for a few minutes, watching him.

'I'm sorry about last night,' he mumbled, buttering his toast. 'I didn't mean to mess up your evening.'

She had no intention of making it easy for him.

'Did you hear me? I apologize.'

She said nothing for a minute, wondering if a relationship with him was really worth all this hassle and hurt. Would it get any better?

'Ellie?'

'Apology accepted,' she said slowly.

'Good!' He laughed, kissing her hand.

'We could get some fresh air,' she suggested. 'It would do us both good!'

He shook his head. 'I'm sorry, I've got things to do.'

'It's Sunday!' she insisted, trying not to raise her voice as he bit into his slice of toast. 'What kind of things?'

As soon as the words had sprung from her mouth she knew she had crossed some kind of demarcation line.

'Stuff!'

She tried frantically to row back from being considered a nag or shrew. 'Yeah, me too.' She grinned. 'But I just thought it would be nice.'

'There's trouble with the band,' he admitted. 'This producer guy's messing us around. Sean and the guys aren't happy about it.'

She could see he was serious.

'I just came by to say sorry. Listen, I've got to try and track down one or two people today, see what they think.' He kissed her, his mouth tasting of coffee and alcohol. 'I'd better get going.'

'That's OK, Rory. Kim and I were thinking of meeting up later anyways.'

She tidied around the place and resisted the urge to watch from the window when she heard the front door bang downstairs.

Chapter Thirty-five

The shopkeepers, traders and business people of South Anne Street all came together on Save Our Street Saturday as thousands of Dubliners enjoyed the welcome August sunshine and blue skies.

'Can you believe it!' joked Scottie O'Loughlin. 'All our prayers have been answered – we couldn't have asked for a better day.'

Ellie grinned as she covered a trestle table with a pretty pink table-cloth she'd found in the flat. She set out ribbon, feathers, flowers and leaves and a variety of trimmings, stiffeners and glue alongside two of the straw hats on hatstands.

She had spent hours last night cutting out a variety of coloured felt shapes in preparation for today. This morning she had collected twenty-four basic straw hats from the wholesaler's in three shades – pink, natural and yellow – which she could use to demonstrate. The millinery suppliers had agreed that she could return any she did not use. Confused, Minouche had slunk round her feet and the table for a while. Realizing she would have no place to sleep and preen, she had taken herself off in a huff.

Scottie had hung a selection of kites from hooks beside his table and had an impressive array of sails, boats and rigging spread out for young hands to try to put together. His old friend Harry Regan had his shirtsleeves rolled up, ready to help.

The Italians had done the street proud. Two huge red and white gingham-bedecked trestle tables were set out with the ingredients to make perfect pizza and pasta, and the Italian flag was flying in the background. Leo and Andrea and their daughter Sophia were wearing their aprons and making a great show of mixing and stretching the pizza-base dough.

The Kavanagh sisters, who had been most unsure about what service their newsagent's could supply free to the public, had a stall stacked up with sweets and drinks and lollipops. Sissy was dressed like a Hungarian gypsy and her sister had confided that, as Sissy's other interest was fortune-telling, she would tell fortunes today for nothing.

'She's really very good,' she whispered to Ellie. 'If there is anything in particular you want to find out . . .'

Gary's print-framing area was spread out over two tables. Frank Farrell had equipped himself with a huge magnifying glass and a few antiques reference books, and set up his table and an old leather chair under a green and white parasol.

'Don't want to get sunburn,' he chortled. He had put on a burgundy jacket and a yellow and red cravat and looked rather dashing, like one of those TV antiques experts.

The deli had laid out everything needed to make the perfect sandwich. There was a demonstration of Aran hand-knitting, and the expensive men's shop was showing how to tie a variety of ties and was hosting a raffle for a new suit. The American diner was mixing up a cocktail of milk shakes and frozen yoghurts.

The Garda Siochana had been highly efficient in ensuring the street was car-free. Once everything was set up, they moved the barricades

214

at both ends of the street to let pedestrians have access. The traders, ready now to show everyone what they could do, wished each other well as people began to come and see what was going on.

'SOS Saturday was mentioned in this morning's papers,' confided Ria, who had placed a neatly folded selection of exquisite clothes on a small table in front of her shop. 'People buy expensive clothes,' she sighed, 'but they have no idea how to fold or hang them so as to keep them in perfect condition. I thought a little lesson in simple elegance and style might be useful.'

'Very useful,' agreed Ellie, who had always considered Ria Roberts one of the most elegant women she'd ever met.

The street began to fill up as more and more curious onlookers came to see what was going on. Scottie had a large crowd of children and their parents trying to master the intricacies of fixing miniature rigging on to model yachts. Harry handed out plastic jars of watery bubbles, demonstrating to the smaller children how to blow them. Frank sat under his parasol as a queue of enthusiastic amateur antiques collectors built up in front of him clutching shopping bags and holdalls filled with their precious treasures.

Ellie couldn't believe the crowds that thronged on to the street.

'Is it a market?' someone shouted.

'No. There's nothing for sale.'

'Everything is free.'

She watched as the television cameras from the country's main news station arrived, the cameramen moving about the street while reporters explained what was going on. Then the Mayor arrived.

Mo Brady, wearing her linen suit and new hat, smiled as the journalists rushed to interview her.

'Everyone on this street contributes to the richness of this city of ours. This street, like many other small streets, is a part of the culture and heritage that is Dublin. On this sunny summer's day the people of South Anne Street are sharing their trade and crafts with us. They ask the citizens of Dublin to join in with them as they try to save this street. Enough small shops and small businesses have closed down to make room for chain stores and huge developments. The time has come for all of us to find a balance, to say no more changes!'

The street was hushed as she spoke and Ellie knew everyone was looking at the boarded-up buildings and the shells of those already gone.

'Save Our Street!' shouted a voice, and the crowd took up the chant.

Mo said nothing for a moment, then: 'I think it's time that people listened.'

She got resounding applause and went down the street afterwards talking to everyone.

The balloon man was handing out balloons and a group of young musicians who had set up in front of the old dance hall began to play.

Ellie was nervous when it came to her turn and couldn't believe the crowd of women and young girls who watched as she demonstrated the various ways to trim a hat.

'Would you like to try?' she asked an elderly lady at the front as she showed how to wrap ribbon around wire and place it in position. Everyone wanted to have a go and Ellie promised they would all get a turn.

'Those who make the most inventive and creative hats will be allowed to keep them,' she said, giggling as a determined nine-year-old covered a yellow straw with a black ribbon and five little black felt cats. Definitely a winner!

The time passed quickly. Drinks, sandwiches and snacks were passed around as the crowds swelled and the queues got longer, everyone patient as they waited their turn. Frank Farrell was becoming quite a celebrity; his line snaked the whole way from one end of the street to the other.

'They'll have to give him his own TV show!' quipped Damien Quinn.

Ellie waved as Mary-Claire and Aoife and Fergus popped down to say hello. Kim was over with Sissy, having her fortune told.

No one could believe how well it was going and how much good humour and interest there was in the fate of their street.

Ellie yawned. Her feet were killing her but she still had a good few would-be hatmakers anxious to create a millinery masterpiece. She stopped in her tracks. Was she imagining it or was that Jerome Casey she saw strolling past her? He wore dark glasses and a panama hat but she was sure it was the property magnate himself coming down to check on them.

At five o'clock the tables were taken down and the street cleared as the crowds drifted away. Ellie packed up her ribbons and bows and feathers. The hats were all gone and Minouche was back, miaowing for attention. Scottie and Harry were deep in conversation as they dismantled their table, discussing how kids were still kids.

'It's been a wonderful day,' smiled Ria, touching Ellie's shoulder. 'I wouldn't have missed it for the world.'

'You are going to stay?' Ellie blurted out. 'You're not going to sell, are you?'

Ria reached for the pearls round her neck.

'I saw Neil Harrington calling on you,' admitted Ellie. 'You shouldn't let him force you into something you don't want to do.'

The older woman looked puzzled. 'I'm not sure exactly what we are talking about, my dear. Neil's mother and I are friends and he was only giving me a bit of timely advice about getting my affairs in order.'

'In order?'

'Yes, well, I'm not going to live for ever. A will is a sensible thing for someone at my time of life, don't you think?'

Ellie was mortified.

'Ellie! Ria!' shouted Damien Quinn. 'Once everyone has tidied up we are all going to Keogh's for a drink to celebrate.'

'After a day like today,' confided Ria, 'I could murder a gin and tonic.'

Chapter Thirty-six

Ellie put the finishing touches to the quirky pale blue and denim hat that she'd made for Kim. Tomorrow they were all going for drinks in Café En Seine then dinner in Milano to celebrate Kim's birthday and Fergus had secretly organized for a cake and candles to be brought to their table. The hat with its stiffened denim pieces was really unusual and should go perfectly with the blue strapless dress with the fitted skirt that Kim had bought in New York. Ellie had made a card and popped it into the hatbox along with a bottle of perfume and a packet of the dark chocolate that Kim loved and would deliver it round the corner to Davy's stockbrokers as a surprise for her friend.

It had been busy all week after the publicity of their very successful street day, and a relaxed night out with her friends and no shop-talk was just what Ellie needed.

'Birthday parties with a load of boring stockbrokers are hardly my thing,' joked Rory as they shared chips from Burdock's on their way home from watching some awful band he wanted to represent. 'Anyway, I've one of the record company execs over from London tomorrow night and I have to entertain them. You go and enjoy yourself.'

'But I want you to come,' she pleaded, trying to get him to change his mind, 'and Kim will be disappointed.'

'Sorry, Els,' he said, turning down the invite and shutting out her protestations with a kiss.

She pushed him off, annoyed. Here she was, dragged from one music venue to another at his whim, tonight listening to the worst band ever in a filthy pub, and yet he couldn't give up a few hours to come with her to something that she considered important. Lately he was always away or doing something and they were seeing less and less of each other.

'Ellie, don't be like that,' he teased. 'You know I hate it when girls moan.'

Milano was busy on Thursdays and it was fortunate they had booked a table for twelve in the packed restaurant. Kim looked gorgeous and hugged Ellie, thanking her for the hat.

'It was such a surprise,' she giggled. 'It's amazing. Everyone at work loved it.'

Ellie could see from the admiring glances of Mick Doherty and Jamie Roche that it was for more than her hat that they considered Kim amazing.

'Fergus, behave!' warned Ellie, noticing that Fergus had taken it on himself to make sure the party went with a swing by topping up everyone's red wine. 'Hey, go easy,' she cautioned her friend. Mary-Claire began pouring glasses of water.

The conversation was relaxed and Ellie found herself enjoying the night out. Kim almost burst into tears when the cake was served and half the restaurant joined in the singing as they all wished her happy birthday.

'I could kill you two,' she threatened Ellie and Fergus. 'Except that I love you both to bits.'

At midnight the party threatened to break up. Ellie found herself yawning.

'The night is young yet,' declared Fergus. 'Let's go to a club.'

'Lillie's,' declared Mick Doherty. The Davy's gang were big fans of the nightclub and had passes to the VIP room upstairs. Ellie had already had far too much red wine but she couldn't be a party-pooper on Kim's birthday, and besides, Fergus had promised to get up and dance. She'd stay for half an hour and then go.

'It's only round the corner,' urged Mick as they followed him down the lane and in past the club's doormen.

'Champagne for the birthday girl!' he called the minute he managed to get the waitress's attention. Kim was impressed and was flirting madly with him. Ellie gave her a birthday hug before Fergus dragged her downstairs to the dance floor. Exhausted after half an hour of trying to keep up with him, Ellie went back to the comfy couches in the lounge to sit down for a few minutes with Kim.

Suddenly she stopped in her tracks. She had spotted Rory. The room was pretty crowded but it was definitely him. He was sitting in the far corner on the red-print couch, having a beer with an attractive blonde, their heads close together as they chatted and laughed. That must be the exec he was meeting. She'd go over and say hello.

'Ellie, let's get out of here,' urged Kim, grabbing her by the arm.

'It's OK,' she tried to explain. 'Rory told me he was going out tonight with someone from the business. It's work. I'll just go and let him know I'm here.'

'No you won't,' said Kim, pulling her away. 'The two of them were snogging the faces off each other ten minutes ago. I saw them, honest!'

Her friend persuaded Ellie to ignore Rory Dunne and not cause a scene but to come back to the bar where Fergus and Mary-Claire and Mick and the rest of their crowd were.

'He's such a cheat and a liar,' argued Polo and Fergus furiously. 'He obviously never expected you to turn up in Lillie's.'

Ellie felt mortified to be let down so publicly in front of her friends. She hid in the loo for a while, embarrassed and hurt. When Kim told her that Rory and the blonde had left, she grabbed another glass of red wine. She danced and drank far too much for the rest of the night, trying to put him out of her mind. At three o'clock they decided to leave the club.

'Come on, we're all going to Eddie Rocket's for something to eat,' offered Kim. Ellie was too tired and upset and after tonight's fiasco all she wanted was to get home.

'Well, you're getting a taxi, then,' said Kim and Fergus, putting her into one in Dawson Street. 'We'll give you a call tomorrow.'

The taxi driver had only just gone past the Dáil when she asked him to stop and let her out at the Shelbourne Hotel as she suddenly felt she needed fresh air. Those were dreaded words to the taxi community and, fearing the worst, he had her out of the taxi in a shot. Ellie leaned against the rails as she tried to collect herself. It had been a wonderful night up to the point when she had seen Rory. He was such a liar. She'd been fooling herself all along. She took in a few gulps of air and began to walk slowly. She should never have drunk so much. Champagne and red wine, never. She tried to step out of the way of a crowd of businessmen standing outside the hotel. The smell of cigars and brandy hung in the air.

'Ellie!'

Her heart plummeted. She didn't want anyone she knew to see her in this state.

'Are you all right?' Neil Harrington asked, concerned, moving away from the group.

'I'm just walking home,' she tried to say gaily.

'You seem to like doing that,' he said dryly. 'Are you alone?'

'Well, no, I wasn't alone. I mean . . . I am now. I was at a birthday thing with friends and we all went to Lillie's after. But now I want to go home,' she explained, holding on to the hotel railings for support.

'I think you should let me walk you home,' he said firmly.

Ellie was about to protest but felt suddenly glad to have someone like Neil offering to escort her.

'Let's go,' he suggested, saying a brief goodnight to his colleagues.

'And what are you doing out at this late hour of the night, Mr Harrington, might I ask?' she giggled, trying to keep up with his long legs.

'Having a farewell dinner with a legal colleague who is moving to Prague.'

'Prague? I've never been to Prague,' she sighed, catching his arm. 'It's meant to be beautiful and romantic, a city for lovers. That is, people who do have lovers!'

He said nothing as they crossed the road.

'You probably have hundreds!' she said argumentatively. 'I have none. I'm being honest! Not even one.'

'I don't believe that,' he said softly.

'Well, it's true,' she said, putting her head in her hands, feeling like she was going to cry or puke and she wasn't sure which would be worse.

Neil stood patiently beside her till the feeling passed.

'Are you OK?'

'I'll live.'

He took her hand as they crossed the road, the two of them watching a cat raid the boxes and bins outside a Leeson Street sandwich bar.

'Nearly there,' he said, coaxing her along as if she was a reluctant three-year-old.

The granite steps of number 44 Lower Hatch Street reared up in front of her and Neil took her key to open the entrance door.

'Will you manage?' he asked.

She gazed up at the steep flight of stairs and the yellow-patterned carpet.

'Forget Prague, it's Paris I want to go to,' she crooned. 'My mother grew up there, did you know that? All the women have lovers there, everyone does and no one cares about it. People don't get hurt. They mind their own business.'

'What floor are you on?' he demanded.

'The second, but I'm just going to sit down here for a little rest,' she said, trying to lower herself on to the granite steps.

'That's not a good idea.' He lifted her to her feet and helped her up the steps to the first landing. She felt like a floppy rag doll as he managed to get her up another floor and manoeuvred to open the flat door and get her inside. Ellie felt herself spinning, spinning, as she pointed out the bedroom.

She woke to her head throbbing and her mouth dry and the sound of a heartbeat, slow and regular. After a few seconds she realized it wasn't her own and that she was lying across someone's chest. For a moment she thought it was Rory, and then she remembered the night before. Cringing, she saw she was curled up on top of Neil Harrington, who was still fully clothed in a navy pinstripe suit, his dark hair standing on end. God, this was awful; by far the most embarrassing thing she had ever done in her entire life. Maybe she could pretend to be asleep and move off him and he would get up and go.

'You awake?' he asked gently, before she could do anything.

She nodded, too ashamed to speak.

'Are you all right?'

Why was he always looking out for her? Catching her at her worst?

224

'Yeah!' she groaned, giving a huge sigh. 'Listen, Neil. I'm sorry about last night. I'm so embarrassed.'

'Nothing happened,' he said quietly, moving her hair back off her face so he could see her better.

'Honest?'

'We're both fully dressed.'

'Why didn't you leave?'

'I wanted to make sure you were OK during the night.'

She moved to get up, to lift herself off him at least. She must have had him pinioned there all night. God, it was too awful to imagine.

'Stay,' he said, pulling her back down beside him. 'You're awake now.'

She felt his lips brush her forehead.

She closed her eyes and fell back into his arms. It was lovely lying here with him. But the pleasurable experience lasted only a minute. God, this was not what she had planned or imagined! What must Neil think of her?

'I must have been like a crazy person last night, Neil, I'm so sorry,' she apologized again, moving away from him. 'I was upset and got drunk and I must have been really stupid and pathetic and talking nonsense, so please disregard anything I said.'

He laughed, sitting up properly and fixing his shirt and jacket. 'You asked me to go to Paris with you.'

Ellie blushed red, red, red.

'And what else?' she said with a sinking feeling, seeing the mockery in his eyes.

'You told me what we'd do when we got to Paris!'

No! No! No!

She knew by the laughter in his eyes that she had not been talking about the tourist trail. Ellie cursed her own romantic imagination and vowed never to drink so much as a drop of champagne again.

He looked pretty shattered. Unshaven, suit crumpled, hair all over the place.

'Did you get to sleep at all?' she asked, shamefaced.

'A little, but you sang, you snored, you told me your plans for Paris. That was the nice bit – and then you snored again.'

'Oh Neil, I'm so sorry,' she repeated, humiliated.

'Listen, Ellie, I'm going to have to go. I need a shave and a shower and a change of clothes back in my own place. I have to be in court in about an hour.'

She sat on the edge of the big double bed, not knowing what to say as he pulled on his shoes and combed his hair.

'Until Paris,' he said when she looked up, reaching to touch her face, outlining her jaw and mouth with his fingers. Ellie, surprised by the shared intimacy, was wishing he could stay.

Chapter Thirty-seven

Ellie retreated to the shop at midday, still hung over and praying that no customer had been looking for her. Minouche was miaowing to be let in and looking for her saucer of milk as Ellie opened the door and pulled up the shutters. She poured herself a huge glass of water and decided that absolutely nothing would be made today. She could tidy and tweak and write up her books and rough sketch, but not a finger would she put to making a hat or it would be a disaster.

Kim had phoned to say thanks for everything and check that she was OK.

'I'm fine,' she lied, 'just a bit hungover.'

She had found Neil's mobile phone under her duvet before she'd left the flat and wondered if he'd missed it. She was tempted to send him a message on it. Thank him. Embarrassing as it all was, she somehow hoped that he'd call on her to collect it. She wanted to talk to him, explain about last night and thank him for taking care of her when she was in such a state.

*

Rory had phoned and she had been deliberately cool and distant with him. She said nothing about seeing him in Lillie's and in return he said nothing to her, only telling her his meeting had been a great success.

'Good for you!' she said, bitterly disappointed by his deception.

She was catnapping behind the counter in the late afternoon, pretending to read a copy of *Marie Claire*, when Fergus came to the door. Judging the state of her pale face, greasy ponytailed hair and sunken eyes, he disappeared down the street to fetch a bacon sandwich and two bottles of Lucozade.

'Get that into you,' he said, watching her eat.

'Ugh,' she protested.

'Any better?'

She nodded. The cure was working.

'You OK, Ellie?'

She didn't know what to say.

'Rory's a bastard, El! I know you like him but he's a rat and you're a princess. It's not going to work. I don't mean to sound like your big brother but he's not good enough for you. He really isn't. I should have kicked his head in last night.'

Ellie began to laugh. 'Fergus, you've never kicked a soul in your life.'

'I know, but if I ever start he'll be top of my list for being such a scumbag to you.'

'I still really like him,' she admitted softly. 'I just kept hoping that he'd be different, that I could change him!'

'Why do lovers always want to change people?' puzzled Fergus. 'It always messes things up.'

'Someone to be true and faithful, is that too much to ask?'

'No,' said Fergus, putting his arms round her and holding her for a while.

228

'What about you?' she quizzed eventually. 'Did you enjoy last night?'

'Yeah, it was great. Good buzz at Lillie's. I met that guy Liam that works with Kim. He's nice.'

'Hey,' she smiled. 'Are you going to see him?'

'Maybe. We might go for a drink tomorrow.' Fergus fussed around, making sure she was OK, and brewed her a quick cup of reviving tea before heading back to his office for a meeting.

Puzzled that there had been no word from Neil, Ellie wondered what should she do about his phone. Obviously he was so busy in court that he hadn't missed it.

Should she bring it back home with her and see if he collected it later at the flat? But then maybe it would look like she deliberately wanted him to call to see her. Should she simply get it delivered to his office? The couriers were always up and down the street. Checking the address in the phone book, she quickly shoved the mobile phone into an envelope with a scribbled thank-you note and paid for it to be delivered.

She was just locking up at the end of the day and talking to Scottie O'Loughlin when Rory appeared. He was wearing his black T-shirt and jeans and carrying twelve yellow roses. Scottie made a discreet disappearance to where he could watch them from his toy-shop window.

'These are for you,' said Rory, kissing her cheek.

'What for?'

'To say sorry about last night, for not going out with your friends.'

'It's all right, Rory,' she said softly. 'I had a good time and Kim enjoyed her birthday. We went to Lillie's after, with a crowd from Davy's.'

'Lillie's?'

'Lillie's Bordello, the nightclub.'

At least he had the good grace to look embarrassed.

'So you saw me,' he said evenly, looking her straight in the eye.

She nodded, not trusting herself to speak, not wanting to cry.

'Yes, Kim and Fergus and Mary-Claire, we all saw you. Couldn't help but see you.'

He didn't even try to deny it or explain. 'I'm sorry, Ellie. Just give me another chance.'

'There's no point,' she admitted. 'It's not going to change things, is it?'

'You're a sweet girl,' Rory said slowly. 'I'm mad about you. You know that. Last night, I don't know why but I just screwed it up.'

Ellie could see that in some bizarre way he meant it. All of it! It was just that with Rory what was meant to be easy and relaxed had become complicated and messy. And she didn't want to do it any more. It was better to end it now before there were any more lies and hurt.

'I'm sorry,' he said as she took the yellow roses and his farewell kiss with absolutely no regrets.

Chapter Thirty-eight

Neil Harrington hadn't listened to a word the judge and his legal colleague had said during a rambling discourse on court procedures. Distracted, he had to ask a junior for his notes at the lunchtime recess before finding time to meet a client and introduce him to his barrister. He grabbed a sandwich and a coffee, then rushed to another meeting. He went to phone Jean, his secretary, and discovered that his mobile phone was missing. Remembering last night, he grinned for a moment. It had most likely fallen out of his pocket and was in the possession of Ellie Matthews, the woman who had scrambled his thoughts all day and left him a physical and mental wreck. Tonight he had the perfect excuse to call to see her after work and collect it.

He was tired and stiff from the awkward position he'd lain in on her bed, but the thought of her lying in his arms all night was pleasing and something he definitely intended to repeat.

Joining the rush-hour city traffic, he circled the Green and found a parking spot on Dawson Street. He locked his car and crossed the street towards the hat shop, stopping for an instant when he saw her standing in the doorway. She looked tired too, he mused.

He watched her for a few minutes. Saw her face light up as the guy in the black T-shirt approached, the way he handed her a dozen yellow roses, heads close, talking, then kissing. Turning slowly, he got back into his car. He didn't need to see any more. He started the engine and drove away.

Rosemary Harrington was in the middle of tying up some sweet peas in the garden when the doorbell rang. She hurried up from the kitchen and out through the hall to the front door, where the shaven-headed courier in his red top and leather jacket asked her to sign for a package.

It was for Neil. She signed for the delivery, wondering was it important. The courier companies regularly delivered to the home address rather than the office further up the square. Perhaps it was something urgent and she had better check? She opened the envelope and was surprised to discover a mobile phone inside. Neil's, by the look of it! There was a simple note attached on pretty yellow business paper. Why would her son be dealing with the hat shop?

Neil
Thank you for rescuing me! This must have fallen down beside the bed last night.
Love, Ellie

Curiouser and curiouser, thought Rosemary. It was from that beautiful young woman who made those gorgeous hats. She slipped the phone and note back inside the packet.

Her son returned home at six thirty and she called out about the package in the hall, reminding him she had a lamb casserole nearly ready for dinner.

232

'I'm going out,' he shouted, grabbing the phone and banging the door, scowling at her just like he'd done when his junior rugby team had lost a very important match.

Chapter Thirty-nine

Tommy Butler searched around under his bed for the box. The cardboard box was well hidden behind a bag of *Marvel* comics and a blue plastic carton holding his favourite DVDs and videos. Lying almost flat on the floor, he reached the container of his treasures: a medal he'd won for swimming and a Fulham football jersey his uncle had bought for him when he was about eight; football boots that were never ever going to be given away despite the fact they were two sizes too small for him, and the globe his grandad gave him for his communion. The globe had fallen off its stand and was a bit dented from rolling around the floor, but to him it was still precious. It made him feel he could hold the world in his hands like Atlas, that fellah Mr McHugh had been telling them about in class. Down underneath it all was his bank book, his post office account and the cards his friends had made for him the time he'd gone into hospital to have his tonsils out. Today he had no interest in sentiment. It was the balance in his bank account he was after. Tommy studied the figure. It was less than he'd hoped. How had he managed to go through his confirmation money and savings so quickly?

Fifty-nine euros and fifty cents was the total in his account.

He sat back up and leaned against the bed. He had been hoping to put the money towards either a new bike or a skateboard. Still, the money would go a long way towards getting a present, a decent present for his granny. Yeah, being a hundred years old was definitely deserving of a great present. Now he just had to rattle his brains and think of something totally suitable and awesome for Lillian Butler.

Mam and Dad were giving her an antique silver frame.

'It's a genuine antique. Georgian silver,' his mam decreed proudly, hiding the present in the sideboard. 'We can get a nice photo of Granny and put it in it, or get one taken at her party.'

Pat Butler had nodded his head in agreement as he sat down to watch the evening news and sports results. 'The perfect present.'

Tommy didn't agree. Auntie Joyce was giving her a photo album, and the cousins from Athlone were talking about a Waterford crystal photo frame or ornament. His big brother, Ray, was giving her hand-made chocolates.

'Old ladies love chocolates. Got a sweet tooth for them.'

Tommy wasn't sure if he should remind his brother that for the past two years or more chocolate had upset Granny's stomach and the only sweets she liked were bullseyes or wine gums, which were hardly good enough for celebrating being a hundred years old. He had tried to talk to his older sister, Vonnie, about it but she was so busy with her new baby that he didn't think she was really thinking when she advised him to buy their granny soaps and bubble bath.

Granny Butler lived in a big old red-bricked building near Ranelagh called the Charlemont Nursing Home with a load of other old ladies and a few men. Nurses minded them and made sure they didn't fall and break their bones because old ladies were always falling! His granny had fallen when she was ninety-seven and that was how she had ended up in the nursing home. Before that she had lived with them, sleeping in the big room across the landing.

He'd missed her when she moved. Missed her stories, and the card games they used to play. Missed the way she used to say that just because he was the youngest and was called after Grandad, it didn't mean to say he was her favourite. No, she'd laugh, it was just that she loved him the most. The most of them all!

Soaps and bubble bath? He had to get her something better than that. He's seen a book about Dublin in the 'rare old times' which seemed to be around the time Granny was born, but studying it in the bookshop he soon realized that Granny with her poor eyesight would no longer be able to read all the pages of print. He needed to get her something that would remind her of all those times – but what?

On Saturday he went downtown and had a bit of a ramble round, hoping to get ideas, resisting the temptation to spend the money on himself and then having to borrow off his parents.

Embarrassed, he wandered through the cosmetic and perfume hall of Clery's searching for the perfect gift, until a lady in a pink dress sprayed him with some perfume.

'This scent will bring back memories of spring in Tuscany,' she gushed.

Tommy grimaced: he'd never been to Tuscany. The scent clung to him throughout the day, even when he went to play football with his mates on the green after tea. In bed that night he could still smell it. Then it came to him. He didn't have a scent that would remind his grandmother of her long life but he could find something else. Something that would remind her of all the good times she'd had in a hundred years. Contented, Tommy rolled over with his quilt tucked round him. Now all he had to do was to think what that something might be.

*

On Sunday he went to visit her with his mam. Sitting in the front seat of his mother's blue Toyota made him feel almost like a navigator as he had to keep up a running commentary on hazards that lay ahead.

'Lady with a buggy, watch out! . . . The traffic lights are just changing! . . . We need to be in the other lane so we can turn!'

Driving with his mam was crazy. His da and big brother refused to go in the car with her and Vonnie had her own little runaround, so it always fell to him to accompany her on excursions that involved more than a trip to the local shops. His mam had a great knack of ignoring the irate drivers around her: she simply turned the radio up loud as could be or put on her Rod Stewart CD. Even Tommy flinched as they turned the corner and scooted up the driveway of the Charlemont Home to the tune of 'Sailing', coming to rest parked up against a flower bed.

'Here safe and sound,' laughed his mother as she got him to carry in a load of things for his nan.

Tommy always kept his eyes focused ahead as he walked past the old people lined up in their chairs and staring at the TV. Some were blocked into their seats like babies in high chairs and some old ladies fiddled with their handbags, but most of them just slept. He supposed that when you got to be a great age all you wanted to do was sleep. You were too tired for anything else. Lillian Butler was in her room and her eyes lit up the minute she saw the two of them. She loved visitors and a bit of chat and she patted the chair and the bedside.

'Give your old gran a kiss,' she ordered, puckering up her lips. Tommy would die if any of the boys in his class saw him kissing a woman, especially an old woman. But his granny had always loved a kiss and a hug and there was no getting away from it.

He could see his mam laughing as he went red.

237

'Now, Tommy love, don't you be shy of telling the people you love how you feel, promise me. I won't always be here to remind you.'

'Yeah, Granny, yeah!'

He sat beside the bed as his mam and his granny nattered away, talking about his dad and Yvonne's baby and the neighbours next door and the conservatory they were building.

'Pat doesn't like it at all!' whispered Mary Butler. 'Not one little bit.'

His grandmother sat in her special chair listening, taking it all in. Her brown eyes were bright in her small face, the wispy white hair standing out round her head as she chatted. Granny Butler was the oldest person he knew. She had lived through the *Titanic*, the 1916 rising, the First World War and the Second World War, Concorde, mobile phones, the first man on the moon, *Star Wars* and James Bond. She was a living breathing history project, as Mr McHugh would say. She remembered everything . . . well, almost everything. One time before she had her fall she had forgotten where their house was, and that she had married Tommy Butler and had nine children. His mam and dad had worried about her and all the aunties and uncles had paid for her to go to a special doctor and had a whole load of Masses said for her, but God was good, as his mam said, for she got her brain back, even if she did have her fall a few weeks later.

'At least she's all there,' was what the family decided.

Looking at her now, Tommy realized she was most definitely all there, as she asked him what marks he got in his spelling test and what homework Mr McHugh had given him for the weekend.

He studied the photos on her locker. Lily Butler had been a right good-looker in her day. Small and dark with those sparkling eyes and a turned–up nose. There was a photo of her on her wedding day with his grandad, with a funny thing on her head that made her eyes look even bigger, and another of her at a christening party wearing a flowery hat. Tommy got up and went closer to look at the photographs.

'Mind you don't knock any of them down, Tommy love,' she warned.

'You look real pretty in them, Granny, really pretty.'

'That's why your grandfather fell in love with her,' smiled his mam.

Tommy studied the array of photos, noticing that in many of his grandmother's favourite pictures she wore a hat or a bonnet or a beret or something.

'You like all these things on your head.'

'I was always a bit of a hat woman, Tommy. Your grandad said I was blessed with my legs and my face but, you know, the old hair let me down sometimes. Ronnie Leary gave me a desperate perm one time! Couldn't show my face for weeks. Tom bought me a beautiful red felt hat. Took me walking down O'Connell Street in it. A man with a camera stopped us and I got my photo taken in it.'

'There it is,' said Tommy, recognizing the buildings, an idea finally taking shape in his mind. A Memory Hat, that was what his granny needed.

A hat should be easy to find. After only a brief saunter round the shops in Henry Street and Mary Street and Talbot Street, and uptown to Grafton Street and Wicklow Street, Tommy began to realize there was a vast difference in terms of price and style when it came to hats, and the fact that he hadn't a clear idea of what he really wanted didn't help. The ladies behind the counters shooed him away when they saw him coming, not even giving him a chance to explain what he was looking for. He had just begun to feel despondent when he noticed the cheerful little hat shop on South Anne Street, with its bright window and the stands with hats displayed. He stopped outside, staring in as he studied the shape and design of each one carefully, twisting and bending as he tried to see the price tag. He noticed the sign above the door. *Ellie Matthews – Milliner. Hats made to order.*

Well, that was exactly what he wanted to do, order a special hat for his grandmother. He stared in the window. The lady was busy with someone. He'd come back tomorrow.

Chapter Forty

Ellie was busy in the back working on Erin O'Donovan's blue goose-feather hat when she heard the shop bell ring. She tucked a few pins into the circle of crêpe and smoothed the blue snippets of feather off her clothes and lap. There must be a customer, she thought as she went to the front. She stopped. The boy was standing there. He'd been watching the place for a day or two from a vantage point across the street. Casing the joint more likely, thought Ellie, preparing to rob her cash or steal her stock. She was lucky she'd heard him sneak in, and her eyes involuntarily flew to the grey steel cash box that lay hidden under the counter.

She wouldn't give in without a fight, she decided. She wasn't scared of him.

'Mrs . . .'

She took a breath. Here it came: the threat, the demand. Funny, he looked a lot younger up close. He might only be twelve or thirteen, his skinny face covered in freckles, his mousy hair standing on end.

'Mrs?'

'Yes?' She tried to appear nonchalant, as if she was used to young thugs coming into her shop every day of the week.

'Mrs, I want to buy a hat.'

Ellie stopped. Had she misheard him or had he actually said he wanted to buy a hat? Purchase one of her creations? She must have misheard. Perhaps he was trying to trick her, put her off her guard. Send her in the back for something while he made off with her stock or the takings, or both. Kids like him could run as fast as hell.

'I want to buy a hat,' he said, more determined. 'A special hat for someone.'

Ellie was taken aback. He sounded genuine.

'I have some money,' he offered.

She shook herself. He was a customer, after all, in search of one of her creations; age and size and the fact that he was a mere schoolboy should not come into it.

'Have you seen one that you would like?'

The boy shook his head. 'No,' he admitted. 'This hat has got to be made special.'

Ellie's eyes widened. 'It might work out quite expensive,' she said gently.

He stood there, still undeterred. 'That's all right.'

She watched as he stuffed his hands in his pockets, his feet shuffling in his trainers. Poor kid. Maybe it was a dare!

'What kind of hat were you looking for?'

'I dunno.' He shrugged. 'Something big and beautiful, with flowers and all kinds of things on it.'

Ellie wondered was he being serious. 'Do you mind me asking who this hat is for?'

'For my granny.'

'Well, maybe your grandmother could come in here herself and choose a hat,' suggested Ellie, proffering one of the fancy new cards that had been designed for her.

'No, she can't,' he said firmly. 'Anyways it's a surprise for her birthday.'

Ellie was taken aback by his determination.

'I want a hat like that.'

He was pointing to a broad-brimmed up-brim with a simple wide bandeau of lemon round it.

'But with all kinds of things on it.'

'What kind of things?' Ellie asked, suddenly curious.

'Things that are special to my gran.'

He suddenly brandished an old sepia photo at her. It was of a young woman wearing a broad-brimmed hat trimmed with roses and ribbon, her dark eyes laughing, her head thrown back, relaxed.

'What a lovely photograph!'

'My gran likes hats,' he said, serious. 'And she likes all kinds of things.'

Perhaps he was genuine and she could let him have a simple base hat with a few artificial flowers to satisfy him.

'Hold on a second.'

She darted in the back and rummaged around. There must be one somewhere. She found it and plucked a handful of roses and leaf stems made of nylon, which could easily be mounted on a piece of pale pink ribbon. She'd show him. Her fingers flew as she attached them lightly with pins. There, done. She carried it out.

'What about this?' she said, placing it on the hatstand on the counter.

He couldn't mask the disappointment in his young face.

'Would your grandmother like this?'

'No. That's not it at all. It's got to be a big hat with all the things my granny cares about on it.'

Ellie was intrigued.

243

'I made a list.'

The list was on a folded sheet of school copy-book paper.

'My granny will be a hundred years old next month,' he said proudly. 'So it has to be the best present in the world. My mam says she already has everything she needs, but she's always loved hats so I thought I might get her a new one.'

'She's a hundred years old?'

'Yeah. She lives in the Charlemont Home. They look after her real well because sometimes she forgets things,' he confided, 'but a hat like that might remind her of all the special days in her life. Help her remember.'

Ellie peered at the scrawly writing. He'd jotted down Lillian's name and age, address, date of her wedding and details of her family. It was a start but it wasn't enough to document a rich life well lived.

Pulling up the stool from behind the counter, she asked Tommy to sit down for she needed him to tell her more about Lillian Butler, his grandmother.

Later, sitting in the shop and trying to think of a design that would suit such a hat, she laughed to herself. Kim would kill her. This went against all her concepts of a business catering for stylish well-heeled customers. Other designers had privileged customers and wealthy socialites clamouring for their services, while she had a kid determined to buy the best for his centenarian grandmother. It was some challenge.

Chapter Forty-one

One hundred years, all put together in a hat. A special Memory Hat. That would be the best birthday present ever, thought Tommy, as he got ready for school.

Finding out all the things that were important to his grandmother over so many years and piecing them together to make the hat would be a bit like playing detective, he thought. He took the small spelling notepad from his schoolbag and began to make notes.

Nine children. That was something no one would ever forget. Tommy wrote down his dad's name and those of all his uncles and aunties. Then there were the grandchildren. Last count there were thirty-seven of them. Now of course there were the great-grandchildren, including his sister's new baby, Dara, which made it twelve so far. Massive. Granny and Grandad Butler had started a dynasty. Before you knew it, half of Dublin would be part of their family. It gave him a warm feeling just thinking about it.

He had pocket money due and if he helped the old lad with cutting the grass for the next few weeks, he could probably earn another few euros to add to his hat kitty. Before you could say 'Tommy Butler' he would have the amount needed to pay for the fancy designer hat his grandmother deserved.

He could see the hat in his mind. The only trouble was deciding what to put on it, like the nice lady in the shop had said. Everything had to be just right. This hat was going to be hard work but for once it was something he didn't mind. He would have to get cracking if he wanted it ready in time as his mam and dad had already started sending out the invitations for Granny's big party.

He would search through the family photo albums to get some clues about his grandmother's life. Auntie Paula, his dad's sister, was usually good for stories and remembered everything. He'd call on her. She'd never married and had no children and loved to get visitors, especially her nieces and nephews, whom she doted on.

Auntie Paula was surprised to see him and made him sit down for a bacon and sausage sandwich and a cup of tea the minute he arrived.

'Just about to have one myself,' she assured him, as she fussed around the kitchen of her red-bricked two-up two-down near the canal. She was wearing a pair of baggy trousers and an old cricket jumper, her plump figure moving around the small kitchen as the smell of rashers filled the air.

Tommy hadn't realized how hungry he was after a day's lessons. He wolfed down the tomato-sauce-smothered snack as his auntie poured out the tea.

'That's what I like to see, a good appetite,' beamed Paula Butler. 'After all, you are a growing boy and need to keep your strength up for studying.'

Tommy blushed. He wasn't exactly doing well in the studying department and was struggling with maths and science. Mr McHugh, his teacher, had suggested him going for extra help after school but it clashed with his football training. He couldn't miss football! He wanted to be a footballer when he grew up so training was more important than a hundred maths lessons in his eyes. He found himself telling his aunt, who nodded sagely.

'None of the Butlers were known for their mathematical abilities, Tommy,' she admitted. 'You just do your best. But maybe that teacher of yours is right – a little bit of extra help might make a difference.'

With very little prompting his aunt soon launched into an account of her own childhood days and going to school. He constantly interrupted her with questions about his grandmother, which she was delighted to answer as Tommy scribbled in his notebook.

Chapter Forty-two

Dermot McHugh looked down at the class of twenty-four boys, knowing in his heart that like himself they were counting the minutes till the bell sounded that would herald the end of the school day. He had spent the past hour trying to instil some sense of the importance of the Land League in two dozen uncaring minds. He had observed them fiddle and shift and doodle and chew gum and secretly read the sports pages of the tabloid newspapers as he rolled out dates and times and places and the significance of their fellow countrymen's secret rebellion against the British landlords.

He could jolt them into shocked attention by announcing that there would be a sudden test on the subject in the ten o'clock history class next morning, but knew he wouldn't have the heart to mark all their papers. Most likely they would mirror exactly what was written in their history textbook. The class swot, Oscar O'Flynn, would hand him immaculate pages of perfect script worthy of a Trinity history scholar, while the rest would as usual do their worst! How had he ended up here trying to teach boys about the past, when it was clear all they were interested in was the future and getting released from school? He had always meant teaching to be a temporary position, something to do until a more interesting and fulfilling career had turned up, and yet here he was, twenty-six years later, languishing in the depths of St Peter's Boys' School. His own class-room, his own pigeon hole in the staff room and the after-school responsibility of running the Chess Club. He blinked behind his glasses.

If he hadn't met and married Laura O'Leary after a whirlwind eight-month courtship his life would be very different now. He wouldn't change loving Laura, or having his two kids, it was just that he had got weighed down with the responsibilities of being a family man much earlier than he had ever expected. His son Aongus sent him a weekly email from Australia: Perth, Ayers Rock, Sydney. The emails kept coming, telling him of his son's wild adventures as he backpacked around the country.

'Isn't it wonderful to see the young enjoying themselves,' his wife kept telling him as she organized their regular summer trip to Kerry. 'I'm so proud of Aongus, going off adventuring and seeing the world.'

The adventuring was expensive and Dermot was carrying the extra few-thousand-euro debt on his own overdraft, his son promising to pay him back on his return to Dublin.

The class were shuffling. Pretending to concentrate, waiting to see if he was going to load them with homework. He was tempted to disrupt their night's DVD and TV watching with a six-page essay but good sense prevailed.

'Just read over the next chapter in your books, boys,' he said as the class finished.

He was definitely going soft in the head, old age creeping up on him, he thought, as he watched them grin and nudge and holler to each other, pushing and shoving through the wooden door.

249

The classroom emptied quickly as he tidied his notes and books.

'Excuse me, sir. I wondered if I could ask you something.'

Tommy Butler stood in front of him. The Butler boy was one of those who usually frequented the back row of the classroom and contributed little or nothing unless it was disruption, so to find him still there minutes after the last class of the day had finished was unusual.

'Yes!'

'It's about history – like you are always telling us.'

He was intrigued.

'I want to do a kind of project.'

Tommy Butler in his classroom volunteering to take on a project was something he had never reckoned on.

'It's like this – it's about someone very old . . .'

'Oh I see, a figure in history has caught your imagination, like Pearse or Parnell or Michael Collins or Churchill.'

The boy looked totally puzzled, the names not even registering.

'No way!' he said. 'No, I'm talking about someone real, a real person.'

'A hero of yours!'

'She's an old woman.'

Dermot looked suspiciously at the boy. What was he doing? Casing some old lady's house, trying to find out how valuable her antiques and furniture were? The mind boggled when it came to the likes of these thirteen–year–olds!

'What woman are we talking about, Butler?'

'A very old woman, sir.'

'I can't help you unless you tell me about this old lady.'

'It's my nan. She's going to be a hundred years old, sir.'

Dermot nodded, relieved to discover he was referring to a Butler family member.

'Well, it's just like we got to mark it, do something special for her. There's going to be a big party and presents and the like.'

'Your grandmother must be a wonderful woman, celebrating one hundred years on this earth.'

'Yeah, well, that's it. I want to do something real special for her, something that will make her remember those hundred years.'

Dermot was totally baffled. This was a very unexpected side to the young Butler fellow.

'Do you mean make a scrapbook, or a family tree?'

'Nah. She's got them already. My idea's way better than photos – it's a hat.'

'A hat!'

'My nan loves hats. Always did, christenings, parties, weddings, but this one's got to be different because it's a Memory Hat. One that will make her think about all the things that happened in her life, remind her, remind us.'

'What an unusual idea!'

'Yeah. The thing is I got to try and organize it. A hundred years is a long time and though I know a lot of things about my gran and my dad and the family growing up, I was wondering, sir, if you could help me?'

'Help you?'

'With the historical bit, sir, not the hat bit. That's already sorted.'

Dermot McHugh considered. He could pack up his bag, send the boy packing and be home in time for his favourite game show, or he could turn on the class computer and begin to search for relevant dates. Tommy looked nervous, hands in his pockets, chin tilted, slightly defiant eyes narrowed, waiting for rejection.

'Where's your grandmother from?'

'Janey, Dublin, sir, where else!'

Dermot smiled. That should have been obvious.

'Sounds like an interesting project. You could learn a lot from it.'

They looked at each other for a moment.

'A timeline might be a good thing – a starting point. World and local history of the last century.'

Tommy looked fazed.

'And of course what was going on in Dublin then, in your grandmother's backyard so to speak, in the "rare old times" as some people call it.'

Tommy Butler looked pleased, interested as the Google search engine kicked in and filled up the screen.

Chapter Forty-three

His teacher had totally surprised him by sitting down at the desk beside him and demonstrating how to use the search engine on the Internet to research the past.

Mr McHugh helped him find out exactly what he needed to know. It was deadly. The teacher even set up a special file for him to store all the information needed for 'project granny' as he called it. Tommy was incredulous as they studied old newspaper articles and photographs, and even a piece of black and white film of a very different Dublin to anything he had ever seen.

'Magic!' It was exactly what he was looking for.

Tommy began to print out all kinds of things about those years, realizing how much his granny had lived through. Although he was a tough nut he couldn't imagine himself living through a civil war and two world wars and having to make to do when everything was rationed during the Emergency. He watched as image after image downloaded: King George V's visit to Dublin, Padraig Pearse, James Connolly and their men taking over the GPO, the first Dáil meeting, the Treaty, the British forces finally leaving Ireland, the Free State, the Civil War that followed as Irish men fought each other, de Valera and Michael Collins, the two leaders, now on opposite sides. The Emergency war years, the last tram running from Nelson's pillar, RTE's first transmission and Gay Byrne on *The Late, Late Show*, long hair, The Beatles, Thin Lizzy, JFK, the first man walking on the moon, Bob Geldof, Bono and U2. Tommy was filled with admiration, for his granny had borne witness to a century passing.

'Some of this background historical information should be very useful,' murmured his teacher. 'Give you a sense of what previous generations went through. You lot have it easy.'

Tommy would normally have made some smart retort to aggravate McHugh but for once he was actually in agreement with him.

From his dad and his aunts and his ma and even his nan herself, he'd found out that Lillian Butler had been one of a family of twelve born in a tall tenement building in Mountjoy Square. At ten years old, on Easter Sunday she had watched wide-eyed as a group of Irish rebels took over the big General Post Office building, guns blazing across the street as they challenged the might of the British Army. Terrified, Lily had run home with her two big brothers to tell her mammy that 'the Rising' had begun. Six hard and bitter years later Ireland had finally won its independence and 'Dev' was sworn in as their new leader.

After finishing school she had worked in Carroll's Guest House on Parnell Street, doing whatever job Mrs Carroll needed, from making beds to cooking a fry-up. At seventeen opportunity had called and she had started working as a waitress in Bewley's Oriental Café in George's Street, serving on tables for crowds of Dubliners in need of a sticky bun and a warm pot of tea. One day a young man called Tom Butler, enticed by the smell of coffee beans coming from the café, had come in and ordered a scone and a mug of Bewley's famous rich roast coffee from Lily. After a week of coming to the café every day and ordering from her, he eventually got up the courage to ask Lily out.

The following year Thomas Butler and Lillian Foley were wed. Married at only nineteen, she had given birth to nine children, his da and all his uncles and aunties. Moving from a flat to a corporation house in Meath Street, she had stopped work to concentrate on raising her family, supplementing her income by scrubbing and polishing and cleaning the floors, windows and carpets of offices and hospitals and houses all over the city.

'Just give me a bucket and a bit of bleach or tin of polish,' she'd joke, 'and watch me go!'

In her free time she sang in the St Laurence's Church choir and knitted jumpers and socks and scarves and throws for everyone in the family, the click–clacking of her needles going constantly no matter where she was.

When his grandfather, Tom, had died suddenly of pneumonia, Lil Butler had put on her best coat and hat and gone to Mr Victor Bewley to ask for her old job back. She was assigned to the fancy Bewley's Café in Grafton Street, where she worked till she was sixty.

Two of her five sons had gone off to fight in the Second World War, Uncle Bernard and Uncle Kevin. Uncle Bernard had died on a Merchant Navy boat somewhere in the North Sea, blown to smithereens by a German U-boat, while Uncle Kevin had driven jeeps and ambulances and lorries and learned how to strip an engine in thirty minutes before he was caught in a land mine with a lorry full of soldiers.

She had seen Nelson's pillar blown up and cheered for president J. F. Kennedy when he visited the home of his Irish ancestors.

'If I'd been a few years younger I'd have fallen for him myself. He was a gorgeous man!' she declared loudly. 'Then, God help us, he was assassinated in Dallas.'

She'd hidden her tears as over the years her children took the mailboat for England in search of work and opportunity, and she'd welcomed her expanding family of grandchildren with open arms. As the family grew up she was content in her own snug home in Meath Street, surrounded by her neighbours and friends and her little dog Belle and a mad budgie called Joey, who used to sit on her shoulder and eat birdseed from her hand. She'd moved in to live with them when she was ninety, Joey coming too, perched in his cage in the kitchen.

'He's the cleverest budgie in the whole of Dublin,' she'd declared proudly, though Tommy remembered the budgie landing on his head and pecking at him like crazy when he was little. He'd hated that mad budgie. But his nan had been heartbroken when the budgie died and had kept his feathers in a box somewhere. Maybe it was still at home, up in the wardrobe or under the bed. Then there was the old case full of photos. He'd get them out, see if he really looked like Grandfather Tom, as everyone said, and if there were any more clues about his granny.

Yeah, it was all coming together.

Why, he had only just started researching his grandmother, listing everything about her, and already there were loads of things to help make up her Memory Hat.

Chapter Forty-four

Men were far too complicated! Ellie decided. Getting involved with them always ended in disaster as far as she was concerned. All her romances seemed doomed and the consequences of following her heart always caused pain and upset.

Why was she always attracted to the wrong kind of men? Guys who were destined to break her heart like Owen, or let her down like Rory, or simply ignore her like Neil. No! She was better off staying single. She should concentrate on work and make a success of the little hat shop.

She sighed . . .

She'd hoped that Neil would phone her, waited and waited for his call. But since that nightmare of a night when she'd disgraced herself he hadn't even bothered to contact her. Who could blame him? She'd seen him once standing in the street talking to Gary at the print shop. She'd stood inside the window, heart racing, wondering if he would drop in on her afterwards, strangely disappointed when he had turned and headed in the other direction.

Her love life was a great big mess. She could advise other women, help give them confidence, make them feel elegant and stylish, add a bit of fun and frivolity to their lives, and yet her own romantic life was non-existent. No. It was far better she forget about affairs of the heart and concentrate on building up her millinery business instead.

'When the leaves fall I'll go to Paris,' Ellie promised herself, 'and visit my aunt.'

She was stitching a piece of rich red felt when Minouche tiptoed over and jumped into her lap. Warm and soft and black, the little cat's fur gave her comfort. She buried her face in it.

Chapter Forty-five

The jade and cinnamon-coloured silk sidesweep was a perfect fit for Constance O'Kelly. It softened her jawline and emphasized her best feature, her eyes. As Ellie had predicted, it toned perfectly with her jacket and dress. The material was of a high quality and expensive, the colour rich and textured, a jade turquoise with hints of peacock almost shimmering through it. This hue suited Constance's skin, while the cinnamon twirls of covered spirals of wire gave the outfit a kick and made it stand out.

'Oh, it's absolutely gorgeous!' Constance smiled, angling herself to the mirror to study the hat from every side. 'It's exactly what I wanted for the wedding.'

Ellie was relieved that the client was so satisfied with her work.

'Thank you so much,' said the older woman. 'I'll go off and have a cup of tea to celebrate.'

'Have one here with me instead,' suggested Ellie. 'I'm just about to make one anyway.'

'Are you sure it's not too much trouble?'

'The kettle is always on the go in this place. It's one of the essential tools of the millinery trade,' she admitted. 'I have a steamer but I still find the kettle is great for steam and heat to shape and stretch the materials, and I get to enjoy a cup of tea as well.'

'This is lovely,' said Constance admiringly as she added a little milk and sugar to the pretty blue china cups that Ellie had invested in. 'You are very like your mother, but I'm sure everyone tells you that.'

'Yes,' grinned Ellie, who was realizing day by day how much her mother had influenced her and encouraged her in certain traditions and in ways of appreciating the finer things of life. They had never been hugely wealthy but she seemed to remember always using good china and her mother creating a world of finesse and charm around them. Madeleine Matthews had a style of her own, which shaped her designs, the business, what she wore and how she decorated their home. Everything she collected or touched seemed to radiate that sense of who she was right up to the time she died.

'You have created a little oasis here, right in the centre of the city. Such style and tranquillity amongst the hustle and bustle.'

'I'm glad you like it. At first I was very nervous about doing up the shop,' Ellie admitted. 'I suppose getting rid of some of my mother's things was difficult. But the shop needed a fresh look, a new beginning.'

'Well, you have succeeded wonderfully, though it must be difficult taking those first steps and moving forward,' mused Constance. 'I find it such a hard thing to do.'

'Are you all right, Mrs O'Kelly?'

'Yes, I'm fine. It's just with Sally's wedding – it's all so awkward. My husband and I are getting a divorce, you know. It hasn't been pleasant, to say the least, and the pressure of the church and the wedding – I just don't know how I'll cope. He even wants to bring her to the wedding.'

'Her?'

'His new girlfriend!'

'Oh,' responded Ellie, feeling immediate sympathy for the middle-aged woman with her sad eyes. 'Well, with that outfit and the hat you will look divine, I promise.'

'It's just so hard being on your own,' admitted Constance, fiddling with her spoon and cup. 'I know it sounds stupid but this is the first time I've ever lived on my own. There was always Shay and the children. Of course they're grown up now and he's gone to live with someone else.'

'It must be hard for you,' said Ellie gently. 'My mother was also alone.'

'Was she widowed?'

'No. My father left when I was very young, in fact I barely remember him. But she was a wonderful mother and made everything we did together fun and magic!'

'All the lonely people,' sighed Constance.

'My mother was lucky. She had this shop, her business.'

'That's what my children tell me,' confided Constance, 'that I should go and do something, study, get a job. The trouble is, I don't know what.'

'My mother always believed that opportunity appeared when you least expected it,' offered Ellie, clearing away the tea things.

Constance O'Kelly got out her Visa card and paid, delighted with her purchase. The young milliner placed her hat carefully in the pretty striped hatbox.

Ellie Matthews was pleased to see that she had made another customer happy. It always did her heart good to know that she was making the right hat for the right person, and that a simple thing like creating a piece of millinery could bring so much joy to both the maker and the wearer.

Chapter Forty-six

Constance O'Kelly slipped out into the garden in her dressing gown to enjoy the early morning peace. She sat under the lilac tree with her tea and toast, while her children slept in their beds.

Today was the big day. Sally's wedding to Chris Donnelly, the man she loved. She couldn't have asked for a nicer son-in-law and she knew that he would make her daughter very happy. The years had slipped by so fast since Sally was a little girl playing on the swing in the garden to her becoming a bride. Her youngest, Jack, had returned from New Zealand three days ago with a bushy blond beard, tanned and healthy, his backpack of dirty washing flung in the hall.

'You're all bronzed and blond and rugged,' she said, showering him with welcome kisses and feeling the muscles on his arms and shoulders, 'and I think you have got even taller!'

'And look at you, Mum! You're pretty blond and neat yourself. You look like you've dropped a stone or two at least!'

Constance had blushed and laughed.

262

'Eating isn't as much fun when you're cooking for one, and I guess I walk a lot more just to get out of the house.'

'Well, it shows. You look great.'

She didn't look great but she supposed she looked a whole lot better than the last time he'd seen her. She had been a hollow shell then, distraught and overwhelmed by all that was happening to her, often suspecting that this, more than his father's disloyalty, was what had driven him away to travel and work in New Zealand.

It was wonderful to have her youngest son with his laughter and good humour home again. Brendan and Miriam had also stayed the night, little Max charging round the house like a tank. She was glad of Brendan's support and for his foresight in realizing that she would appreciate her eldest son being there now that Shay had gone. She had offered to take everyone out for supper to a restaurant but they'd refused and insisted on a barbecue on the patio with cold beers and sausages and hamburgers and chicken kebabs, baked potatoes and salad instead. Sitting there in her jeans and T-shirt, she had realized that all being together round the old garden table, surrounded by her tubs and pots of summer flowers, was the nicest possible way to celebrate Sally's last night as her single daughter. Max had flitted round the flowers like a honey bee and collapsed exhausted after his meal, Brendan carrying him upstairs to bed in his shorts. The rest of them had sat out under the stars and chatted till long after midnight.

Constance had slept for a few hours only; the combination of emotion and nervousness about seeing Shay and Anne-Marie in the church together had woken her.

'She is not sitting at the top table,' Sally had promised. 'That's for you and Dad and Chris's parents. Anne-Marie is seated at a table nearer the back with Leo and Grace and a few of the cousins.'

'Didn't your father object?' asked Constance, curious.

263

'Of course, but I told him take it or leave it. She is at the wedding, which is what he wanted. Chris and I have the final say about the tables and who sits where – even bloody Dad knows that!'

'Good!' she laughed.

'I told him my two brothers were itching to walk me up the aisle,' joked Sally. 'Anyway Anne-Marie is sitting beside Sheila and that boyfriend of hers.'

Constance knew that Sally and Chris had done their utmost to persuade Shay to leave his girlfriend at home but her husband had dug his heels in, determined to flaunt his new relationship in front of all their family and friends. She just had to accept it and avoid contact with either of them as far as possible, which, given the day, was going to prove pretty difficult.

She pulled in a deep breath and said a silent prayer for the courage and wisdom to get through the day.

The morning passed in a whirlwind of crazy things to do. Immediately after breakfast and showers, herself and Sally and Miriam went to the hairdresser's in Blackrock for a wash and blow dry and a manicure. Constance blinked when she saw herself in the mirror, her hair shining and glossy, clipped shorter. The beige and blond highlights had given her skin and face a new definition and softness. Sally looked stunning, her blond hair coiled loosely back with the clips that would hold her veil and headdress. Miriam, open-mouthed, was staring at her polished pink nails.

'I haven't seen my hands look this good since Max was born,' she admitted wistfully.

Afterwards they collected the bridal bouquets, checking every-thing was right before Alice, their florist, headed up to the church to do the arrangements there.

Arriving home, they discovered that Max had emptied a box of cornflakes all over the kitchen and hall floor, unbeknown to his father and uncle, who were drinking coffee and engrossed in a rerun of *The Rockford Files* on the TV.

'Oh, I'm so sorry,' apologized Miriam, scooping her son into her arms. 'I'll hoover it up!'

'No,' laughed Constance, 'I'll do it. You've got to keep those nails perfect.'

Truth to tell, it felt good to have a small child running round the house again doing mischief and messing things up a bit. Last night with all the bedrooms full she could almost feel the heartbeat of the house return, regular and strong like it used to be when she was busy raising a family. Poor house! Stuck instead with a lone, angry middle-aged woman. She cleaned up and promised herself to show Max how to make chocolate cornflake hedgehogs once he was old enough.

Everyone helped themselves to the mushroom risotto with Parmesan and salad before they all got changed for going to church. Emma and Suzie, the bridesmaids, had joined them. Constance was conscious of the minutes and seconds ticking away as Sally and the girls went upstairs to change.

'Constance, are you all right?' asked Miriam softly.

She nodded dumbly, trying not to show the emotional turmoil she was feeling at Shay's absence and the stress of seeing him with another woman in the church.

'Brendan and Jack and I are all here,' promised her daughter-in-law. 'Everything is going to work out fine.'

'I know. It's just me being foolish.'

She could hear the girls joking and laughing upstairs in the big back bedroom, sounding just like they did when they played with their Barbie dolls, or were dressing up to go to discos. Where had the time gone?

Jack was squeezing himself into his tuxedo, which made him look even more handsome now that he had agreed to trim his beard and long hair for the sake of his sister's wedding photographs.

'I don't want people asking in the future, "Who is that wild man from Borneo at your wedding?"' teased Sally.

'Mum, have you seen my silver cufflinks?'

'Try the top drawer!'

Miriam and Brendan were having a bit of a struggle to get Max into his little waistcoat and trousers and bow tie.

'It's just like Daddy's,' pleaded Miriam as Max tried to turn his tie into a helicopter and flung it across the bedroom.

Constance stepped into Sally's room, where Emma was intent on fastening the tiny buttons and hooks up the back of the bride's fitted corset. Sally's face was all aglow.

'You look absolutely beautiful, pet,' she said, hugging her daughter close. 'The dress, your hair, make-up, everything is perfect.'

'I kept it light and natural-looking,' said Sylvia, the make-up girl, who had come to give them all a hand. 'When I'm finished with the bridesmaids in a few minutes, Constance, I'll be in to do you.'

She was about to demur, but remembered that today needed more than just her usual dash of foundation and some lipstick. Sally and the girls had insisted on the professional touch.

'That would be lovely,' she beamed.

Though nervous, Sally was on an excited high as she twirled round and showed off her dress and train. Marcus Foley had served her well, the design perfectly complementing her figure and long neck and cascading to the floor in a tumble of magnificent Irish lace.

'Sally, you look so beautiful,' Constance said, trying not to cry. 'You are the most beautiful bride ever.'

Emma, a nurse, passed her a tissue from the box on the bedside locker, and gently rubbed her shoulder, even off-duty her caring skills evident. The girls looked wonderful in their co-ordinating deep rose and dusky pink bridesmaid dresses, the colours picked up in the simple beribboned floral sprays in their hair.

'Everything's going to be fine, Mum,' smiled Sally. 'Promise.'

Looking in the long bedroom mirror, Constance could see that Sylvia had worked a transformation, subtly highlighting and shadowing the contours of her face and finishing it off with a glow of bronzer.

'You're sure I'm not too old for it?' she asked anxiously.

Her eyes looked huge and wide courtesy of eyeliner, a blend of eyeshadows, and two coats of a mascara that made her eyelashes fuller and longer than they had ever been.

'Dad's going to be here in the bridal car in a few minutes,' Brendan shouted up to her.

She could feel the panic rise in her, for she had no intention of seeing her ex-husband until she got to the church. She felt good in her outfit and the colour seemed to bring out the honey tan she had developed in the garden. She slipped on her shoes and took a deep breath as she lifted the lid of the hatbox and carefully fitted the most delicious swirls of jade green and cinnamon on to her head. The hat immediately gave her height and the sense of poise and style that only wearing an individual creation could generate. She loved it. Spinning round in her new finery, she suddenly felt confident and composed. Nothing was going to spoil today.

Chapter Forty-seven

Constance held her head high as her son Jack escorted her up the aisle of the Church of the Assumption on Booterstown Avenue, noting the admiring glances from her sister Una and brother Jim and a load of her women friends. The jade green dress with its jacket detail and unfussy bodice felt great, and the two contrasting shapes of her hat gave her a virtual lift, and unaccustomed height. For the first time in a very long while she felt graceful and elegant, a proud and confident mother of the bride!

Sally arrived twelve minutes late, looking radiant on Shay's arm as he led her up the aisle to Chris, the anxious groom, whose face lit up the minute he saw his bride. Sally looked so beautiful, slim and blond, holding a bouquet of cream roses and baby's breath and ivy, her gown trailing behind her, every little detail hand-sewn.

Constance steeled herself not to break down and cry and destroy all Sylvia's good work as Shay, after handing over their daughter, stepped into the bench beside her. She could sense his nervousness and noticed the band of perspiration on his upper lip. They stood and sat and knelt down to pray like two statues, neither looking at or making eye contact with the other, as in front of them their daughter took her wedding vows. Father Luke was wonderful; obviously au fait with the embarrassing family situation, he was totally discreet in his words of wisdom to the happy couple.

'Never go to sleep on your anger,' he advised. 'Stay up all night if you have to and sort it out. And remember, always be kind to one another.'

Constance could feel a tightness in her throat. Stealing a look at her husband, she wondered when had that kindness disappeared from their own marriage?

There were photos outside their parish church, then a forty-minute drive to the Wicklow countryside and the country house where the reception was being held. Guests checked in quickly and the staff welcomed them warmly as they congregated in the sunshine, giving a huge cheer when Sally and Chris arrived in a vintage Rolls-Royce.

Kildevin was the ideal location for the reception, as it provided the intimacy and welcome of an old Irish country house. From the warm comfort of the magnificent drawing room with its huge marble fireplace to the cosy library and the breakfast room set in the quaint glass orangery overlooking the herb garden, the house was a gracious home-from-home to all who visited. Cosy armchairs and snug couches were scattered around the place and outside Lutyens-inspired benches provided a resting spot for walkers. The huge ballroom was well capable of seating their one hundred and seventy guests as they dined watching the evening sun go down over the lake.

Sipping a glass of welcoming champagne in the sunshine on the lawn of Kildevin House, Constance could finally feel herself relax.

'You look wonderful!' Catriona said, paying her a genuine

compliment. 'The jacket and dress is gorgeous and your hat's magnificent. I haven't seen you look this well in years.'

'Thanks,' she laughed, 'I must have looked like the wreck of the *Hesperus*!'

'No, I don't mean that,' chided Catriona, almost reading her mind. 'What I mean is you look different, so much younger, more stylish.'

'Sure it's not mutton dressed as lamb?'

'No,' protested Catriona, hugging her. 'You should have heard what Tadhg said when he saw you coming into the church.'

Constance beamed. She wasn't used to getting compliments and she just had to learn to accept them.

The compliments flew all day and she was almost in danger of levitating from the ground. Perhaps some of it was sympathy, as she knew everyone realized that her husband's lover, Anne-Marie, was floating around the place. She had caught odd glimpses of her in a tight-fitting pink sheath of a dress, tottering around in what looked almost like stiletto heels, her thin thirty-year-old face defiant as Shay introduced her to their family friends. It was all so awfully public and humiliating. Constance, determined to give the pair of them a wide berth, steeled herself to remain composed and enjoy having so many friends and family members around her.

'Hello, girls.' She smiled, walking in the other direction as she spotted a few of Sally's friends down near the abundant rose-beds, which were bursting with a myriad array in every shade of pink.

Emma, the bridesmaid, introduced her to everyone, Constance hoping she wasn't interrupting anything.

'Sally looks amazing!' gushed Chloë Higgins, the wild tomboy schoolgirl who over the subsequent years had become a trainee barrister. 'You must be so happy for her.'

'Yeah, you look stunning too, Mrs O'Kelly,' added Niamh, 'and your hat is a wow!'

Sally's friends were a great bunch of girls.

'And you lot would give the supermodels a run for their money!'

'Yeah, it's great to have a chance to get all dressed up to see your best friend walk down that aisle,' confessed Emma, 'though it'll be years before I do it!'

Constance laughed and left them to their champagne and an approaching group of young men in tuxedos, who were friends of Chris's.

During the wedding meal, Chris's father, Paddy, was an entertaining dinner partner on the top table and regaled her with accounts of his work all over the world on major engineering projects.

'When the children were young, Maggie and I would pack up and take them everywhere with us – Egypt, Nigeria, the Pacific, the Emirates and even South America – but once they hit secondary school we had to put down some roots here. We bought the house in Clontarf and Maggie kept the home fires burning while I worked.'

'Didn't you mind being away from home so much?' Constance probed.

'I suppose it was rough on the family but it was what I was used to. Now they're all grown up and Maggie and I can think of our-selves. I'm retired and we've bought a small place in Cyprus and a little boat. We've always had the ambition to sail.'

Constance cast an envious glance over at the tall grey-haired woman trying to make conversation with Shay. She could tell by the way he was buttering his bread that he wasn't even listening. She suppressed her irritation with him as Paddy Donnelly invited her to visit their Cyprus home any time with Sally and Chris or even on her own.

'We have plenty of space and only use it a few months of the year.'

'That would be lovely,' she said, realizing the idea of a short sojourn on a sunshine island far from Dublin was very appealing. 'I might take you up on that.'

Sally and Chris were so happy and wrapped up in each other that it reminded her of her own wedding day. She glanced over at Shay, wondering did he remember. She could see he was nervous as the coffee was being served, and then the best man called for the father of the bride to say a customary few words.

For the first time since they got married she had absolutely no idea what he was going to say, and she could sense a similar nervousness about her daughter as Shay rose to speak. Anne-Marie stood up at the back momentarily to take a photograph of him. Constance held her breath as he began. His speech was short and polite. He was charming and polished as usual, thanking everyone for coming and complimenting all involved in the wedding's organization before talking about their daughter.

'I remember when Sally was seven,' he went on, 'finding her wearing her communion dress and one of the net curtains tied on to her head. She was madly kissing her teddy bear, Oscar. When I asked her what she was doing she told me she was getting married to the bear. Hopefully the experience will prove useful for my new son-in-law, Chris, who I can assure everyone is not a bear!'

Sally blushed and Constance laughed despite herself, remembering poor old Oscar. At the end of his speech Shay congratulated Sally and their new son-in-law and to her surprise he graciously thanked her for helping to raise such a wonderful daughter. Everyone clapped and Constance took a big gulp of wine as they all drank a toast. She looked up the table and said a silent 'thank you' to Shay, as Paddy stood up slowly and in his warm welcoming speech outlined what a great addition to the Donnelly family Sally was.

'She's a girl after my own heart,' he smiled, 'and if Chris and herself are even half as happy as Maggie and I have been over the years, they will have a wonderful life together!'

Constance gave a silent prayer of thanks that Sally's new in-laws were so nice and that she wouldn't have to struggle with cold, distant people like the O'Kelly family that she had married into.

Almost as soon as the speeches and the cutting of the wedding cake were finished the tables were pushed slightly back and the band appeared. She watched proudly as Chris and Sally took to the floor. As the first tune ended Chris asked her to dance, while Sally managed to grab her father and get him away from his tête-à-tête in the corner with his girlfriend. Chris was the perfect gentleman and managed to steer her almost to the opposite end of the floor. Constance chatted easily to him and then did a few twirls round the floor with Paddy, a big ballroom-dancing fan, before Jack did the decent thing and asked his poor old mother up to dance. Brendan good-naturedly also took a turn round the floor with her.

'Where's Miriam?'

'She's trying to get Max to settle down and sleep. She's in the room with him still. I think he's acting up a bit, probably exhausted after such a long day.'

'The poor wee man. Listen, Brendan, I'll go and see how he's doing,' she offered. 'I don't mind putting my feet up for a few minutes. What's your room number?'

'Number 105. They put us on the ground floor so we'd be close by. It's very near reception and they promised to listen in to the baby alarm.'

'I'll send Miriam out,' she promised.

The door was slightly open and she knocked and went inside, where Max was lying stretched out rosy-cheeked on top of the double bed.

'Granny,' he called the minute he spotted her.

'How are you, pet?' she asked, sitting down beside him.

'We've played games, been to the bathroom umpteen times, drunk gallons of juice and read at least five stories,' smiled Miriam, 'and, as you can see, we are still bright as a button even though we are exhausted. We won't give in!'

Constance suppressed a laugh, for Brendan had been the exact same as a child.

'Max, would you like Granny to sit here for a while and play and read you some stories?'

He nodded slowly.

'Then we can let poor Mummy go and see Daddy while we have a good time!'

'Don't go, Mummy,' he protested.

'Poor Daddy's down there all on his own,' Constance added, 'and I need to put my poor sore feet up after all that dancing, so what about I stay with you?'

Yawning, the three-year-old agreed as Miriam slipped out of the bedroom.

'Now, Max, it's just you and me, so what are we going to do?'

At the bottom of the bed his plastic collection of dinosaurs lay abandoned. Constance sifted through them, trying to find his favourite. They were all shapes and sizes, from Tyrannosaurus Rex to Brontosaurus and Pterodactyl.

'What about a dinosaur story?' She racked her brain trying to think of one that would work, opting for a new version of Goldilocks and the Three Bears, which involved dinosaurs and a boy called Max. Soon the dinosaurs were up and down the bed, wondering who had eaten their porridge and sat in their big big chairs and lain down in their enormous squashy beds. Max held the Brontosaurus to his chest as it laid down its long neck to sleep in its bed. His eyes gently closed as he relaxed against her and slept.

The night was warm and once his breathing was regular and deep she walked out of the open patio doors to the terrace, listening to the sounds of the distant music and the croak of frogs from the lake. There was someone outside; she could hear them talking on the phone. Perhaps they were in the next-door room or were simply standing a few feet away. It was impossible for her not to overhear the conversation.

'She's a hell of a lot younger than he let on and you should see the outfit. She must have spent a fortune. Designer all the way though she's not the one paying.'

Constance's heart sank. She should have shut the door and stayed inside beside her sleeping grandson but, fascinated by the speaker, she was riveted to the spot.

'They put me down the back of the room like I was a naughty schoolgirl, but you know me, I don't give a toss! Shay wanted me here and that's all that matters. I'm the new lady in his life and his kids and brothers and sisters and aunts and friends better get used to it.'

Constance couldn't believe it. Anne-Marie was on the phone somewhere out there in the darkness, talking about the wedding. She couldn't help herself: holding her breath, she listened.

'What that snobby wife of his thinks doesn't matter any more! Shay wants her out of that house and his life as soon as possible.'

Constance could feel herself shaking. Though sorely tempted to respond, she stayed silent as the voice moved away, then closed the glass door to the darkness. She seriously considered climbing into bed beside Max and hiding away for the rest of the night, but anger got the better of her and, fixing her make-up in the bathroom mirror, she decided to rejoin the wedding party. No woman like Anne-Marie was going to stop her enjoying her daughter's wedding.

Her legs felt almost like jelly as she hurried down the corridor. Shay had such a nerve to do this to her, to embarrass her in such a way. The dancing was in full swing and she waved to her daughter-in-law on the dance floor, signalling that Max was asleep.

'We'll check him every twenty minutes,' said Brendan, busy smooching with Miriam.

Helen Kilmartin spotted her, and guided her outside towards a couch in the bay window.

'Are you OK?'

'I could do with a drink.'

A few minutes later a waiter returned with their order of two gin and tonics as Constance confessed to her eavesdropping.

'I don't believe that little b—' responded Helen, adding some more tonic to her glass. 'The audacity of her!'

'It's been so hard putting on a brave face all day, pretending that I don't care!' Constance admitted. 'But hearing her talk about the house, and my life, I just can't believe it.'

'Well, you did a great job of hiding your feelings. Everyone's saying that Shay must have been cracked to leave you for such a bit of a thing.'

'Did you see her?'

'Of course.'

'And what did you think of her?'

'She's pretty, though a bit of a tough nut, and she obviously makes Shay feel young again, ready to take on the world, turn the clock back. I see he put a bit of colour in his hair.'

'Did you notice? It's so pathetic.'

'Anne-Marie boosts his ego, gets him to join the gym, do things differently, go to new places, start over.'

'He's Max's grandfather, for God's sake!'

Helen burst out laughing. 'I don't think that's ever stopped anyone from making an eejit of themselves.'

'Thank God I have Sally and the boys and little Max,' sighed Constance, leaning her head back against the comfort of the plush burgundy headrest. 'And good friends like you. I don't know what I'd do without you all.'

'Listen, Constance, promise me you'll try not to think about them for the rest of the night,' urged Helen.

'I promise,' she said sincerely.

'Come on. The band's playing inside, let's dance!'

Constance smoothed her hair and took a deep breath as she joined the rest of the wedding party.

Chapter Forty-eight

Mo Brady loved a bit of a fight, not a physical punch-up but a good verbal argument to get the council members going. The cut and thrust of political life stirred her in a most unexpected way. When she was a child she'd loved the story of Joan of Arc, the young woman who had fought and died for the people of France. Banners flying, guns blazing, that was the way Mo always liked to do business. She wasn't one for whispering and scurrying around corridors doing deals and reaching secret agreements behind people's backs. No, she was upfront. She said what she meant and was often accused of wearing her heart on her sleeve. Tonight was going to be one of those nights, she could feel it in her bones.

The City Council Chamber was packed and it looked like it was going to be a long session. On the agenda were new traffic plans for the city, the upgrading of the public buildings on Parnell Street and Bachelor's Walk and the redevelopment of South Anne Street.

She listened as they went through the first items, voting for the preservation of the four-storey Georgian houses on Parnell Street.

Two or three of the members were vociferous in their belief that the buildings were not worth saving and should be bulldozed.

'Keep the façades and knock the rest,' suggested Councillor Billy O'Shea. 'Brand new offices or brand new apartments – that's what the people want.'

'I totally disagree with you, Councillor.'

Mo's heart sank. Kathleen Taylor O'Malley had the floor, which meant they could be here for the night.

'Architectural heritage must be preserved at all costs,' she insisted, as she began to read from a long list of the period details of the properties. Coving, cornices, plasterwork, door frames, fan hall-lights, beams, ironwork balustrades, fireplaces. The list went on. Three of the men got up and left. Mo could guess they were heading for Dwyer's pub round the corner. Mo was half tempted to join them as Kathleen got into her stride.

'The tenement days in Dublin are long gone, Kathleen,' interrupted Billy, 'and I'll not ask any young couple to live or work in archaic surroundings. By God, I won't!'

A huge row erupted in the council chamber as neither of them would budge from their stance.

The time ticked by till they came to the order of business that interested Mo most, the plans for South Anne Street. She sat forward on her leather chair, blinking as she looked around.

Mo had studied the plans carefully, got the environmental impact reports and examined the developers' plans with a fine-tooth comb. As far as she could see, they were buying up every available property on the small street and hoped to acquire even more. The galleria shopping mall, with its escalators to the five floors and underground parking, which hoped to attract a major fashion store to its modern commercial development, was well advanced. However, Casey Coleman now seemed to want to develop another large retail unit on the other side of the street. She thought of the toy shop, the cheese shop, the beautiful hat shop, their painted shopfronts and style all adding to the charm of the street.

All the information was back and she knew the city manager had enjoyed a rather heated meeting with the head of Casey Coleman Holdings and his legal representatives as he sought to discover the true extent of their property holdings on South Anne Street and their plans for these properties. She looked round, waiting to see which of her colleagues would start the ball rolling. There must be objections. Dolores Coffey was half asleep; it was long past the seventy-five-year-old councillor's bedtime. Finbarr Flood from the Green Party was not lifting his skinny neck above the parapet. Mo straightened herself in her seat, scanning the carefully prepared papers in front of her as she stood up to speak.

'I have a mandate from the small traders and business holders in this street,' began the Lady Mayor, waving the sheets with the thousands of signatures that had been collected on Save Our Street Saturday. 'They call themselves SOS – Save Our Street – and having talked to them and met with them and learned of their problems and the pressures they are under I have to say that this council must listen to them. They are the voice of the people, the citizens of Dublin. A street like this will disappear unless we here in the council are prepared to safeguard its survival.'

She adjusted her glasses, realizing that she had their full attention and so far without objections.

'As councillors we are not against the redevelopment of Dublin and it becoming a modern European city, but we must ensure we keep our own separate shopping identity and support these smaller indigenous businesses. These are the ones that give colour and life and a sense of place to this city of ours. We must protect and upgrade them while there is still time, before they disappear for good.'

Richard Doyle was nodding and she knew she had his support.

'We must try to retain our small individual retailers and ancillary businesses. These are what make up the heart of Dublin, the city we all love so much!' She stopped for a minute to get her breath, have a look around.

Gerry Simmonds and a few others were taking detailed notes.

'Millions of visitors came to our city last year to enjoy this ancient Viking town that has become a modern city but with a heart. I walk these streets almost every day and this little street is in my neighbourhood. These businesses are the lifeblood of the city and we cannot afford to kill them off, close them down and replace them.

'The developers have got a massive permit already and I would be most reluctant to see even one more centimetre of planning granted to them in this vicinity. This should be made clear to them. Any shops they have taken over should be expected to reopen in keeping with their original type of street frontage. Perhaps in time we should consider a grant to small traders to encourage them to upgrade and maintain shopfronts and signage, etc.'

'My Lady Mayor, I must remind you of the late hour,' interjected Des King, turning in appeal to his party members seated around him.

'I agree it is late, late in the day for us to preserve our city streets, but I call for an immediate vote on this proposal,' Mo said with a sweep of her hands. 'It's the least we can do to Save Our Streets.'

There was a round of applause with a few objections. Gerry Simmonds stood up to say what high-quality developers Casey Coleman Holdings were and how their proposal would enhance the city.

'That is accepted,' she interrupted, 'but it's their ability to retain small local businesses that is our concern today.'

Twenty minutes later it went to a vote. Mo was nervous as she looked round at the faces of her party rivals. She could feel her stomach churn as she tried to read their minds, hoping that her fellow councillors would support her.

Over the past few years in politics she had learned that you can't win every battle, can't carry every issue, but this was one she firmly believed in.

She held her breath, whooping with excitement when the motion was passed with a large majority. The council also decided to set up a separate group to determine the cost of introducing a grant and to study best practice in maintaining small shops and businesses. Victory was theirs. The little man had won!

'Good on you, Mo!' shouted the other councillors afterwards as the Lady Mayor, exhausted from talking to two or three of the journalists present, made her way to the mayoral car. She couldn't wait to get back home and have a cup of tea with Joe and the kids and tell them all about it.

Chapter Forty-nine

Ellie was rapt in concentration, attaching a fine piece of netting on to an unusual hat made of two circles when she heard the shop bell ring. The circles hat was for Geraldine Callaghan, whose husband was one of the country's well-known property investors. It was an exquisite concoction and had taken days to make as she had hand-dyed the crill fabric, the netting and the bands to get the exact shades of aquamarine and turquoise she wanted. The materials were difficult to work with but had been turned into two whorls of colour that would sit on Geraldine's auburn hair and show off her magnificent turquoise satin suit with the faint circular pattern along the skirt's hem and on the lining edge of the jacket. She had purchased it in Milan.

'Brian will love it,' she had crowed, the minute she tried on the hat. 'Oh thank you, it's so perfect.'

'Just let me finish it off, Geraldine, and I will have it ready for you this afternoon,' she'd promised, as the wealthy young woman dashed off to meet a friend for lunch.

Ellie glanced in the mirror. It was the boy again.

'Hold on, I'll be with you in a minute!' she called out as she put Geraldine's hat down carefully and went to greet her youngest customer.

'Hello,' he said, lifting a plastic bag up on to the wooden counter. 'I did what you told me and went back researching all about my grandmother and the times she lived in. Found some things that might be useful.'

'Well, that's a great help, Tommy.'

'My teacher helped me do a timeline and I found old photos and things.'

Ellie watched as he spilled out some of the bag's contents, fazed as to what she was supposed to do with it all.

'Your grandmother seems to be a very interesting woman,' she said as she fingered the items. 'What's in this?'

She lifted the lid of a faded box, which might previously have held talcum powder or sweets. Tiny blue and green-tinted feathers nestled on tissue paper.

'These are feathers from her budgie, Joey. She really loved him,' declared Tommy proudly. 'They were hidden up in the old wardrobe but I found them.'

'Interesting,' she murmured, wondering if the child really wanted her to put them on his grandmother's hat.

'And this was her cap and apron from when she worked in Bewley's Café.'

The lace was faded and slightly stained but she was sure that with careful washing and a little gentle bleaching it could be restored. There were also some beads, and a printed scarf.

'You've found a lot, Tommy,' she praised him.

'I want the hat to be right, to look right,' he insisted.

'I have to finish something for a customer this afternoon, so can you leave this lot with me? It will be a great help to look at the photos, see what kind of a person your granny is.'

'Sure, and these pages are ones I printed out about her life and the family and all.'

'From 1906,' she noticed, impressed. 'Listen, I am going to put all these items away safely in this hatbox, with a base I've already made. Will you call back on Saturday and I'll have a design or two ready for you?'

'Defo,' he promised, going out of the door with a big grin on his face.

Ellie couldn't help herself grinning either. She'd heard that the City Council had refused Casey Coleman's request for further developments on the street. From what she understood, they were finally recognizing the value of small shops and there was even talk of introducing a grant to encourage small businesses to stay in the city centre and upgrade their premises. She was so glad that she hadn't let smart solicitors like Neil Harrington or property developers like Casey Coleman Holdings buy her out and close her down or drive her out of the thriving business she was developing.

Madeleine Matthews would be proud to see the small hat shop she had opened so many years ago continuing to trade. With such an eclectic mix of customers, Ellie never knew what each day would bring. She loved it. This was her business. Her shop with her own designs! It was up to her to grow it, make of it what she wanted.

She was enthralled by the centenarian Lillian Butler, who, judging by the photos of her as a young woman, had been blessed with a heart-shaped face and twinkling brown eyes, peeping out from under a knitted cloche hat or big wide sunhat, either gazing up at her beau, Thomas, or shyly holding his hand. In one photo she stood surrounded by her nine children on the steps of a shabby staircase, in a black hat with a huge feather on it. Could one piece of millinery possibly give any sense of a life so full and well lived? But it was what the boy wanted, and she intended doing her darned best to please him and the old lady.

A silk lily was an obvious choice not just because of her name but to commemorate the Easter of 1916 when she had run down Sackville Street with her brothers and sisters and witnessed the start of the Rising. Perhaps the lace, a small piece from the hem of her apron, stiffened and starched, would make a ribbon or a flower. What about beans – coffee beans, polished and mounted like stamens or beads? The feathers, something to symbolize her nine children, the war years . . . It was a puzzle what she could do to tell of a rich life on the tiny canvas of a millinery piece. The boy had too much esteem for her, expected too much, yet she was determined not to let him down.

Chapter Fifty

Neil Harrington had walked up the street at least twice and had partaken of a creamy latte in the coffee shop before he finally found himself standing outside the gaily painted hat shop. Flowers tumbled from the pots on either side of the door, and the striped awning had been slightly opened, which added to the continental atmosphere that Ellie had managed to create.

The window was filled with five hatstands, which displayed a variety of millinery confections. Even to his untutored eye they looked delightful, and three simple clumps of violets growing in silver pots sat tastefully between them. Without thinking he found himself pushing at the door, startled by the tinkle of the shop bell only inches above his head.

He stood for a second waiting before she appeared.

'Oh,' said Ellie, surprised to see him. 'It's you.'

For an instant he was discomforted, put off his stride.

'Yes. I was passing and I said I'd call in.'

Her dark eyes flashed at him quizzically under that thick

glossy fringe. She was obviously wondering what he was there for.

'I actually came in to get a hat.'

Her lips began to lift up into a smile.

'Well, it's for my mother. She loves these kinds of things. I thought it would be nice for her to have one of yours, upcoming designer and all that.'

He wondered for a moment where those words had come from, and why he had blurted them out, but now it was said it didn't seem a bad idea really. Rosemary Harrington led a very busy social life, what with being on the fund-raising committee for a hospital and organizing charity balls and events for a number of societies. It had almost become a full-time occupation since his father had died and she always seemed to need outfits. Another hat wouldn't go amiss, and besides, she had out of the blue mentioned the possibility of getting a hat from the young hatmaker on South Anne Street. He would surprise her with one.

'Yes. She most definitely needs one.'

Ellie stood across from him, near enough for him to pick up on the light floral scent that clung to her. She suddenly became businesslike.

'Well, when does your mother need this hat?'

'Soon.'

'How soon? Is it a rush job?'

'No! No,' he retreated. 'It's not urgent, but I thought that with the good weather and garden parties and the races, and there's a christening coming up . . .'

'I see. Did you have anything in particular in mind?'

He was totally flummoxed. He racked his brains trying to remember the kind of things his mother wore, but for the life of him he couldn't. He even did a mental playback of family albums, searching frantically for an image of his mother with some kind of item on her head.

'She's mad about hats. The house is full of them.'

'Maybe she has enough then,' she suggested gently.

'No. Most definitely not! She gets tired of them. Always wants something new and fresh.'

Ellie's eyes widened.

'Neil, have you any idea what your mother would like? It would be a help.'

'I'll leave it all up to you. Your good hands and all that.' He suddenly felt pleased with himself.

'Have you looked at the ones in the window?'

She walked past him. He could smell her shampoo as she reached for the furthest hatstand and presented him with a concoction of pink and purple. Most definitely not his mother's style!

'Or there's this coloured band that can be very effective. It sits across the head and these tiny pieces of cream and white almost look like they are floating. It's a wonderful style.'

He studied the band as she passed it to him, noticing how small her fingers were, her nails unpolished and buffed.

The two other styles were definitely more suited to a wedding.

'Listen, I'll just slip in the back. My mother had a collection of basic designs to show customers. Starting points, she used to call them. It's good to show people if they are not sure what they want, as choosing a shape is important. The book is somewhere there. Give me a minute and I'll find it. I'll get my pad so we can rough out something for your mother. I'll be back in a jiffy.'

He sat on the small chair waiting for her, for once unsure what to say or do as the black cat in the window licked her paws and stared at him.

Ellie returned, books in hand, and pulled up a stool beside him.

'Neil, will you have a look through this.'

He began to turn the pages.

'How are you?' he asked.

Her eyes widened.

'If you mean have I had any more drunken nights where I have disgraced myself, the answer is no.'

'I didn't mean to be judgemental,' he apologized. 'I just wanted to know if you are all right.'

She blinked and turned her head and for some reason he suspected he'd upset her further.

'Ellie?'

'Never better actually,' she said, dazzling him with a smile. 'The business is doing well. People are beginning to know about the shop and I love what I do. Things are going great, and fingers crossed I'm off to France in another few weeks.'

'France?'

'Paris.'

He swallowed hard, trying to concentrate on the ridiculous drawings on the page. Obviously off to Paris with that boyfriend he'd seen her with. Maybe if he wasn't such a stuffy old fool and had sent her yellow roses and romanced her, things would be different. Too late as per usual.

He stood listening to her talk for another few minutes, just to hear her voice and watch the way she scrunched her nose.

'Neil, are you listening?' interrupted Ellie. 'I think it's a really nice idea about getting your mother a hat but I do think it would be better if she came in to talk to me herself and order something she really wants. I'm not even sure of her hat size.'

'But you've met her,' he insisted. 'Besides, I want to surprise her.'

'She's very stylish, in a classic kind of way,' mused Ellie aloud. 'Probably something very simple and elegant, maybe a black and white or black and cream or beige, a slight down-brim that's not too wide.'

'Perfect,' he said, noticing the way she frowned when she was concentrating.

*

Fifteen minutes later, after her promise to phone him when the hat was ready, he found himself back out on the street.

He'd missed twelve messages on his mobile and was late for a client meeting. He hoped that his secretary, Jean, was looking after Jerome Casey in his absence. He'd spent the past forty minutes talking about his mother and women's hats just so he could see Ellie, and he hadn't even had the courage to ask her out to dinner.

Chapter Fifty-one

Making the Memory Hat, as Tommy called it, was the most difficult commission she had ever undertaken. Ellie groaned with regret at her own stupidity for saying yes and encouraging Tommy Butler to believe in her. She had racked and reracked her brain for inspiration and was determined not to produce something God-awful and cluttered for this wonderful old lady.

From the photos it was clear Lillian Butler had always loved hats, spent her meagre money on one when the occasion demanded, worn them with a rare confidence, for hats had been part of her life. She had kept in style and adapted to the latest fashion and trends, even wearing a jaunty beret. Already Ellie had covered half a pad in designs but she was not happy with any of them.

'Don't tell me you are still at it!' joked Fergus, who had called in to collect her.

She nodded dumbly, for she was meant to have been ready at least half an hour ago to go to the cinema with him.

'Don't tell me we are not going to *Les Parapluies de Cherbourg*!'

'You go, Fergus. Honestly, I have to try and work on this.'

'I'm not going to the Film Centre without you. What would I be doing at a foreign film if you weren't with me?'

'I'm sorry.'

'No harm done, we'll do it another time,' he said, moving over towards the kettle. 'Do you want a coffee?'

'Oh, that would be sweet.'

She listened as Fergus rattled on about how wonderful and interesting Liam Flynn was compared to other guys he'd gone out with.

'You do like him, El?'

'Of course,' she beamed reassuringly. Friends always needed to be told that the people they fancied were the brightest, the most beautiful and the best in the world.

'He's a bit wound up.'

'Fergus, he's a high-powered trader.'

'I know,' he said proudly, rooting around for something to eat. 'Any biccies?'

'There should be some chocolate chip and a packet of digestives in the tin.'

Later, nursing a hot milky coffee, she confessed to Fergus about the position she found herself in.

'That Lily sounds a real Dublin character. Lived here all her life, raised a family, moved from place to place, street to street, all over the city. She's part of the place like the Liffey, the Castle, Christ Church. A true Dub.'

'I know, she's had an amazing life. It's just that I don't know what to do to capture her spirit. It's like I have hit a blank wall and can't think of anything.'

'Well, a lily or lilies sound good, nice and simple. The obvious.'

'Yes, but that's not what Tommy wants. He wants something more than a classic expensive-looking hat. He wants magic and blow-your-mind kind of stuff. I can't disappoint the kid.'

'A conundrum.'

'To put it mildly.' She sighed. 'Tommy would hate a plain ivory lily, he'd expect colour and bells and whistles, though I suppose cream or ivory would give me a good canvas to work on, a perfect background.'

Suddenly Ellie jumped up, hugging a very surprised Fergus, who almost spilt his mug of coffee all over his trousers.

'What's that for?'

'That's for lighting the torch, for giving me the idea. Fergus, you are just wonderful! Now I know why I love you so much.'

'Hey, well, that's great.' He laughed smugly. 'I'm glad I am good for something!'

'Drink up your coffee. If we race we might still make it to the Film Centre.'

She had stretched the material as far as she could, then using a light brush had retraced the pattern she had drawn out in fine pale browns and white. Once the material had dried she would shape the hat on the block and leave it for a few days before she began to assemble the trimmings that would capture centenarian Lily Butler's life and the spirit of the one-hundred-year-old Dublin woman. Ellie was strangely excited about the old lady's hat, as it was like assembling a work of art, a collage of the different experiences that make a life. What would she put on a hat to symbolize her own life? she wondered. She fingered the round coffee beans. They were like polished beads, their colour rich and dark. The bird's feathers were exotic, adding a splash of colour, the blue-green remnant of silk ribbon like a river in flow. This hat was different from anything else she had ever designed or created and she would not charge for the hours of work, for she knew Tommy's funds were limited. The boy was a strange kid, different from what she had first expected, his rough tough exterior hiding the sensitive young man he really was. She smiled to herself, thinking of his face as he gave his grandmother his gift, knowing that her time was being well spent.

Chapter Fifty-two

The shop was busy and Neil Harrington was tempted to turn round and come back at a time when he would have her to himself. Get the chance to talk to her privately.

She was fully occupied, attending to some young fellow who was red-faced with embarrassment, his brown hair standing on end as he kept telling her how much he loved some hat.

'It's lovely, flipping great. My nan will love it. Just wait till she sees it.'

Ellie's eyes were shining as the thirteen-year-old proceeded to tumble a load of dirty-looking notes and coins on to the counter, some rolling along the wooden floor as the kid scrambled after them.

'Hello,' Neil said, trying to get her attention, hoping to get her to look at him the way she did at that scruffy kid.

'Oh Neil, you've come for the hat. I have it ready for you.'

He stood patiently, wishing that she would get rid of the young intruder.

'It's in the box!'

Two hatboxes lay on the floor near his feet. Curious, he lifted the lid off one.

It was a wide hat and covered in the most extraordinary things. A hotchpotch of items circled the wide brim – fruit, feathers, flowers, lace, even a medal – and God knows what other items were scattered upon it. He'd never seen anything like it. Embarrassed, he replaced the lid. He knew for sure that his elegant mother wouldn't be seen dead in such a creation, no matter who the designer was. In trepidation he lifted the lid of the other box, immediately recognizing the sophisticated style of the plain black hat with the simple line of creamy white colour that circled its brim, and he knew his mother would approve.

'Do you like it?' she asked anxiously.

'It's perfect,' he admitted, 'and I know my mother will adore it.'

'I thought it might suit Rosemary,' she laughed, pleased with his reaction.

The pesky kid was still there and making no move to shift, and his heart dropped when two anorexic blondes in skin-tight leather pushed past him and began to try headpieces on their hair, talking aloud.

'I'd better pay you for this,' he said, taking out his credit card, and not even flinching when she said how much the hat was going to cost. He remembered why he hated shopping and wondered what kind of price she was going to charge the kid.

'Have you got this in pearl?' interrupted one of the blondes, pushing her skinny hips between them and trying to get attention.

'Sorry, I'll be with you in a minute,' replied Ellie as she dealt with his payment.

He considered asking her for coffee, but could see she was too busy. The kid glowered at him as if he was luring away his mate. No, it would be better if he came back another day. Got her on her own.

'Thanks,' he said, lifting the hatbox lightly by its string.

'I do hope Rosemary is pleased,' she worried. 'If not tell her to come in and see me.'

'I guarantee that she will love it,' he reassured her. 'It will be a lovely surprise for her when she gets back from Parknasilla at the weekend.'

Chapter Fifty-three

Tommy Butler had wrapped up the hatbox in a big black plastic bag and he held the present as if his life depended on it. He'd had no intention of trawling the streets with a big sissy hatbox or a woman's shopping bag. No, he had come prepared with a bin bag and now, glowering at the other passengers on the 11 bus, he dared them to guess what he was carrying. He could imagine what the neighbour-hood lads would say if they knew. He'd b....... burst anyone who laid one f...... finger on him or his grandmother's hat on his way home!

They had the TV on and his mam was cooking chicken curry when he let himself in quietly and sneaked upstairs to his bedroom. The smell of onions, garlic and spices was wafting through the house. Tommy was starving.

First things first: where could he hide the present without squash-ing it and without his mam or Ray finding it? The bottom of the wardrobe was the only safe place as his mam often hoovered under the bed or dusted the top of the wardrobe. He turfed out all his foot-ball boots and his sports bag and flung them under his bed temporarily so he could place the plastic bag with the box carefully in his wardrobe. He put a football jersey and a pair of shorts on top to disguise it. A mixture of relief and pride punched him in the gut as he sat on the bed.

The hat had cost him every last cent of his pocket money and the remainder of his confirmation money but he didn't begrudge it for a minute. He would forgo chocolate, the cinema and games rentals for the next few weeks in return for purchasing such a gift. Even with all the money he had spent, he guessed that the shop lady had under-charged him for the beautiful hat she had produced. Ellie Matthews, the hatmaker, had a kind face and a good heart and he knew she was being sincere when she wished his grandmother all the best on her hundredth birthday.

Chapter Fifty-four

Arriving home from a visit to the dentist, Constance O'Kelly was shocked to discover Shay standing in the bathroom of their Blackrock home, his broad frame leaning against the sink as he rooted through the overhead medicine cupboard.

'What are you doing here?'

'I was wondering if there was any of that painkiller the doctor gave me the last time I pulled a muscle in my back. It should be here somewhere.'

She studied his face. He looked pale under his usual golf club tan. A little puffed around the eyes, always a sign he was eating and drinking too much.

'In trouble again?'

'No,' he protested. 'Just a bit of a twinge but I want to have it in case I need it. Anyway I had to collect my dress suit.'

'It's hanging in the back wardrobe, still in the wrap from the cleaners.'

Constance had given some consideration to taking the garden

shears to every item of clothing that Shay possessed, but sanity had prevailed and she had simply moved them to the small, musty wardrobe in Jack's room. There they shared space with their son's rancid trainers and football boots and unwashed jeans, alcohol-soaked shirts and a hotchpotch of vile-smelling boys' socks.

'I'll get it in a minute but first there's something I wanted to talk to you about.'

Constance stood on her own maple floor suddenly feeling nervous. What was this about?

'Can we sit down and talk?'

She was about to make some negative remark when she saw that her husband was serious.

'All right, Shay. Let me put the kettle on and make us a cup of tea.'

As she fussed around in the kitchen with the teabags and mugs and milk she wondered what he wanted. He looked tired.

'Things cannot stay the way they are, Constance. We both know it.'

She said nothing. Her lips and mouth were still slightly numb.

'I know how hard it has been for you,' he admitted, 'how tough this year has been.'

She held the warm mug in her hands, trying to remain composed.

'But you living here on your own in this house is madness. I'm still making the final payments on the mortgage, along with the insurance and our VHI, and now I have the rent on the apartment in Donnybrook too.'

'That was your decision, Shay.'

'I know. I'm not arguing that. But the bills have doubled. Electricity, heating, house insurance! The money is due for the alarm on this place next week and you'd better organize to pay it.'

'With what?' Her laugh was suddenly uncontrollable. 'I have no income.'

He put his head in his hands. She noticed that he was wearing new denim jeans and what looked like trainers.

'That's your problem. You live here and you must decide if safety and security are top of your priorities.'

'I think having an alarm on the house is a bit of a priority, Shay. If you remember, you've spent the past fifteen years going on about it ever since your golf clubs and my handbag were stolen from the hall.'

'I'm just informing you,' he said, tossing her the bill, 'that the payment is due.'

'Well, it will just have to be cut off then,' she snapped, 'since I don't have the money to pay it.'

'Constance, there is no point fighting about it. We are where we are. Although I pay the mortgage on the house, it belongs to both of us jointly. I'm not arguing about it. It's just that it no longer suits our needs. The kids are grown up. We had always planned as we got older to sell it. You know we had.'

'I love this house,' she insisted, looking out towards the garden.

'I know you do,' he said. 'It's a great house. But now times have changed. You need the money. I need the money. Can't we somehow resolve this without being at each other's throats and resorting to bloody barristers?'

She wanted to be angry with him but instead felt sapped, drained. She'd had enough of being angry and fighting. Was this man with his scared face, paunchy stomach and Nike runners really worth it?

'I'll think about it,' she offered, standing up and putting the mugs in the dishwasher.

'And I'll pay the alarm people,' he said.

She stood in the kitchen, listening to the sound of Shay moving around upstairs just like old times. His heavy feet thumped on the overhead floorboards, doors banging as he got his suit. Then suddenly he was gone, the hall door slamming, the silver BMW reversing out of the driveway. She wondered where he was going in the dress suit, and immediately regretted her own stupid curiosity. It didn't matter where he went as she wouldn't be with him and that was something she was going to have to accept.

Shay and herself were no longer a couple. No longer partners. Their worlds were totally separate now and she just had to get used to it.

'It's good that you could sit down and talk,' said Helen, serious, when Constance phoned her later that night. She listened for an hour as her friend replayed Shay's visit, her financial problems and the true depths of her despair. 'Things can't go on the way they are.'

'I know,' Constance sniffed, jaw aching after a root filling and heart-broken after thirty years of marriage.

'You have got to get your life back on track without Shay,' she admonished.

Constance knew her best friend was right. Helen had been widowed over ten years ago. Paul's death from kidney failure, though not unexpected, had been tragic. Helen had been left to raise their two sons on her own. She had never complained or raged but had earned the respect of everyone around her by simply getting on with it. Helen was right. Deep inside, Constance knew she was no different from a million other women who found themselves, for one reason or another, suddenly alone. Her world had altered and now so must she. Looking to the past was doing nothing but causing her hurt and pain. Somehow she had to look to the future.

The summer was almost gone, apples on the tree in the garden, the Michaelmas daisies brown and withered, the nights chilly as Constance folded away her summer clothes and covered the barbecue. There was a massive amount of work to be done in the garden and she wasn't sure she had the energy or the enthusiasm for it. Jack had taken off weeks ago and wouldn't commit to being home for Christmas.

'It's only a day or two, Mum,' he'd protested. 'Flying home from Thailand for turkey and plum pudding is hardly worth it.'

She had buried her disappointment, trying to understand his wanderlust and lack of need for home and family.

The blissfully happy newly-weds, Chris and Sally, called at the weekends, and she made a point of going into town once a week to meet Sally for something to eat at lunchtime or after work. It was wonderful to see Sally so contented.

There had been more good news: Miriam had announced that she was expecting again. The arrival of another grandchild, a little brother or sister for Max, would be a blessing.

'What are you going to do for the winter?' quizzed Helen. 'You are not going to sit here on the couch hibernating, watching *EastEnders* and *Coronation Street* every night!'

Constance hadn't the heart to admit that that was exactly what she had been planning.

'Lots of people sign up for evening classes. It'd be good to do a course on something that interests you, take up something, do something new,' Helen continued, waving a booklet listing the evening courses being run all over the city. 'The last thing you want to do is stagnate now that Shay's gone.'

Constance had studied the booklet later that night, surprised by the range of courses on offer. When the children were younger there had always been reasons not to do things, what with homework and exams and study. In addition, Shay had been the type who liked his meal ready when he got home and for Constance to be available if he had to entertain a client or attend a function. Those days were past and Helen was right: she was a free agent and didn't have to suit anyone any more except herself.

In trepidation she had phoned the information desk in Trinity College to enquire about the art history course they were running. It sounded very interesting and the young man on the phone was so enthusiastic about it that before she had time to think she had signed up and paid for it.

'I must be gone mad,' she chided herself. 'Why, I won't know a soul.'

Helen had simply smiled when she told her.

'Well, it's a start.'

Chapter Fifty-five

'Are you ready, Tommy?' shouted his ma from downstairs. 'You can't keep us waiting. We can't be late today of all days.'

Tommy glanced at himself in the bedroom mirror. He had gelled his hair and was wearing the new shirt his ma had bought him, pale blue with a T-shirt under, and his jeans.

Yeah, he didn't half look good.

'Your father is going crazy, Tommy. He's sitting out in the car. For heaven's sake, will you hurry it up or he'll drive off without you,' she threatened. 'And then you'll have to get the bus.'

'I'm coming,' he roared, 'so tell the old fellah to keep his hair on.'

He grabbed the black-plastic-wrapped hatbox from the bottom of his wardrobe and carried it gently down the stairs. The front door was open and the rest of them were all sitting in the car. He closed the door and, releasing the lid of the car boot, placed the box carefully inside.

'What are you doing?' asked his brother, eyes gawping, curious, his large box of handmade chocolates on his lap.

'I was just putting Nan's present in the back.'

'What did you get her?'

'You'll see when we get there.'

'Go on, tell me.'

'No. You'll see soon enough. It's a surprise.'

'Rubbish,' jeered Ray. 'Something stupid and useless!'

'Will you two stop fighting,' ordered their mother. 'I've had enough of it. Today is a day of big celebration for your grandmother and all the Butler family and you two boyos better behave.'

The two of them glared at each other, knowing by their mother's warning tone that she meant it.

Tommy grinned. He had no intention of spoiling his grand-mother's day. He was so excited about it himself. All the family were coming. Aunt Maggie and Uncle Phil from Liverpool and their five kids and three grandchildren, and Uncle Matt and his wife and four kids had flown in from Canada. His cousin Peter had come from Sydney with his girlfriend, Melanie, and of course the Irish cousins were going to be there in full force. None of his grandma's own old friends was alive but obviously the people in the home with her and a few others had been invited along. He had cadged an invitation for Mr McHugh and given it to him on Wednesday after history class, and had posted the one to the hat lady, Ellie Matthews, though he wasn't really expecting her to turn up.

'Are you OK, Pat?' asked his mother. Tommy was aware that he had never seen his father so quiet when driving anywhere.

'I'm just watching the traffic.'

Normally his father would be blowing the horn, moving lanes, try-ing to edge the car past the lights, revving the engine for the off once the green signal came. He supposed it must be hard when you realize that your own mother is a hundred and that you are pushing it too, almost over the hill.

'Sure!'

His father gave a huge sigh.

'I'm just worried that all this fuss and the party and seeing everyone might be too much for her,' he admitted slowly. 'Give her a turn, a heart attack or a stroke even.'

Tommy's eyes flew to his mother.

'Pat Butler, do you think for one minute that your blessed mother is the type to keel over because people make a fuss of her? Well, if you do, you are wrong. Lily loves fuss, loves to be centre of attention. With all the children and grandchildren and great-grandchildren flying in from all around the world and all over the country to see her, she'll be in her element! Don't you dare give everyone the glooms today.'

Tommy could see the weight lift off his father's massive shoulders as he listened to Mary Butler's good sense. Only a few minutes later he gripped the wheel and honked at the car moving slowly beside him, not even indicating as he pulled across.

Yeah, the king of the road – his da was back on track!

Chapter Fifty-six

Lillian Butler still found it hard to credit that today she was a hundred years old. A century ago, in an overcrowded room on the third floor of a tenement house on Mountjoy Square, her mother had brought her into the world. Her parents had struggled to raise their brood during terrible times. Sometimes she could remember the smells and the noise and the neighbours of her childhood days as clear as a bell and other times she struggled even to recall her mother's face. It was all so long ago.

'Morning to the birthday girl!' chorused Teresa, one of the kitchen staff, as she roused her for her breakfast by singing 'Happy Birthday' loudly and giving her a big kiss and a tin of wine gums – her favourite sweets. And it had been like that all day, the staff and nurses bursting into song, congratulating her for reaching a hundred years of age, as if she had done anything to make it happen. She enjoyed their hugs and kisses and gifts and cards, asking Nurse Barry to read them to her, as her old eyesight was so bad these days. She enjoyed her usual early morning bowl of porridge and a slice of brown toast, marmalade and a cup of milky tea.

'Wouldn't you like anything special today, Lil?' the cook had asked.

She had shaken her head. This was her usual breakfast, and birthday or not she wasn't about to change it. The nurses had bathed her. Yesterday Josephine, the hairdresser, had come in especially to wash and set her hair, ready for today's party. The nurses teased it into shape as they helped her to dress.

She had never imagined herself living so long, a hundred years on God's good earth, watching her children grow up, then their children and now she even had great-grandchildren. Twelve at the last count! Her only regret was that Tom was not at her side to share this day and see the family they had reared. He had been the best husband a woman could want. Tom had kept a roof over their heads and put food on their table, never complaining as they both struggled to raise their family. They'd had their fair share of ups and downs but had stuck it out, making the best of what was given them. She smiled to herself, remembering it all.

Her daughter had helped her pick out the pale blue chiffon dress with its floaty skirt.

'It looks lovely, Ma. Makes you look younger.'

'Ninety-nine!'

Poor old Kitty! She'd never had a sense of humour and still didn't get the joke.

'You look very elegant, Lil. You will do your family proud today,' Angela, the matron, congratulated her, presenting her with a magnificent bouquet of flowers and a huge card signed by all the residents. One of the others had reached a hundred last Easter but poor old Bill was bed-bound and had to be fed and minded by the nurses.

'And here's your telegram and cheque from the President,' laughed the matron.

Lil blushed. Imagine the President writing to her as if she was someone famous or well-to-do!

'Lil, I hope you don't mind me interfering but you have a busy day ahead. All your family are coming in today to join in your celebrations but myself and the staff want to make sure that you don't overtire yourself.'

'I'll be good,' she chuckled.

'Yes, but I want you to have a nap after a light lunch.'

Lil agreed willingly, for then she would be right for the party. She wanted nothing to spoil this special day.

Chapter Fifty-seven

Tommy whistled out loud, 'Wheweee,' as he lifted his black bag into the hallway. The Charlemont Old People's Nursing Home had been transformed for the day with flowers and balloons everywhere, and big banners in reception and the corridors saying '100 years'. One of the young nurses pointed them in the direction of the huge dining room where the party was to be held.

He noticed as he walked past the sitting room and day room that the residents – well, that was what his ma liked to call them – were all dressed in their very best, cardigans and dresses and blouses and skirts and jackets. He supposed it must be a very big thing to them, the residents, to have someone make the hundred mark! Maybe they were all trying to make it and it was just that his grandmother was the first past the winning post.

'Lil's sitting pretty in her chair up there,' a staff nurse told them. 'Matron is with her and a few of the family have already arrived, Mr Butler. Your brother from Canada and his family are there.'

Pat Butler grinned. It was ten years since he'd seen Matt and only two of his kids had ever been to Ireland before. He was silly to have worried: today was going to be one of the Butler family's finest as they all assembled to pay tribute to his ma, a wonderful woman.

His grandmother looked lovely. Her hair was all nice and softly curled and looked even whiter than ever, like a halo around her small face as she kissed and hugged and welcomed everyone. Auntie Paula and his cousin Brian were fetching everyone drinks from the small bar the family had set up. There was wine and beer and sherry and vodka, and Coke, orange and big bottles of red lemonade. The presents were all put on a table in the centre of the room, and he shoved the hatbox on the ground slightly under the tablecloth beside two huge floral arrangements. His cousin Andy was taking photos of everyone with his grandmother on a fancy digital camera.

'Go on, smile with Nan.'

'Give Lil another kiss!'

Lillian Butler was lapping it all up and wiped tears from her eyes as six great-grandchildren were deposited on her lap and around her.

'I only wish poor Tom was here to see them all,' she smiled.

Tommy helped himself to a sausage roll and some vol-au-vents. Some had prawns in them but he preferred the cheese and ham ones. There was loads of grub, for the Butlers all had big appetites. The Canadian and Australian cousins were grand, asking him to come and visit them when he was old enough.

'What do you do for fun around here?' asked Aaron Butler from Alberta, the same age as himself and about a foot taller.

Tommy racked his brains, thinking of playing football in the road or up in the park with the lads and walking to the cinema or the chipper. Somehow it didn't sound as good as it really was.

'I do snowboarding and ski in the winter and kayaking once the weather gets warm!' said Aaron.

Tommy stuck out his chin. 'Yeah, well, we don't get enough snow here for that kind of thing but we all hang round, messing, if you know what I mean.'

More and more people were arriving, and the room was filling up and buzzing with sound. He was surprised to see Mr McHugh had arrived and was engrossed in talking to his ancient old uncle Donal.

'An event like this, young Thomas, is part of social history and not to be missed. Thank you for inviting me along to join the celebration.'

Everyone was getting on really well and the glass of sherry had given his nan two rosy cheeks.

'We'll all eat first,' bossed his aunt Kitty, 'then everyone here will get their turn to go up and say happy birthday to Mammy and give her their present and good wishes.'

Tommy watched as the Butler family moved like a pack of migrant wildebeest towards the buffet table, arming themselves with plates and knives and forks. He decided to hang back and remove the plastic covering off his gift, for he was dying to be first in line for his granny to see what he'd got her. He tilted open the lid to take a satisfied peek.

Janey! He couldn't believe it! Inside was a scummy black and white hat like you'd wear going to a funeral. His da would kill him. He turned it over in the box, crouching down as if the Memory Hat might miraculously appear underneath. He felt like crying as he looked round the room. Where was his hat?

Ray was stuffing himself with chicken goujons and potato wedges when Tommy grabbed his mobile phone off him and took off.

'Give me back the phone!' threatened his brother, as Tommy disappeared into the quiet of the corridor with his hastily rewrapped black plastic disaster.

Please let her be there, he begged, knowing it was almost closing time as he rang the number that was written in curly writing on the side of the lid. She had to be there!

Chapter Fifty-eight

A mix-up with the hatboxes! Ellie couldn't believe it. How had it happened? Tommy Butler was talking nineteen to the dozen on the phone and near to tears by the sound of it.

'I've got the wrong hat.'

What had she done for the fates to conspire against her like this, she thought, as she listened to his anxious voice.

'Where's my nan's hat?'

Her heart sank as he explained, and she began frantically to rummage through every box in the shop. It must be here somewhere.

'Where are you?' she asked.

'I'm at Nan's party,' he shouted back, sounding totally defeated.

She could sense his utter disappointment and knew that the promise of another hat would be no good. She had to find his hat and try to swap them round.

'Tell me about the hat you have in the box?'

'It's a stupid black one,' he insisted.

'So it's pure black?'

'No, there's a bit of white on it.'

She recognized the description immediately. He had Rosemary Harrington's hat, which meant that she had his. She racked her brain. Neil's mother had said she lived beside Merrion Square. She pulled out the phone book, searching through the H's. Not there, obviously ex-directory. Shit, shit, shit!

'Listen, Tommy. I think I know where your hat is and I'm going to try and get it. It's only a long shot.'

'Please, Ellie, please try and get it,' he pleaded. 'The party's on. Everybody's eating before they do the presents.'

She grabbed her jacket and purse and the invitation from the noticeboard, locking the shop as quickly as she could. Almost throwing herself in front of a cab on Dawson Street, she begged the driver to take her to Merrion Square.

Once there, Ellie walked up and down the row of Georgian houses trying to find the right one. Offices, solicitors, an art gallery . . . Almost frantic, she grabbed hold of a tall young mother with blue eyes who was about to cross over to the park with her little boy. She recognized her from somewhere.

'Sorry, do you live here? Do you know where the Harringtons live?'

The three-year-old looked at her as if she was crazy as his mother burst out laughing.

'That's us, I'm Rachel Harrington – well, I was. We met before at the opera.'

'Oh! Oh, I see . . . I'm looking for your mother actually.'

'Good timing then! We've just driven up from Kerry. That's why we're going to the park, to stretch our legs after that awful long journey. Mum's inside.'

Ellie felt like she was going to collapse with relief as she climbed the front steps and rang the bell.

She tried to brush her hair off her face and appear more composed and calm as she heard footsteps approaching.

'Ellie, this is an unexpected pleasure!' Neil Harrington was standing in front of her. 'Would you like to come in?'

'I'm sorry to disturb you, Neil, but it's about your mother's hat.' She sounded so stupid and lame. 'There's been a mix-up with the hatboxes and the thing is, I think you've got somebody else's hat and they have yours – well, I mean your mother's.'

She was doing her best to sound rational but could tell from the expression on his face that he thought she was some kind of raving lunatic, turning up at the weekend on his doorstep.

'The wrong hat?'

'Yes, exactly. Has your mother worn the hat yet?'

'No, it's still upstairs in the box. I haven't had the opportunity to give it to her yet.'

'Oh, that's good.' She gasped with relief. 'That's great.'

'So do you want me to do a swap?' he teased.

'Yes, but I haven't got the other hat yet. Please, Neil, could you get the box and the hat quickly!' she begged, resisting the urge to run up the stairs herself and find it.

'This all sounds very urgent!'

'Well, it is,' she confessed, thinking of poor Tommy Butler waiting. 'It is actually a matter of life and death. I have to get this hat – your hat – to the right person. It's actually a very elderly person, who could as we speak be nearing her end.'

'Dead serious!' Neil quipped.

'I promise to return the one you ordered immediately.'

She watched as he loped off up the stairs and reappeared a few minutes later with a familiar box in his grasp.

'Thanks,' Ellie said, retrieving the Memory Hat, which was resting snug in a bed of tissue. 'I'd better get going.'

'Where do you have to go?'

'I've got to get this to a little boy I know.'

'I thought you said it was for an elderly person?'

'It is,' she admitted. 'I have to get this hat to him to give to his grandmother. It's her hundredth birthday today and there is this big party for her.'

'And the boy wanted to give her the hat. Let me drive you!' he offered.

'I was going to—'

'Don't tell me you are going to walk!'

'No, get a taxi.'

'Well, I'll be your taxi,' he offered, grabbing a set of keys from the hall table and pulling on a cord jacket. 'I insist.'

Ellie gave a huge sigh of relief, somehow knowing that she could rely on Neil Harrington to get her to where she was meant to be. She placed the hatbox carefully on the back seat and sat in beside him, rooting in her bag for the invitation.

'Where are we going?' he asked.

She gave him the address.

'I'll drive like the clappers,' he promised, reversing his Mercedes across the road as Ellie took out her phone and began to dial the number Tommy had called from.

Chapter Fifty-nine

Tommy Butler was gutted with disappointment as he watched the family begin to file up and give his grandmother her hundredth birthday presents. All his planning and organization had been for nothing. He felt like someone had thumped him. His dad's older brother Donal was filming everything on his camcorder.

'A souvenir to help us all to remember this very special day,' he told everyone as he made them 'smile and tip their present towards the lens!'

Everyone stopped talking and watched and clapped as Lily Butler received her gifts and greetings.

Tommy loved his old nan and was so proud of her being head of the family, and the way her eyes twinkled and smiled as one by one his uncles and aunts and cousins brought up present after present. There was a big wool rug and a crochet shawl, silver photo frames, photo albums, bedjackets, slippers and a cushion for warming her feet; a huge magnifying glass that his grandmother was very taken with, and potted plants and bunches of flowers; fancy boxes of perfumes and bath oils and all kinds of lotions; a book of Irish poetry with a CD, so Granny could listen to it, and a set of rosary beads from Father Mac. His granny loved to talk to God and was always praying for the family's intentions and exams and careers and love life and their good health, which was the most important of all.

Tommy melted away to the back of the crowd, not knowing what he was going to do when his turn came. Imagine if his nan had opened the box and seen the black funeral hat. Janey, his dad would kill him! He could end up giving her a heart attack.

No, he had to get away, get out of here. He pushed past the two nurses in their uniforms and got out to the corridor. He'd walk slowly past the desk. Then out the main door and leg it, hatbox and all.

'Hey, Tommy!' interrupted his brother. 'Ma wants you inside, it's our turn.'

'I'm not going in,' he said, defiantly staring at the acne-marked skin of his brother.

'Ma said if you don't get in she'll kill you.'

'Well, I'm not budging.' Tommy looked at the lino on the floor, reckoning that if he ever lived to be one hundred years old this day might well rank in his top five worst days ever.

'And Dad will murder you,' threatened Ray.

'You go in and give her your stupid box of chocolates!'

'Well, they beat your rubbish present, whatever it is. Go on, give us a look.'

Ray did his best to grab the bag from out of his brother's hands, letting loose with a flying punch, the two of them tumbling to the ground and trying to beat the hell out of each other.

'J...., Mary and Joseph!' screamed their mother, appearing from out of nowhere and grabbing hold of them. 'Is this where I find the two of you, rolling around the ground like two eejits?'

They stopped instantly, compelled by her freezing blue gaze.

'Wait till your father hears about this,' she warned.

321

'Sorry, Ma,' apologized Ray, running his fingers through his hair and fixing his tie. 'I was only trying to get him to come in.'

'You go in, Ray, we'll be along in a minute.'

She stood beside Tommy, saying nothing as he got his breath back.

'What's going on, Tommy?' she asked. 'You've been acting strange for the past few weeks.'

'I was planning something for Nan, that's all, a good surprise, but it didn't turn out the way I wanted it.'

'Look, your grandmother is a very old lady, things don't mean that much to her any more. What she likes to see is all her family around her. That is worth more than anything. So forget whatever it is that went wrong. The family present is inside and your grandmother is waiting for us all.'

Tommy sniffed. His ma was right, like she always was. Today was about his grandmother, not him. He was just following her back into the dining room when he spotted a commotion at the reception desk. It was the hat lady and a tall man and they had a hatbox with them. His box with the Memory Hat, his grandmother's special birthday present.

Ray gave their grandmother his box of handmade chocolates with the big gold ribbon around it.

'Sweets for the sweet,' smiled his mam. Vonnie had gone up next with the baby and her present of a big squashy pink pillow that would help support Granny in the chair and in bed.

'Just what I needed for my bad back!' declared Lily, plumping it up for the camera. She had loved the beautiful silver photo frame with the enlarged photo of their family with his nan on the day of Tommy's confirmation.

'It's an antique,' joked his dad. 'Irish silver from the year you were born, and today we will take a photo of you with all the family to put in it.'

Now it was his turn, and Tommy proudly lifted the big blue and white hatbox and carried it towards her. He could see her wondering what it was.

'Open it!' shouted everyone.

His nan's hands were shaking so bad he had to help her lift the lid off the hatbox but when he saw her face he knew he had brought the best present ever.

'It's a hat,' she said softly. 'A new hat. 'Tis years since I've had a new hat.'

'Do you like it, Nan?'

'Oh, it's so beautiful,' she enthused, her gnarled fingers touching the delicate circle of cream with its shimmer of colours. 'One of the finest hats I've ever seen.'

'It's a Memory Hat,' Tommy explained, showing it to her. 'See this, Nan? If you look close, these are all the places you lived since you were a little girl.'

All around the circle of the hat base what seemed like a vague pattern turned out, when looked at closely, to be delicate drawings of Mountjoy Square, Meath Street, Leeson Street.

'My homes,' she chuckled. 'Look at our steps and the front doorstep where Jessie and Kitty and Pat and Paula used to play.'

'And this flower.'

'The lily – my mother's favourite flower.'

'It's an Easter lily,' Tommy reminded her.

'Aye, the patriots. We never forgot them,' she said firmly. 'We wore one every year to commemorate the Rising.'

'And there are nine silk roses,' he explained, 'one for each of the family – your children, Da and all his brothers and sisters. And see these smaller leaves? They're for us, your twenty-four grandchildren, and the little baby buds are your great-grandchildren. The tiniest one is Vonnie's new baby!'

'All my beauties!' she marvelled, almost overcome.

'Do you remember when you worked in Bewley's, Nan?'

'Those were the days. Sweet cake, hot scones, cherry and almond buns and macaroons and walnut cake, everything fresh! Tea and coffee for everyone.'

'This is a piece of lace from your uniform at Bewley's.'

'Well I never, my old uniform!' declared Lil, peering at it. 'I thought the moths had got it long ago. You know that's where I met my Tom.'

'I remembered that too. These are the rich roast coffee beans Grandad liked so much.'

'A cup of coffee and a cherry bun – that were his favourite.'

From a tiny piece of brown felt, the polished and lacquered beans stood up almost like petals.

'That was from the lining of one of Grandad's jackets, Nan. I found it in your old sewing box.'

Lil Butler stroked it softly, with tears in her eyes.

'This is something of Uncle Terry's and Uncle Mick's, from when they fought in the war.'

'God be good to them,' she said, touching the narrow ribbons.

'And do you recognize these?'

'Ah sure, they're from me darling boy Joey! He was a magnificent bird, the most intelligent creature that ever lived! His little feathers are worth a hundred of them old ospreys if you ask me.'

Then his grandmother lifted the hat on to her head, the shape perfectly framing her face, her hundred-year-old brown eyes still a-sparkle as she turned her head from side to side to show off the Memory Hat.

'Come here, Tom. Thank you for buying me such a wonderful hat. It's the nicest present of all.'

Tommy looked down at her as everyone cheered and laughed. She thought he was his grandad! Her mind was confused once more, forgetful.

He wanted to say, 'Nan, it's me, Tommy,' but for some reason he said nothing as she reached for his hand.

'I always knew you were a good one!' she whispered. 'Best of the bunch.'

Tommy could feel the lump in his throat as Uncle Donal took a photograph of the two of them, with Lily Butler proudly wearing her new hat.

Ray and Vonnie both clapped him on the back and admitted he had bought the best present ever.

'Tommy, you always manage to surprise us,' quipped his mam, wrapping her arms round him, her eyes welling with tears. 'Your da and I are right proud of you. It was a lovely thing you did for your grandmother, so thoughtful.'

Tommy hated it when his mam got soppy but he felt like she did – proud of himself. Even the hat lady came up and gave him a kiss, and said what a grand fellow she thought he was.

Moments later there was a gasp of amazement as one of the staff carried in the enormous birthday cake with one hundred candles on it. Everyone pushed forward to see it and sing 'Happy Birthday' at the top of their voices. Tommy and the younger ones in the family helped his nan to blow out all the candles.

'I'm all out of puff,' she joked.

It was the best birthday party ever, his nan even getting up and having a little dance with his da and each of his brothers, moving slowly round the floor in her floaty skirt with her hat still proudly on her head. Uncle Aidan lifted her off her feet, he was so tall.

A man from the newspapers came and took her photo, as Tommy tried to explain about the Memory Hat. His nan posed like she was a model.

'I am very impressed,' said Mr McHugh when he shook his hand. 'And, Tommy, I took the liberty of printing out and making up a small booklet about the past hundred years – your grandmother's time. I did it in big print for her and I'll give you all a copy. Most of it is what you have on your computer file.'

Tommy was astounded. Old McHugh might be a dry old stick but maybe he was nice with it.

The hundredth birthday party for his nan, Lillian Butler, was the best day ever and seeing her surrounded by all his family and wearing his Memory Hat was something he would never ever forget.

Chapter Sixty

Ellie almost collapsed with relief. Neil held her in his arms and told her everything was going to be OK as they watched Tommy go up and give his grandmother the Memory Hat. Ellie was so happy and proud that it had all worked out, and Tommy and Lily were clearly delighted.

'Well done,' said Neil as they joined the family party. Later they danced the Hucklebuck, the Birdie Song and a Butler family version of 'The Walls of Limerick' to the tune of 'Riverdance', and ate vol-au-vents, cocktail sausages and chicken tikka. They managed two plates of birthday cake while sipping congratulatory glasses of champagne.

' 'Tis the least we could do,' insisted Mary Butler, inviting them to join them, 'after all the trouble you went to over Tommy.'

'The hat is a gorgeous piece of work!' declared Lily Butler appreciatively, squeezing Ellie's hand, when Tommy introduced her as the hatmaker lady. The curious centenarian demanded to know who the handsome gentleman with her was.

'Just a friend,' she smiled.

Ellie was so happy that she had not let her youngest customer down. Of all Lily's vast brood of grandchildren and great-grandchildren, Tommy was clearly his granny's favourite.

'She's a great old girl,' remarked Neil, standing beside Ellie, watching as Lily Butler took another few steps around the dance floor with her youngest son, Pat. 'I wonder will the two of us be as good as her when we pass the century mark?'

'I doubt it,' she laughed. 'Our generation are big softies. Lily and her crowd had it tough.'

As the music slowed Neil pulled her closer. She rested her head against his chest, aware of his breathing and his face against her hair. Ellie was struck with the very serious realization that she really, really fancied him.

After another twenty minutes they decided to leave the Butlers to enjoy the rest of the evening as a family.

'Come on, I'll drive you home,' offered Neil as they said their goodbyes and collected the other hatbox from Tommy.

Neil put it carefully in the boot of his car.

'It wouldn't do to get them mixed up and give your mother the Memory Hat,' giggled Ellie, realizing she felt slightly tipsy once the fresh air in the car park hit her. She should never ever touch champagne. Ever.

They were both silent in the car and Ellie had to admit to surprise at what good company Neil had been and how relaxed he'd been with Tommy's family. He was actually very charming, and kind, and sexy, and what was the phrase Lily had used to describe him? 'A true gentleman.'

As they drove in the darkness listening to Frank Sinatra, she wondered would he ask her out, ask her for a drink, a meal, but he said nothing as they pulled into Hatch Street. She could sense he was staring at her.

'Ellie, thanks for bringing me along to something totally different on a Saturday night,' he teased. 'Not my usual scene, but I did enjoy it.'

Ellie cringed. It was awful. She had probably messed up some big date of his or dinner with that girl Gayle he was seeing. No wonder he'd wanted to get home!

'Neil, thanks so much for turning up trumps and helping me and driving me there and being nice to Tommy and everyone. It was way beyond the call of duty and I'm sorry if I've ruined your night.'

'Shh,' he said, reaching forward and kissing her. Ellie was momentarily stunned, then she found herself responding to him.

'I wouldn't be here with you if I didn't want to be,' he said, pulling her closer. 'I can promise you that.'

Ellie felt giddy.

'And besides, getting to meet someone like Lily was very special,' he admitted. 'Seeing her with all her sons and daughters and grand-children and great-grandchildren around her – it makes you think, Ellie. That's what it's all about.'

She nodded in agreement, feeling his arm round her neck. She tilted her face towards his, wanting him to kiss her again.

'We're not meant to be on our own,' he said slowly, staring at her in the dark.

Ellie could feel her eyes well with tears, thinking of how alone she really was.

'Are you OK?'

She sniffed. 'It's silly, just me feeling a bit sad and emotional.'

'I didn't mean to upset you,' he said, stroking her hair and the side of her face.

'I know.'

He kissed her again and Ellie felt the warmth of his breath and tasted his lips as she kissed him back. It was just as she remembered. Perfect. They kissed and kissed until she felt dizzy and giddy and wanted more.

'Ellie, are you sure?' he asked.

She considered, blowing her nose on a tissue. She wanted him to come inside, to have him finally kiss and stroke her and talk to her and hold her and stay with her.

'I know I'm emotional after Lily and upset about things, Neil, but I really do want you to stay . . .'

'Giggly, sexy and sad!' he sighed. 'Too much champagne! I should get the picture!'

He thought she was drunk again.

'No, it's not that,' she protested uselessly, as he pulled away from her.

Ellie felt the happiness of the past few hours she'd spent with him deflate, like a big red balloon becoming smaller and smaller till it was nothing. Everything good between them suddenly gone! Blown away like thistledown.

He kissed her on the cheek. Ellie was tempted to pull his dark head down towards her again as they said polite goodnights.

'I hope that Rosemary likes the hat,' she called after him, watching the tail lights of his car disappear into the darkness.

Chapter Sixty-one

Constance carefully replaced her beautiful wedding hat in its protective striped hatbox. It would always remind her of that perfect September day. The wedding, the house full of her children and grandchildren instead of the empty shell it had now become. Everything was so still and quiet. Although she could hear the radio going in the kitchen and the clock ticking in the hall, the house was silent, as if waiting for something. Waiting for flesh and blood, children and mess and noise and laughter and loving to fill it again. Her breath caught in her throat – for she could never again provide these things. She wanted to cry for all that had passed, slipped through her fingers like sand, babies, toddlers, teenagers now all grown and gone, getting on with their own lives while she sat in empty rooms surrounded by old toys and books and mementos.

Helen and Sally and the boys and even Shay were right. Things couldn't continue like this. She had to let go of the past and begin to move forward, create a new life of her own, let this house live and breathe again and be what it was meant to be. A family home!

Sally had persuaded her to consider going to Cyprus with them for Christmas. Chris's parents had insisted that she would be more than welcome. Her lecturer, Don Sullivan from Trinity, had said that it would be very useful as the museums in Cyprus held some of the finest examples of early Greek and Roman art to be found.

On her morning walk around the neighbourhood she had discovered someone was building ten two-bedroomed duplexes on a site just off Seapoint Avenue. They were compact and easy to keep, with balconies and a sea view. When Helen and herself had gone to view them, Constance had been surprised by the light and the magnificent sweep of Dublin Bay that would greet the occupants every hour of the day. The kitchen, small and neat and full of every mod con, was divided from the living space by an island so that even the cook could watch the boats sail up and down the shore. The gas fire lit with the touch of a button, and the duplex was altogether more appealing than she would have imagined.

She swallowed hard, put on her glasses and reached for the telephone directory to search for the name. Dialling quickly, her voice shaking, she began to talk to the auctioneer. It was finally time to sell the house and move on.

Chapter Sixty-two

Ellie Matthews busied herself arranging her new autumn and winter stock: red felt and cosy wool, velvet ribbons and coloured holly berries and silk hand-sewn leaves. The days were already shorter, with a nip in the air and showers of rain that made everyone grab their umbrellas or run for cover.

Molly Ryan had supplied her with bright orange and yellow blooms and some winter-flowering pansies from her stall to decorate the shop and doorway.

Ellie had made a delicious aubergine wool toque with a rim of fur and a gay little spray of winter berries, which she placed on a stand in the centre of the window. She was down on the floor, packing away the remaining autumn stock, when she realized there was a customer in the shop.

'Hello!' he called, peering down.

It was Neil Harrington.

Embarrassed, she shoved the boxes out of the way and pulled down her black and white kitten-print skirt, conscious of his staring at her.

'I like the cats,' he teased.

'It reminds me of Minouche.' She nodded over to the black cat lounging on a cushion on the chair.

'How have you been keeping?'

'I'm fine,' she lied, not admitting she had waited and waited for him to call her and had finally given up, accepting Kim's advice to try to put him out of her mind, 'as a pure physical attraction did not a relationship make'.

'The shop looks great,' he said, looking around him, 'and I see that the jeweller's and the sandwich bar down the street are having a bit of a facelift too, following your good example.'

She wasn't sure if he was teasing her.

'Yes, with this new grant available from the council, everyone's got a bit more confidence in the street. There's a new kids' shop opening in December where the old gift shop used to be. It should be lovely.'

'See what you started?'

'Mo did it!' she said firmly.

'Our mighty Lady Mayor, more power to her.'

'What about your clients?' she ventured.

'Actually, as you can imagine, they are not best pleased. Jerome is not used to not getting his way but he is astute. He'll still have his galleria and he'll now accommodate some individual designer shops, which should only add to the street.'

'Thank heavens.'

'Anyway, I resigned from dealing with that part of his business a while ago. Felt there was a bit of a conflict of interest. The proper thing to do and all that.'

Ellie hadn't a clue what he was talking about but she did like it when he was being all lawyerly. She wondered should she offer him a cup of coffee, but then maybe not. Silence hung between them and she wished one of them would say something.

'Actually, Ellie, the reason I called in was on a matter of personal business,' he said, looking at her.

'Personal business? That sounds serious.'

'Yes, hat business.'

She had to stop herself smiling.

'I need a hat.'

'Neil,' she giggled, 'if your mother wants to change that hat or get a different one, it's no problem, honestly. Just tell her to come into the shop. I've some lovely stock in for the winter.'

'No,' he interrupted. 'My mother is quite delighted with my purchase of the black one. No, I'm afraid this time I'm the one who needs a hat,' he said, standing directly in front of her.

Ellie felt uncomfortable. She had never made a man's hat and wasn't sure it was an area she wanted to explore.

'What kind of hat?' she asked, curious, stepping closer to him.

'I need a hat for this stupid big head of mine!' he said.

Ellie began to laugh.

'I'm not sure that I'd have anything big enough.'

'And that doesn't even cover half of it,' he admitted.

'Neil, you don't have to keep buying hats just to talk to me. I've been here all the time. You know that!'

'I know,' he said softly, staring down at her. 'I've been such a fool, Ellie. Wasted so much time I can't believe it. I've never ever met any-one like you.'

She held her breath.

'I know we got off to a bad start but from the minute I saw you at the door of this shop I knew you were the one I wanted. I'm crazy about you.'

Pushing Minouche off the chair he sat down slap bang in front of her. Ellie couldn't believe it: Neil Harrington looking at her like that, making her heart lurch and her pulse race.

'I think I might need to measure you,' she said softly, realizing just how much she wanted to touch him, run her fingers through his dark hair. He pulled her on to his lap and kissed her. This time, unrestrained, she kissed him back, totally forgetting about customers and the window and the busy street outside.

A long time later, she touched her burning cheeks, Neil teasing her as she fixed her skirt and tried to tidy her hair.

'About Paris!'

She blushed. She thought he'd forgotten all her drunken ramblings.

'Are you going with him?' he said, suddenly serious.

'Him?'

'The guy in black with the yellow roses.'

'But there is no him.' She explained about breaking up with Rory, unbelieving when he told her that he'd seen them together.

'I thought you two might be a pair,' he said slowly, searching her face.

'No. There's no one,' she promised. 'I'm going to visit my aunt Yvette.'

He reached for his briefcase on the floor. 'I got you this,' he said, passing her a parcel. 'Open it!'

She recognized the wrapping paper: it was from the art and print shop down the road. Nervously she pulled it open and lifted the framed print from the bubble wrap. It was an old illustrated print, a map of Paris, featuring a squiggly drawing of the Eiffel Tower, Notre Dame, les Invalides, the Seine.

'It's lovely,' she said, reaching up to thank him with a kiss.

'That's where I want to take you,' he said, pulling her into his arms and making sure she understood exactly what she could expect.

The rain started again, dripping down off the canopy and spattering on to the flowers below, as Neil Harrington told her that he loved her. Ellie Matthews felt her heart race as she told him what she'd suspected for a very long time – that she loved him too.